SACRED GROUND

ADRIENNE ELLIS REEVES

SACRED GROUND

ARABESQUE®

SACRED GROUND

An Arabesque novel

ISBN-13: 978-0-373-83009-1
ISBN-10:   0-373-83009-2

www.kimanipress.com

Printed in U.S.A.

This book is lovingly dedicated to
Lee Caswell Ellis

4/6/27–12/21/05

My thanks to Edward Darby, Sr., for his intimate knowledge of rural South Carolina and sharing it with me. My appreciation also to Alice Stamps who provided me with essential information about South Carolina woodlands and forests.

In the middle of this work, my brother became ill and later died. The fact that the book eventually reached the publisher is due in no small part to the patience and efficiency of my daughter, Debbie Reeves, to whom I give my heartfelt gratitude.

Chapter 1

The rain poured down as it could only in March. Steadily, persistently, undeviatingly, straight down as if it would never cease, taking all of the warmth, liveliness and hope out of the air.

Gabriel Bell sat glumly, his right hand barely touching the steering wheel of his Lexus, wasting the phenomenally overpriced gas with which he'd filled the tank this morning. The car inched forward, one vehicle in the endless line stretching in front of him heading south on the New Jersey Turnpike.

"Some beginning to what's supposed to be our big adventure," his fifteen-year-old brother, Drew, complained, moving restlessly in the passenger seat.

"Yesterday at breakfast we talked about leaving today," Gabe said. "Remember that?" He slid a glance at the man-child next to him.

"Yeah. So?"

"You had nothing to do after school but finish packing your

things so we could get an early start this morning. Early. No later than eight, we agreed."

"I couldn't help it if the guys came over to say goodbye, and I did some stuff while they were there." Drew was defensive.

"Right. Then you fell into bed and didn't get up until seven and spent the rest of the morning running around the apartment finding your CDs and video games." Gabe kept his tone mild. No point in getting himself upset over this skirmish. What he intended to do was win the war.

"How'd I know it was gonna take so long to find things?" Drew said indignantly.

"There was no rain this morning when we were supposed to leave. So deal with it, Drew. Complaining won't make the rain stop or the traffic go any faster."

Maybe he should've taken the Garden State Parkway. It was definitely more scenic but I-95 would take them the straightest way from New York City to South Carolina. To a place he'd never seen and, as Drew had said, to their big adventure.

As if the very idea of thinking about it energized the atmosphere, there was a sudden acceleration in the line of cars and they resumed their usual highway speed.

"Yes!" Drew said and sat up straight.

"It's still raining, so there must have been an accident holding everyone up. Watch for it on your side." Anticipating Drew's reaction if he did see signs of an accident, Gabe moved into the far right lane.

A few miles down the road, Drew exclaimed, "Man! Look at that. Someone must have been hurt really bad!"

The whole passenger side of a small blue car was smashed against a guardrail, apparently pushed there by a large SUV that skidded on the wet pavement. The ground was littered with broken glass around which flares were set. A highway patrolman was sitting in his car out of the rain and writing in his notebook.

"How'd they get mangled together like that?" Drew asked, turning back to get one more look.

"I'm not sure, but it looks like the SUV was trying to pass but he skidded on the wet road and hydroplaned into the blue car."

"They prob'ly had to get more than one ambulance," Drew said thoughtfully.

Although Drew said nothing more, Gabe noticed that he kept glancing over toward the speedometer.

"What?" Gabe asked.

"It's still raining hard and I was wondering how fast you're going," Drew replied.

"You've got a right to ask. It's your life as well as mine. I'm staying at fifty until we get past this rain."

The rain began to lighten a little at the same time that Gabe saw a restaurant exit coming up.

"Let's get off here for lunch and maybe by the time we're through, the rain will have gone."

"Sounds good to me." Drew was always ready to eat.

A busload of people began entering the restaurant, cutting between Drew and Gabe. They milled around chattering and looking at a few craft items for sale in the lobby. Gabe couldn't see Drew for a few minutes. A group of men moved and there he was, looking anxious.

"What happened to you? I thought maybe you went back to the car," he said.

Gabe slung an arm around his shoulder for a second. "I got caught in the middle of this crowd. Let's try to beat them or we'll be here all afternoon."

Drew was the prime responsibility in Gabe's life now, and every facet of his young brother's existence had become magnified for Gabe since the death of their parents two years earlier. Pop had caught the flu, which had turned into pneumonia, and in a few short weeks it had taken him away. While the family was still dazed by the suddenness of his death, Ma had gone the same way before the winter was out, after being caught in the freezing rain while waiting for the bus.

When Gabe had come out of the cloud of grief that had overwhelmed him, his first thought of the future had been gratitude that he hadn't married Olivia Eagles after all. It had been a close call but he knew she wasn't the kind of woman who would have welcomed a teenage boy into their home. Single and unencumbered, Gabe had vowed to make Drew the center of his care.

Although he was twice Drew's age, Gabe had loved his little brother from the moment his mother had laid him in Gabe's arms at the hospital.

"You've always wanted a brother." She was smiling and teary-eyed at the same time. "I expect you to take care of him."

Gabe thought of their mother as he and Drew were ushered to a table in the restaurant and served the soup of the day that their waitress had recommended.

"I like soup when the weather's like this, but this sure isn't like the chicken-noodle soup Ma used to make."

"That's why I never get soup in a restaurant," Drew said. "This chili isn't so bad."

"Ma would've loved this trip. She always wanted to go places," Gabe said.

"Yeah, you're right. It's funny that Pop never did, but it's because of him that we're going to South Carolina."

It had been on another afternoon three weeks ago that Gabe had received a call while he was deciding between using the ground round steak for hamburgers or for meatballs to go with spaghetti. Drew was supposed to check in any moment; Gabe would let him call it.

The phone rang. "You want hamburgers or spaghetti and meatballs for dinner?" Gabe asked.

"I prefer spaghetti and meatballs as long as there's herbs and garlic in the sauce," a man said. "Is this Mr. Gabriel Bell?"

"Sorry. I was expecting my brother to call. I'm Gabe Bell. What can I do for you?"

"My name is Jasper Moultrie, Mr. Bell. I'm an attorney and I have information to give you regarding your great-grandfather's will. When would it be convenient for me to see you?"

"Whose will?" Was this a new kind of scam? Gabe wondered. At work, in the papers and on television, there were always warnings about the ingenious ways con artists were thinking up to get your money. He didn't know anything about a great-grandfather.

"Ezekiel Bell was his name. He had a son named Edward who had a son named Booker. Your father, Mr. Bell."

Moultrie's voice, quiet yet authoritative, made Gabe sit down at the table with the phone, prepared to give serious attention to what the attorney was saying.

"How do you know all this?" he demanded.

"That's what I'd like to explain to you, Mr. Bell. I could come to your office on Chambers but I think you'd prefer hearing the details and asking questions in the privacy of your home. When may I come over?"

He even knows where I work, Gabe thought. Maybe he'd better see this guy right away in case there really is something to this will he should know about. "How about tonight? Is that too soon?" he asked.

"That's fine. Shall we say eight-thirty?"

"Fine. I live at—"

"I know the address, Mr. Bell. See you soon."

"You're in someone's will? Does that mean you'll get some money?" Drew asked when Gabe told him of the call.

"I don't know what it means, Drew. I just hope it's all aboveboard."

At eight-thirty, as Gabe let Mr. Moultrie in, shook hands, introduced him to Drew and offered him a seat, he felt his skepticism fade away. Tall, his white hair setting off his dark brown skin, his features regular, and his dark eyes shadowed with glasses showing a world of experience, his presence nevertheless displayed a liking for people and a willingness to smile.

"I haven't been in an apartment like this for years." He glanced appreciatively at the high ceiling, the built-in bookcases, the tall window overlooking the boulevard, the long hall through which he'd entered. The dark blue sofa and the upholstered chairs were well-worn and comfortable. "They don't build them like this anymore," he said.

"I was raised here, so was Drew, and when our parents died, I moved back in."

"Wise move. I only get to New York occasionally when I have business here. I live in Charlotte, North Carolina. You ever been there?" His glance took in both Gabe and Drew, who were sitting on the sofa.

"Never been south, except once I went to D.C.," Gabe said. Drew shook his head negatively.

A little smile touched Moultrie's mouth as he placed his black briefcase on the floor. He settled himself in his chair and straightened his pant legs. His hands steepled, his eyes smiling, he began his story.

"If it's all right with you, Mr. Bell and Drew, I'll give you some background on this will. Your great-great-grandfather was Ezekiel Bell Sr. His mother and father had been slaves but he was born free in South Carolina in 1870. All his life he heard stories from his father, Elijah, his grandfather Moses, and other elders who talked about a place that was special to the Africans in that part of South Carolina who'd come from the same area in West Africa. They called it 'De Land.' It held a treasure that was linked to where they'd come from."

He paused but there were no questions. Gabe and Drew made an attentive audience.

"'De Land,' they said, was watched over by 'sperrits' and the men in the Bell family beginning with Elijah."

"Did they know exactly where that place was?" Drew asked.

"Yes, but it didn't belong to them. Getting hold of it and then keeping it was the responsibility of Elijah and his descendants."

This sounded too much like a script for a Harrison Ford movie to Gabe for him to take it seriously. At least Drew was entertained.

"The stories caught the imagination of your great-grandfather, Ezekiel Bell Jr., and he asked questions about it. He was a smart boy and in his belief, he made 'De Land' his life work. He learned to read and write, earned money any way he could and saved every cent. His intuition had led him to 'De Land.' He'd dreamed about it and recognized it when he saw the remnants of this old plantation in Orangeburg County. He married Sarah who was a hard worker like him and understood his dream.

"Every few years they'd purchase more of the land. As the years went by he found several ways to increase his income. He bought a few acres to raise cows, hogs and even chickens for the market. He learned all about building houses when he built his own, and hired himself out to build for others.

"Meanwhile he and Sarah had a family—Elizabeth, Robert and Edward. Finally he'd purchased fifteen acres, and the special woodland the Africans had spoken about belonged to him."

"I don't get it," Drew said. "What made it special? Did it have oil or something?" He sat forward, his hands on his knees.

"What made it special for him," Mr. Moultrie explained, "was how the older Africans had felt something mystical about it. They used words he didn't understand. His father said they meant *sacred ground* and they said it with reverence."

Sacred ground? Superstition or a legendary folktale, Gabe had to admit the attorney was spinning an interesting story at this point.

Mr. Moultrie continued. "There was another fact about this sacred ground that was unique. Ezekiel had felt a calling to purchase the property. He knew he couldn't sell it but had to hold it in trust for a particular person." He paused.

Gabe felt the hair rise on his arms as Moultrie's calm gaze rested on him.

"You, Mr. Bell."

Gabe tried to speak but his mouth was dry. "Me?" he croaked. Drew was looking at him with the same astonishment he was feeling. "How could it be me?"

"Because it had to be passed to the eldest grandson in the sixth generation who carried the Bell name."

"How am I the sixth?" Gabe was trying to make sense of what he was hearing.

"Elijah Bell began the saga. His son, Ezekiel Sr., was the second generation and Ezekiel Jr. was third. Edward was fourth. Booker, your father, was fifth, and that makes you the sixth."

"What happened to all the other children who must have been born in six generations?"

"Some died single, some had only daughters, not sons. Do you know of any relatives you have on your father's side?" Moultrie asked.

Gabe shook his head. "Ma had four sisters and five brothers and most of them had children. Pop always said that was enough family for anyone. When I asked Pop about his family he said there was only his brother, Jacob, but I didn't even meet him until after Drew was born. He was single and teased Pop about having two sons, one for Pop and one for him," Gabe reminisced affectionately. Uncle Jake had been a favorite in the family.

He couldn't sit still any longer. "Excuse me, Mr. Moultrie. Would you care for something to drink? Coffee, tea, juice, water?"

"Water's fine."

Gabe took bottled water from the refrigerator, poured some over a glass of ice for Moultrie and grabbed two bottles for him and Drew. He felt like he was in Oz and had to anchor himself with something familiar before he heard the rest of this bizarre story.

"Let me tell you how I came to be involved with this matter," Moultrie said after he'd sipped some water. "Then we'll get to the details of the will. I was born and raised in Swinton, South Carolina. Went to university in Columbia and to law school in Philadelphia. Eventually I established my law practice in Charlotte, North Carolina. Once when I happened to be home, I had a surprise call from Ezekiel Bell asking me to do some business for him, which I did. Six months later he told me that had been a test to see if I'd kept his confidence."

"He didn't trust you?" Gabe asked.

That brought a smile from Moultrie. "As you get to know more about your great-grandfather, you'll see he had a subtle mind. Apparently he'd listened to see if there was any whisper about the transaction in the community. From then on I carried out all his business. He said he didn't want a local person and that he felt fortunate to find a person from Swinton who worked elsewhere."

Gabe had been doing some estimates in his head "He must have been very old."

"One hundred years old when he died several weeks ago."

"A hundred!" Drew whistled silently. "I've never known anyone that old."

"South Carolina has a lot of centenarians, Drew, as you'll see," Moultrie said.

"Any question about the soundness of his mind?" There was nothing casual about Gabe's question.

"None at all. In his late years, he wasn't as physically active as he'd been but he never lost his mental faculties, I can assure you. In any case, the bulk of the will had been written when he was in his seventies. There were only a few items to add later, primarily about the identity of the heir after I had traced you down at his request." He paused and turned his benign glance on Gabe and Drew. "Any more questions? No?"

He took several papers from his briefcase. Drew's eyes followed his every movement.

"As these documents go, Mr. Bell's will is quite brief. He insisted on only the specifics and omitting as much legalese as possible."

Gabe was motionless as Moultrie read the will, glancing up every now and then.

"'I, Ezekiel Bell Jr. of the city of Swinton, the state of South Carolina, do hereby make, publish and declare the following as and for my last will and testament, hereby revoking all wills and codicils made by me at any time, and directing that my executor, or substitute executor, serve without bond.

"'First, I nominate, and appoint my attorney, Jasper Lee Moultrie, as executor of this, my last will and testament, and direct that he pay my funeral expenses and just debts as soon after my decease as possible.

"'Second, I give and bequeath to my great-grandson, Gabriel Riley Bell of New York City, New York, for the period of three full months as soon after my death as possible, my fifteen acres of land, which include my home at 305 North Grayson Road outside of Swinton, South Carolina.

"'Third, Gabriel Riley Bell is to reside in the furnished house at 305 North Grayson Road and to examine its contents closely.

"'Fourth, Gabriel Riley Bell is to explore, discover and carry out the treasured destiny this property has held for six generations.

"'Fifth, Gabriel Riley Bell may not rent, lease or sell any portion of this particular property.

"'Sixth, Jasper Lee Moultrie, executor, will provide living expenses of two thousand dollars a month for the three months.

"'Seventh, upon the satisfactory completion by Gabriel Riley Bell of Article Four, the executor will so declare and will then deliver to Gabriel Riley Bell the entire estate consisting of the aforesaid fifteen acres of land in Swinton, South Carolina, the house and contents that are on the property, and any other parcels of land belonging to the estate at the time of my death.

"'Eighth, I give and bequeath to Gabriel Riley Bell the sum of one hundred thousand dollars with one half to be held in trust for his brother, Drew Booker Bell, until his twenty-fifth birthday.

"'In witness whereof, I have hereunto set my hand and seal on this eighth day of June 2005.

"'Signed and declared by the said Ezekiel Bell Jr., and for his last will and testament in the presence of us, who at his request, in his presence, and in the presence of each other, have hereunto subscribed our names as witnesses.

"'Marshall G. Hamilton of Swinton, South Carolina, Jane Ann Hamilton of Swinton, South Carolina, Jasper Lee Moultrie of Charlotte, North Carolina.'"

Moultrie silently handed Gabe a copy of what he'd read. As he reached for it and settled back on the couch, Gabe felt his breath return. He'd been oxygen starved. Drew scooted next to him so he could read the will that talked about fifty thousand dollars for him. He had to see the words to believe it.

"So I'm to go to Swinton and live in this house on the fifteen-acre property for three months during which time you'll give me living expenses of two thousand a month?" Gabe asked, his eyes still on the document.

"That is correct."

"That's clear. What I don't get is the fourth article. As a result, I assume, of examining the contents of the house, I'm supposed to discover and carry out a treasured destiny that's been waiting or hidden for six generations?"

His voice rose in disbelief as he repeated the words Ezekiel had written. "What does that mean?" His gaze fixed itself on Moultrie but his expression said that whatever Moultrie answered it would be subject to disbelief.

"Sounds like it means buried treasure." Drew, excited at the prospect of finding a cache of jewels, clutched Gabe's arm.

"I can't tell you, Mr. Bell," Moultrie said sympathetically. "I do know that most of what you'll need is in the house so as soon as you get there…it'd be wise to thoroughly search each room. Drew can help you."

"But what are we to look for? A map, a key, a box, or what?"

"Mr. Bell said you'll know it when you see it."

There was another provision stipulated in the will that was perplexing to Gabe. "Why the sixth generation? That's a long time to wait. Supposing there hadn't been a grandson with the name Bell in the sixth generation?"

"When I asked the same question, Mr. Bell said the oldest African had foretold it."

Other questions that Gabe or Drew brought up usually came back in one way or another to the same vague statement. Gabe began to think Moultrie knew as little about this "treasured destiny" as he did. Great-Grandfather had trusted even his attorney just so far with ancient secrets.

There were only three issues to be decided about the will as far as Gabe was concerned. If he took the whole matter seriously, as he decided to do after Moultrie left.

The first involved his job with the state in the accounting department. He'd gone there right out of college and was content to do a competent job that would advance him up the ladder in a reasonable number of years before retirement. Consultation with human resources and his department head resulted in an agreement that he could take two of the weeks as vacation and the rest as a leave of absence without pay but without a loss of benefits. Since benefits was his main concern because of Drew, Gabe was satisfied.

The second issue was that Drew had been slacking off in school and worrying Gabe seriously for the first time because of the group of kids he'd begun hanging with.

Intervention of some sort was called for and Gabe had been racking his brains as to what it should be. There was no way he was going to allow Drew to slide further down the slippery slope of disengagement from school.

Three months away from his school would at least change his environment. Gabe went to the school counselor, who helped him make arrangements for lessons and exams.

The third issue was the least important to Gabe. He asked himself again if he would be searching for gold. But it would be an adventure unlike any that had come his way in his uneventful life, and it would help Drew.

The day he'd notified Moultrie that he'd arranged matters with his job, the attorney urged him to get to Swinton as quickly as possible. "Remember the house is fully furnished. All you and Drew need are clothes and personal items like your computer, books and music."

A week later they were on their way with a check for two thousand dollars in Gabe's wallet.

Chapter 2

"This is a whole lot better'n yesterday." Drew drummed the side window in rhythm with the beat from the radio.

"You can say that again," Gabe agreed.

His spirits had been rising ever since they'd awakened to see clear skies from the windows of the Richmond motel where they'd decided to stay when, instead of the rain stopping as Gabe had prophesied, it had increased right up through the early dark. After breakfast they'd gone through Virginia and were now in South Carolina.

The total mileage from New York to Swinton was around seven hundred miles and Gabe could have made it in one long drive. Friends of his had boasted of driving more than that, stopping only for brief naps by the roadside. That wasn't his style. He wanted to see where he was going and what the land was like. South Carolina was certainly different from any place he'd seen before.

The sun shone through huge trees whose branches arched over long approaches to houses set back on lots, and it shone as well through tall, straight trees that marked the boundaries of fields.

Some of the fields were already green. Some were still brown.

"What's that white stuff over there?" Drew pointed to a large field where dry brown plants had balls of white sticking to them.

Gabe slowed the car. "That's cotton."

"It grows like that?" Drew looked at him disbelievingly.

"You've seen pictures of it in books and on TV, haven't you?"

"Yeah, but—" He turned to look again at the fluffy balls.

"But it's different when you see it in real life, isn't it? I wish Pop had told us about his South Carolina people. Those unknown relatives of ours had seen cotton fields. Maybe they'd even gone along those rows picking and filling sacks to be taken to the cotton mills. Or maybe they worked in the tobacco fields. Remember those funny-shaped tobacco barns we saw?"

Gabe hoped Drew was picking up information that he'd remember. For himself, he was ashamed of his own ignorance. If nothing else good came out of this adventure, his New York insularity had been revealed to him. There was much more to be seen and to be appreciated beyond the five boroughs of Manhattan, Brooklyn, the Bronx, Queens and Staten Island.

They passed small towns where there'd be rural sections where empty houses and other structures had fallen in upon themselves and were covered with vines. He'd read somewhere that the green plant that clambered up trees and smothered them was a parasite called kudzu. It was extremely difficult to get rid of. He noticed there were a number of houses with trees, shrubs and flowers around them, but the houses were standing alone except for a garage and perhaps a shed. He wondered who lived in those dwellings and what their lives were like without other people close by.

The contrast between the South Carolina countryside and what he saw daily in Manhattan was fascinating to him.

Signs told him he was coming up on Florence where he knew he'd have to feed the hungry gas tank. Might as well feed his always-hungry brother, too, before he began complaining. He could leave I-95 here and pick up 20 West, get a glimpse of what Columbia, the capital, was like, then go southwest and make his way to Swinton.

"Are we gonna eat anytime soon?" Drew asked right on schedule.

"We're stopping in Florence for gas and we'll eat there." He filled the tank at the first Shell station he saw then drove away.

"Hey! There's a McDonald's right next door," Drew pointed out.

"I see it. Let's go someplace a little nicer. Aren't you tired of fast food?"

Drew shrugged and began looking earnestly on both sides of the street. "I just wanna eat sometime soon," he grumbled.

They came to a small shopping area that had a homey look with its trees, benches, and turn-of-the-century lamp fixtures.

"There's a restaurant next to that bookstore," Drew said. Gabe turned in and found a parking place. He took his new casual jacket from the backseat and slipped it on. After they visited the men's room and came out into the nicely decorated dining area, Gabe felt a sense of excitement. This was the final leg of their trip. Their next stop would be Swinton.

Business was brisk, with a stream of people at the buffet counter. Many of the tables were already occupied and there was a buzz of conversation throughout.

"The food looks good," Drew said as he picked up a tray and silverware. "I'm sure hungry."

"Get whatever you want." Gabe was behind Drew and had already decided on the steak and baked potato combination, a green salad and cherry pie. A lady farther down the line was having some problem at the cash register. As Gabe leaned a little forward to see what was happening, his attention was caught by the profile of a young black woman just past the third person beyond Drew.

She turned slightly to look at the vegetable casserole she'd passed and seemed to be making up her mind whether to order it.

Her skin, the color of creamy milk chocolate, was flawless and the contour of her face seemed perfectly designed. He couldn't see her eyes but a turquoise earring sparkled in the lobe of a delicate ear and matched the jacket she was wearing.

As she shifted her shoulder bag, her left hand came into view. It was bare. *I've got to see her face,* Gabe thought.

The line began to move swiftly as a second cashier was added. Drew and Gabe had to answer questions from the server about their steaks and by the time they'd received their meal, the young lady was nowhere to be seen.

"I don't see an empty table in this section," Drew commented, and led the way around a partition into a smaller area where the tables and chairs were bunched together.

Gabe was suddenly struck from behind by a tray and felt something damp landing on the left arm of his new jacket.

"What the—" he began and turned while trying to keep his tray of food upright.

The girl in the turquoise jacket was trying to keep the rest of her food from sliding off her tilted tray while apologizing at the same time.

"I'm so sorry." Big hazel eyes glanced up at Gabe and a deep flush reddened her face.

"Here, let me clean the potato salad off of your sleeve. Someone bumped me and before I knew it my tray hit you. I'm so sorry."

She needed her hands free but there wasn't an empty table nearby. Among the diners watching the fiasco was a woman who took the tray and offered a clutch of napkins.

Gabe wanted to be anyplace but where he was. Everyone was looking at them as the girl bent and wiped at the oily salad, making the spot worse than it had been. Where was Drew? He could at least come and get Gabe's tray so he could move.

"It's all right," he told the girl. "Don't bother with it." Gabe didn't think she even heard him, she was so upset as she kept rubbing.

"Little accident?" Drew said with a broad grin as he came up beside Gabe and took his tray. He rarely had the opportunity to see his big brother lose his cool.

Annoyed at being the center of this kind of attention, Gabe captured the girl's hands. They were slender, soft and smooth.

"It's only a cotton jacket and it'll wash out," he said firmly, letting go of her hands and taking a step away.

Gabe saw she was nearly as tall as he when she straightened up to discard the damp napkins. The profile he'd seen of her at the counter hadn't prepared him for the interesting tilt of her eyes, the generous shape of her mouth, the nose that fit perfectly with her other features and above all, a sense of strength and determination. No wonder it had been so hard to make her stop her cleaning job.

"I'll be glad to have the jacket cleaned," she said. Her voice was businesslike as she met his eyes but her face still had a rosy flush.

"That isn't necessary, but thanks." Wanting to put an end to the already overlong scene, Gabe turned away and walked over to the table where Drew was waiting.

"Eat your food so we can get out of here," he growled as Drew welcomed him with a smirk. "I'm tired of being the afternoon's entertainment!"

He'd wanted to meet the girl in the turquoise jacket, but did it have to be a disaster?

If this muddle was an indication of things to come in the

next three months, he might as well turn the car around and head back to New York.

A few hours later, Gabe was convinced this might be one of the weirdest decisions he'd ever made in his thirty-five years as he slowed his car to a mere crawl, trying to avoid the potholes in the one-lane country road, which was already guilty of layering what used to be his sparkling black Lexus with dust.

The fact that the afternoon sun held a softness that he'd never experienced in New York City in March didn't make him feel any better, and even though it illuminated spectacular trees, which stood like ancient sentinels, their branches arched over long approaches to houses both stately and modest, his earlier enjoyment waned each time his tire hit another pothole.

When he'd seen the detour sign a few miles back, he'd had no idea it meant going from a four-lane highway onto seven miles of dirt road. Surely this couldn't last much longer. Glancing in his rearview mirror, he saw there was a line of cars behind him. If they were in a hurry it was just too bad. He wasn't taking a chance on injuring his car by going any faster than the fifteen miles per hour his speedometer was registering. Now he understood why there'd been a hand-printed Drive Carefully warning taped to the metal detour notice.

Up ahead he thought he saw another bright orange sign. He accelerated to twenty miles per hour and sure enough, after a slow and careful turn to avoid another large pothole, he was able to get back on the highway.

When they'd left Florence, Drew had grumbled, "I wish we could've stayed on I-95 and gone to Florida. At least it has Disney World. But what's South Carolina got?"

"Lots of alligators. They used to fascinate you."

"That's when I was a little kid." Drew twisted his mouth in scorn.

"Fort Sumter is outside of Charleston. That's where the Civil War began."

"Who cares about history? Anyway, we're not going to Charleston." Drew turned away from Gabe and fidgeted around in the passenger seat until he found a comfortable place to put his long frame, and in a few minutes had gone to sleep for the umpteenth time since they had left Manhattan and Gabe had pointed the Lexus south.

Gabe was trying to hold on to the notion of adventure this South Carolina trip might have for him and Drew, when he saw a green sign on the right: Swinton, Next Exit.

His heart beat faster and he touched Drew on the shoulder.

"Wake up, Drew. We're almost there!"

Drew sat up. "It's about time," he grouched, trying to hide his excitement as he rubbed his eyes.

Gabe took the exit smoothly and paused at the light. Seeing nothing on the left except more fields, he turned right when the light changed. Cars passed him on the left while he took in the scattering of gas stations and small businesses interspersed with modest frame houses that hadn't yet been overtaken by the town as it expanded toward the highway.

"Today is March 4," Gabe observed. "Look at that sign by the bank. What does it say the temperature is?"

"Fifty-five degrees at 3:00 p.m."

"You have any idea what the temperature at home is?"

"Yeah. I heard on the radio it's 30 degrees and cloudy," Drew said.

Although it wasn't the intense yellow of a summer sun, the light that fell on the brick library, the two-story town hall, the steeple-white Baptist church and the residences that began to appear had a pleasant glow.

"I like this better," Gabe said. Cold weather had to be endured if you were living in Manhattan but he'd always looked forward to its departure.

"Where do people down here swim?" Drew turned to look at a group of several brick buildings that, according to the sign, comprised Swinton High School.

"The high school might have its own pool and there's probably one in the park. I saw some lakes on the map, and of course you know we're not that far from the Atlantic Ocean." Gabe glanced at Drew to see his reaction.

"How far?" Drew's expression didn't change but Gabe heard the interest in his voice.

"I don't know exactly, but you can look it up on the map when we get to the house," he said casually.

After a few more blocks Gabe made a right turn. This was undoubtedly Swinton's shopping center, with clothing, furniture and other stores, as well as a movie house and several restaurants on both sides of the street.

A blue sign with an H in the middle of it indicated that Swinton had a hospital.

A left turn put Gabe on Grayson Road, where he crossed the railroad tracks. The character of the area changed. The houses were farther apart, accommodating sizable gardens and fruit trees. Chickens roamed some yards and four horses looked up from a field as the car went by.

"Aren't we looking for an address on Grayson Road?" Drew asked.

"Yep. Moultrie said it was 305 North Grayson Road."

"That means it's in the country where they've got horses and cows," Drew wailed.

Gabe looked at the speedometer. "I doubt it's country in the way you mean it."

The road sloped down around a bend and over a bridge shaded by limbs of tall trees, which grew on both sides. Up a little hill and the houses began again, some small, some large, with neatly trimmed lawns. Gabe stopped as a yellow school bus slowed to a stop and the door opened to let out a string of elementary-age students.

At the light, the bus turned the corner and after another block or two, a church, a barbershop, a hardware store and a variety of other small business establishments filled the streets. As he passed each corner Gabe looked to the right and left, noting that the area was larger than it first appeared.

The people going in and out of the stores were nearly all black, as were the drivers that passed him and lifted a finger in greeting.

At the third light, Grayson Road branched right and became North Grayson Road.

"We must be almost there," Drew said. "It should be in the third block."

On the corner of the first block was the Grayson Community Church, an impressive brick building with a smaller structure at the rear. More houses clustered together in the first two blocks. In the middle of the third block Gabe stopped the car at the curb.

He got out and walked around to where Drew was already standing. Awestruck, they stood together looking at 305 North Grayson Road, their home for the next three months.

Chapter 3

An imposing house occupied the center of the block. Five wide steps led up to the deep porch with its four stately columns. Two large windows on either side of a substantial-looking front door were matched by four smaller ones on the second floor.

The house gleamed dazzling white in the late-afternoon sun and its glistening black shutters completed a picture that caught at Gabe's imagination. It had never occurred to him that his great-grandfather's house would be so grand.

He wondered who cared for the lawn, the shapely shrubs and the flower beds. The two-car garage was on the left of the house and painted the same white with black shutters on its two small windows.

Stunning as the house was, Gabe saw that it was just the beginning of the property. Surrounding the lot on which the house stood were acres of trees. The growth was thick and the trees looked tall and healthy. Gabe had no idea how many acres he was looking at but the entire property in its prime condition spelled money.

"All this is yours?" Drew asked in disbelief.

"Seems unreal, doesn't it?" Gabe just looked, trying to take it all in. "But that's what we're here to check out." He felt as bewildered as his brother.

They walked up the five steps and across the shiny porch to the door. Gabe selected the new key on his key ring and hoped it would work. What an irony it would be if after two days of driving he wouldn't be able to get in the house. The key grated at first but on the second try the door swung wide.

He pushed open the screen and stepped into a dark hall. Automatically he felt on the wall to his right and snapped on a switch. Light poured down from a chandelier, revealing a wide hall with hardwood flooring, a winding staircase and a room opening off each side. There were also small tables and a closet.

Drew went around Gabe to explore the room on the right. "Look, Gabe, he had one of those old-fashioned sofas like Grandma had."

"They were very popular in Grandma's day. It was a sign of class if you could afford one. You see how long they lasted." There were several chairs that complemented the sofa, as well as tables with heavily shaded lamps.

"Looks like something from a museum, not a room you'd be comfortable in," Drew commented.

"This was the parlor and it was only used for formal visiting. It's not like our family room. Let's see what's across the hall."

"This is more like it." Drew zoomed in on the television that had its own corner, picked up the remote control and pushed the power button. The screen lit up and Drew scanned all the channels. "He's got cable. Cool," he said.

The room was a combination of old, heavy chairs, a massive bookcase, a contemporary love seat, floral draperies that let in the light when pulled and an oriental rug in the middle of the floor.

The item Gabe liked best was the fireplace. He could imagine how cozy the room would be in the winter with the drapes closed and a warm fire lighting up the place while you looked at some show on TV or read a book or had a conversation with friends while music played in the background. He looked around again. Was there a radio or CD player? If not, he and Drew could get one.

Opening off from the living room was a dining room with a table and chairs for eight, a china closet and a matching sideboard.

"This looks almost like the china closet we have only it's bigger." Drew traced the wood framing the door and Gabe knew he was thinking of their mother and how much she had treasured the dishes given to her from her family. She'd said once or twice that someday those pieces would belong to Gabe's wife or Drew's wife. She was keeping them for her daughters-in-law.

Gabe moved over to stand next to Drew. "Our great-grandmother probably has some china in here that was passed down to her. Just like Ma."

The dining room led into the kitchen, which had a wide window over the sink. Gabe pulled the shade up to reveal a large room painted a soft yellow. It held an electric stove, a large refrigerator, a dishwasher, a kitchen table with four chairs and a small TV on a bar.

A stall shower and toilet had been put in at the end of the hall near the back door. The washer and dryer were nudged into a corner separated by a partial wall from the bath facilities.

"All the bedrooms must be upstairs," Drew said. "Looks like they put one down here just for convenience."

"When Great-Grandfather built this house it was thought proper to put bedrooms on the second floor if you could afford a two-story house. The downstairs was public but the upstairs was private. Just for the family." Gabe counted the steps as they went up. "It's only sixteen steps. That won't bother you."

"'Course not," Drew shrugged. "I'm just sayin'."

Of the four bedrooms they saw, one had been turned into an office. There were files, maps, crowded bookshelves, a desk and a chair or two. All the rooms had clothes closets, dressers, big double beds, tables with lamps and knickknacks. The large bathroom had a long tub with claw feet.

Everything was of good quality and Gabe was impressed, yet always in the back of his mind he heard Jasper Moultrie say that he was to examine each room of the house closely. Otherwise he'd never find what Ezekiel Bell had left for him to discover.

When they explored the backyard they found a paved area which led to a neat shed that Gabe surmised held the lawn furniture.

A garden plot ran half the length of the garage.

"What's all that stuff?" Drew looked at a few shoots pushing through the soil.

"Maybe you can find out and tell me," Gabe said, "but I'm impressed. Maybe Great-Grandfather had someone take care of it, because what could a man who'd been one hundred when he died a few weeks ago do with a spade and a hoe?"

By unspoken consent they walked beyond the garden to where a wire fence closed in the rest of the land. The heavy six-foot fence was topped with barbed wire.

"He lived in this little old town almost in the country so what's with all this barbed wire? I don't get it. I think he must've been crazy. What's in there other than those trees?"

The expression of bewilderment on Drew's face was so much like their mother's when something hadn't made sense to her that Gabe had to swallow several times and question himself once more if he'd done the wise thing or if he'd been a little crazy, too, like Ezekiel, at whose command he now stood here with Drew.

There was a gate wide enough for a tractor or a truck to drive through. Gabe searched among his keys and found one that fit.

"Let's go in and see if there's anything other than grass and shrubs inside," he said as he unlocked the gate and pushed it wide. There was nothing but grass, low shrubs edging the space and wildflowers. Drew went one way and Gabe went the other but it was the same all over with slight depressions here and there. They covered the space then met and sat down on a rough wooden bench that stood on the right side of the cleared plot.

Birdsong and soft breezes blowing through the woods were the only sound in the late-afternoon air. Yet there was no sense of isolation. In fact, Gabe glanced around once or twice, so strongly did he feel the presence of someone.

Probably it was Great-Grandfather, who'd surely sat on the bench many times contemplating his land.

"It's like he had his own private park," Drew said, eerily echoing Gabe's feelings.

How could she have been so clumsy? Makima Gray was disgusted with herself. Mama used to say to let Makima do it because she didn't drop things or stumble or spill food even when she was a little girl. All her life she'd been naturally agile and careful.

She didn't know how to explain what had happened. In the restaurant, she'd glimpsed at the tall man in the black jacket behind her in the line. He'd been talking to the teenage boy in front of him. He'd also been staring at her.

The small area she usually sat in had been crowded and thoughtlessly she'd turned to its opposite side when disaster struck. Her long shoulder bag had hit against a chair, upsetting her balance, and the young girl behind her had knocked her elbow with a muttered "Sorry," as she went by.

One dish slid off the tray before she could catch it. Feeling like an idiot, she'd looked up to apologize and met the startled glance of the tall man whose black jacket was now decorated with her potato salad.

Thoroughly humiliated, she heard herself babbling on and on as she wiped at the salad with napkins a lady handed her.

The man had stood, tense and silent, until someone relieved him of the tray he was still holding.

He grabbed her hands to stop her dabbing at the stain, refused her offer to clean the jacket and stalked away.

Every time she thought of the incident she mentally kicked herself, again. Thank goodness it had happened in Florence, not here where everyone knew everyone else. Otherwise she'd never live it down.

It was time to get on with her work and put her personal misadventure behind her. As it was, she'd lost her appetite for what was left of her meal and had left the restaurant immediately. She didn't want to run into him in the parking lot. He was probably on his way to Florida and she'd never see him again.

She thought she hadn't noticed his features but as she drove home she found that his broad jaw, firm mouth, wide forehead, expressive dark eyes and heavy eyebrows had painted a picture in her mind. He had cinnamon-brown skin and his fingers were long and well shaped.

There was no getting away from it. The man she'd made a fool of herself in front of had been very attractive.

She wasn't supposed to be on duty on Saturday, which was why she'd gone to the morning conference in Florence, but when she'd arrived home, Stanley Worden, a volunteer, had called to ask if she could fill in for him.

"The only scheduled activity is an extra quilting bee. It seems the ladies were a little behind on their present project. They promised to be out by six. Can you do it, Makima?"

Stanley was usually dependable and she thought working at the center might help take her mind off Florence so she'd agreed.

She took a folder from her bottom drawer, one of many numbered from one to ten. All were entitled Grayson Medical Clinic.

She was working on number ten. Perhaps with recent events the tide had turned and she wouldn't have to go on to number eleven. This was her goal and her daily prayer.

Her project had begun three years ago. Her youngest sister, June, eighteen years old, had been coming from Orangeburg where she and three friends had gone to watch a football game at South Carolina State. A drunk driver had hit the car on the passenger side where June had been sitting. Everyone else had minor injuries but she had suffered the full brunt of the impact.

The only local facility for such trauma had been the volunteer fire department, which did its best to stabilize June so she could be taken to the hospital in Swinton. The multicar midnight freight train delayed them still longer and June's life had ebbed away by the time they arrived at the hospital.

Since that day Makima had made the establishment of a medical clinic in the Grayson community her priority so no one else would lose a life because the hospital was thirteen miles away on the other side of the railroad tracks, and where emergency care would be available twenty-four hours, seven days a week.

Her work had been tireless.

"Don't you think that's too big a project for Grayson to take on?" Gerald Smalls had asked when she'd sought his help.

Gerald was well-meaning and pleasant, but Makima knew he rarely volunteered for hard work. That hadn't kept her from asking. He was well liked and had a lot of friends.

"It's a big project, Mr. Smalls," she'd replied. "All I want you to do is talk to your friends about it. We need to spread the word so when we have the first big rally, hundreds of people will come. You can do that, can't you?"

"Be glad to, and I'll get my wife to talk it up, too."

The first rally was held three months after June's death. Her father, Arthur Gray Jr., recalled how his father had settled in the rural area of Swinton at the turn of the century, arriving from Mississippi with his wife, Ruth.

"They were looking for a better place to make a living and raise a family. They believed in hard work and used their money wisely. They bought land when they could, educated their children and helped many other people who came here. This community was named Grayson after them and it grew and prospered. Now because of this tragedy, we have an opportunity to do what they did. Working hard as a community we can give Grayson its own medical clinic so that our people won't have to go into Swinton for every health need, especially our senior citizens who don't always have rides."

Makima had asked business leaders, ministers and teachers to speak. After all the questions had been asked and answered, she closed the rally with comments from the families whose children had been in the car with June. She'd asked her mother to speak but wasn't surprised when she said she couldn't.

A second rally had been held four months later and this time her mother had been the first to speak.

"I want to thank you all for coming out this evening. This is a special day. I want to show you the first large deposit of money for the Grayson Medical Clinic. Here is the check from the insurance company." She waved it in the air as the filled auditorium exploded in applause. When it was quiet again she explained the money would be put in a certificate of deposit so it could be earning interest during the time it would take to pull the project together. "This is our seed money and we have faith in God that He will water this seed until its work is finished."

So much had happened since that day. Some of the grants Makima had written had paid off. Foundations had made some contributions and in Grayson itself, many organizations had held fund-raisers.

The reason she'd gone to Florence had been to speak to a possible donor following the public-health conference. Not only had the donor made excuses for refusing to give funds to the worthy cause, he'd also had the nerve to flirt with her. It's no wonder she'd been easily upset at the restaurant.

The remaining hurdle for the project was land. She wanted a piece of Mr. Zeke's property. She'd spent many hours with him and Miss Sarah, his wife, before she'd passed away. Miss Sarah had often called her "my little girl," and had given her the run of the house.

As a child, Makima had followed Mr. Zeke around, and when she grew up they'd spent time together when he was working on one of his many projects. He'd explained to her how he'd fashioned parts of the house and how he loved working with wood.

When she'd started her drive for the clinic, she'd asked if she could use part of his property. "I have a feeling this is where it's supposed to be," she told him.

"We'll see," was his answer.

As the months went by she became deeply involved in the legal and medical requirements for a clinic, necessitating long conferences with a number of people in the business, and visiting the kind of clinic she thought would be appropriate. Many other community people helped, but she was the prime mover even though there was a board made up of Grayson residents.

Occasionally she'd talk with Mr. Zeke and mention the land she wanted to buy for the clinic. "The land's not going anywhere," he'd say.

The last time she'd spoken with him was a few weeks before his death. He hadn't been ill and that time he'd said, "It'll be here." His death had been a shock to her and the rest of his friends. She'd been prepared to give him a down payment on the land and to get something in writing for the two of them. Now it was too late.

The whole town knew that his heir was a distant New York relative.

Makima was certain that she'd be able to negotiate with him because a New York man would have no interest in living in a small Southern place like Grayson.

She just wanted to be the first to meet him before anyone else had the same idea.

Chapter 4

The chirping of birds outside the window awakened Gabe with their unfamiliar sound. He never heard birds outside his apartment window. They must have been in his dreams.

Then he remembered. For the next three months he'd be awakening in his great-grandfather's bedroom where he could look out of the window and see acres of land and trees.

Yesterday when they'd unpacked the car he'd chosen this room for himself in the hope that it and the office next door might give him some clue about what he was supposed to find.

Drew had taken the back bedroom and wondered where there'd be space for his belongings.

"The dresser drawers are full of blankets and the closet has clothes in it already," he'd told Gabe.

"Put it all on the bed in the other room, because we'll have to go through everything. Put it in neat piles, Drew. Don't just throw the things on the bed," he'd added, knowing his brother's tendency to do just that.

Now he stretched, put his clasped hands beneath his head and contemplated his immediate future as he watched the trees moving gently in the March wind.

Had anyone told him a few months ago that he'd interrupt his and Drew's lives to come to a nowhere town in South Carolina, he'd have told them they were out of their mind. Yet here he was, expected to look for something in this big house filled with the accumulated living of two people. He didn't even know what it was he'd be looking for. How could he recognize it when he saw it? Drew thought it'd be a treasure like a chest of jewels or money, but Gabe didn't think it would be anything so obvious.

Ezekiel's mind was more subtle than that. His will had told Gabe that he was to explore, discover and carry out the treasured destiny the property had held for six generations. The word *destiny* was the most intriguing part of the whole business.

He'd marched along in his ordinary life not doing anything unusual from day to day, just going to his job, doing some volunteer work, hanging out with his friends Calvin and Webster, having two unsuccessful love affairs, and that was all until Pop and Ma had died. Their deaths had been the major events of his life and had left him with Drew and a new sense of responsibility.

Those were the facts of his existence so far. But destiny seemed to have a different meaning, like a course of action that had been determined way in the past and couldn't be changed. You were chosen and you couldn't escape it. You could turn and shake and wriggle and run but it caught up with you because it wasn't happenstance. It was destiny.

Gabe felt the hair on his arms stand up. Destiny was a powerful word, a concept not to be taken lightly, he thought, as he lay in the bed of the man who had devised the term for him, Gabe.

Today was Sunday. He wasn't a churchgoer except in the past when, on occasion, he'd escort his mother, but it might be a good idea to take Drew and walk over to the Grayson Community Church for its eleven o'clock service.

He needed to know the people here and what they could tell him about his great-grandfather. The best way to begin in this small town was at the church.

Also, he needed all the assistance he could get from whatever source if he was to carry out his destiny.

Makima got to church at ten-thirty. She loved being in the main auditorium by herself. She would sit in the corner, close her eyes and absorb the sense of peace and tranquility the sanctuary gave her. Her forbears had obtained the land and built the first church on this spot. Sometimes it seemed to her that she could feel their presence and their joy at how the church had grown to serve and nourish the community.

It was here that she'd finally come to terms with the senseless death of her sister. It was here that she came to pray over the knotty problems encountered with the clinic project. And it was here that she'd come for healing after Reggie had walked out of her life.

She hadn't slept well last night. She'd dreamt that the flirt from the foundation had followed her to the restaurant and had tried to get her to sit at his table at the same time that the tall stranger in the black jacket had snatched their food away. She'd made herself wake up, got a drink of water, and eventually had gone back to sleep.

She hadn't felt rested, so she'd paid special attention to her appearance as a way of getting herself in the proper mood for church. She dressed in a navy blue two-piece knit with white trim, navy pumps and perched a stylish confection of blue straw and ribbon on her hair.

Now as she sat with a bowed head, she prayed for a peaceful

mind and spirit so she could ascertain God's will for her next step about the clinic. Surely it was His will that such a facility be built, since its whole purpose was to serve the people. That being so, surely He would make it possible for her to obtain the land Mr. Zeke had promised her. She asked God's blessing on her negotiations with the New York man, the heir to the property.

Makima lifted her head as she heard the first footsteps of people coming for the morning service. She slipped out the side door and made her way to the vestibule to her place as part of the welcoming committee whose function was to greet the worshippers.

An unbroken stream of people came up the steps where they were welcomed, handed a program and ushered through the double doors, which now stood open. Once the choir marched in they would be closed.

Makima greeted Miss Selina Moore, who was walking with a cane this morning. "Let me help you to your seat. Arthritis bad again?"

"It sure is, honey, but I wasn't going to let it keep me from coming out. Your folks all right?" Miss Selina was a retired teacher who'd taught school when Makima's father had been the principal.

"They're fine. They had to go to Orangeburg today but I'll let them know you asked about them." She settled Miss Selina in her favorite seat and hurried back up the aisle.

The vestibule was crowded with almost-latecomers. Deacon Miller called her over.

"Makima, I want you to meet someone. This is Mr. Zeke's great-grandson, Gabriel Bell, and his brother, Drew Bell. They've just arrived from New York.

"Gentlemen, this is Miss Makima Gray. She knows everything about our church and about the community, too."

Makima felt the blood drain from her face as she met the eyes of the tall stranger from the restaurant. Only her iron will and pride kept her on her feet as she extended her hand to the Bells and made a polite response.

"Shall I show you to your seats?" she asked as people moved in behind them.

"No, thanks. We can seat ourselves," the tall one said formally. He was evidently as shaken as she was. The boy was different. He was trying to keep from smiling and there was a sparkle in his eyes when he looked at her.

A few moments later the choir marched in and the vestibule doors were closed. Makima usually sat in the front of the church to be on hand if needed, but now she crept into the last row and was thankful to make it there before she collapsed.

She was numb.

How could this have happened? The man she'd spilled her salad on was the same man she had to persuade to sell her a piece of the land he'd inherited.

Was this some cosmic joke being played on her?

She opened her bag after a few minutes to look into her compact mirror. She was still colorless so she made quick repairs and settled down to try to compose herself. It was useless. All she could think about was that Gabriel Bell lived right here in Grayson and now that she'd seen him here, somehow she had the impression that he was not going to be the kind of person who took one look at Grayson, tucked in his tail and ran back to the city.

He'd looked solid in his dark gray suit, white shirt and blue tie. A man not interested in staying would hardly have made it his business to come to church the day after he'd arrived.

She wondered what he'd thought when he saw her and realized from Paul Miller's introduction that she lived in Grayson.

She closed her eyes. Images have power, and probably his image of her kneeling at his feet and dabbing ineffectually at his jacket would always be with him and associated with the name of Makima Gray. She'd have to change that.

She began to look around for him and his brother. Had they sat in the central section or on one of the side sections? There they were just four rows in front of her in the central section.

Gabriel sat up straight; she liked that in a man. His dark hair was cut short, his neck well trimmed. When he'd looked at her, his eyes hadn't been as cold as they'd been in the restaurant. His primary emotion, like hers, had seemed to be astonishment.

The church secretary read out the names of visitors and invited them to stand and be recognized. There was warm applause when Gabriel and Drew Bell stood. Later when the minister came to the pulpit he greeted them again.

"Mr. Ezekiel Bell was a founding member of this church," he told them. "Everyone called him Mr. Zeke. He was known throughout the community as a caring man who would help anyone when help was needed. His wife, Miss Sarah, taught school here many years and together they contributed a great deal to Grayson. He was a magnificent craftsman, as his house will testify. He lived well beyond his three score and ten years, for which we are all grateful. He will be missed and we are happy to welcome you, his great-grandsons, to Grayson."

When the service was over, people were going to want to meet him and his brother. It was her job to see that it happened.

Personal discomfort had to be put behind her. She was in God's house doing God's work.

When the final prayer was over, she straightened her shoulders and went to the aisle. She ignored Gabriel's look of surprise.

"I'd like to take you around and introduce you to some people," she said with a warm smile. "Miss Selina Moore wants to meet you because she was a dear friend of Miss Sarah's and they taught school together."

Mr. Nelson came next, then Mr. Weber who had the only

drugstore in Grayson, and after them enough people that Makima felt it was time to move the Bells out of the church. Gabriel was friendly and relaxed but Drew was looking dazed. Maybe they didn't do this in New York churches.

As they came out onto the steps, a stylish young woman flashed a smile at Gabriel, stuck out her hand and said, "Hi, I'm Alana Gray, Makima's sister, and I've been waiting to meet you." She was one of a small group of young people.

"Glad you waited," Gabe said, returning the handshake and the smile. "I'm Gabe Bell and this is my brother, Drew."

"I'm Bobby Gray, Makima's brother," said the man in the group. "And this is Valerie Wolf and her brother, Jeff."

Valerie was a petite brown-skinned girl with a Cupid's-bow mouth and long eyelashes. Jeff looked to be about Drew's age.

Alana seemed to have taken over the conversation with her exuberance as she explained that they were all planning to go to a movie in Swinton later and then get something to eat and asked if Gabe, Drew and Makima wanted to join the party.

Gabe glanced at Drew and, seeing that he and Jeff were talking, excused himself but said Drew might want to go.

"I have another engagement," Makima said. "I won't be through in time to go with you. What're you going to see?"

Jeff named the movie that had good reviews in the action-suspense category, and arrangements were made to pick Drew up at five o'clock.

Gabe turned to Makima. "Thanks for the introductions," he said warmly. "I enjoyed it. I didn't expect people to be so friendly. I'm looking forward to a real visit with Miss Selina so I can hear more about my great-grandmother."

"Now that she's retired she truly appreciates visitors, Mr. Bell."

"Please call me Gabe. That's what I go by at home."

"Gabe," Makima said, "could I make an appointment with you?" She shifted her bag from one hand to another.

He looked surprised. "Certainly. What about?"

"It's a business matter and will take some time. Are you free tomorrow?"

He looked even more puzzled. "Just name a time that's good for you and I'll make myself available."

Chapter 5

"Drew, I'm so proud of you, man," Gabe said as they walked home from church. He nodded to a couple who spoke to them in passing.

"Why? What'd I do?" Drew said in surprise.

"You kept your cool when we were introduced to Miss Gray and acted like you'd never seen her." Drew was growing too fast for the investment of a suit but he looked fine in his tan slacks and navy sport coat.

Drew's face lit up and his laugh was one of pure youthful enjoyment. "Yeah, that was something, wasn't it? She looked like she was gonna faint. I sure didn't want to make her feel any worse, so I just played along with you."

"You handled it like a man and I know she must have appreciated it."

"I'm not a clunk all the time, you know." Drew hid his pleasure with bluster.

"All that stuff the preacher said about Great-Grandfather was pretty cool. I kinda wish I could have met him." There was a wistfulness in his voice that found an echo in Gabe.

They crossed the street and as they came to their block, Drew said, "This might not turn out to be too bad. I didn't expect people to be so friendly. Jeff sounds like he's okay. He's just four months older'n me and he likes swimming, too."

Gabe felt relieved. One of his concerns in coming to South Carolina had been about Drew finding friends. He'd have to check Jeff out, but meanwhile all systems seemed set to go.

"Your turn to fix lunch," he reminded Drew as they were upstairs changing their clothes.

"Do I hafta?" Drew grouched automatically.

"Yeah, you have to. There's plenty of food in the refrigerator. Call me when it's ready."

Gabe had decided to use this opportunity to introduce Drew to cooking responsibilities since he wouldn't be going to school on a regular basis.

He'd made arrangements with Drew's school for home studies and tests. He didn't know how that was going to work out but at this point it wasn't high on his list of priorities.

Drew produced monster sandwiches and chocolate-chip cookies for lunch. He drank a quart of milk while Gabe had apple juice.

"Not bad," Gabe said when the meal was over.

"Best thing is no dishes to wash." Drew gathered up the paper plates and napkins and sailed them into the trash can. That was a compromise Gabe had agreed to. Dishes were only for dinner. Paper ware for everything else.

Valerie and Jeff came by for Drew promptly at five, assured Gabe they'd take care of him and gave him Valerie's cell number. The movie started at six, then they'd eat and should be back around ten, Valerie said.

Gabe went up to the bedroom and began a thorough search through every piece of clothing in the tall dresser. Each shirt, underwear, pajama set, pair of socks, handkerchief and scarf was gone over. He'd told himself at the outset that he must be methodical, so he took his time.

His CD player provided music for the laborious task and meanwhile he let himself relive what had happened at church.

Walking to church with his brother in the March sunlight and then being met by all kinds of people who smiled and said, "Hello," as if they knew him had lulled him into a pleasant sense of comfort. It had taken one critical instant to snatch him rudely awake.

The deacon who'd officially welcomed him and Drew was about to let them proceed into the sanctuary when he called a woman over to meet them. Gabe scarcely heard the introduction, he was so shocked.

All he could take in was that the girl who had spilled potato salad on his jacket and embarrassed him to the max lived right here in Grayson. She was standing right there in front of him. What were the odds of that happening?

Thankfully Drew hadn't said anything. The girl looked like she was about to faint so he cut the moment short and went on into the church. Drew had said, "That's the same lady from the restaurant, isn't it?" Gabe had nodded a yes.

The service began and since it was so similar to his mother's church service, he knew when to make the right responses as part of the congregation.

He'd been touched and surprised by the minister's remarks about Great-Grandfather. There was something to be said after all about small towns where people stayed all of their lives.

The minister began his sermon. Gabe couldn't have said what it was about because he was thinking of the girl whose last name was Gray.

How awkward was it going to be with both of them living in Grayson? He thought the deacon had said the girl knew everyone in the community. That meant she had status and it also meant they'd be bumping into each other while he was here. That could be a problem.

Did she have a job? He could find out and avoid the place. He didn't mind being cooperative for the brief time he'd be in Grayson. She, on the other hand, had a life here. He'd keep a low profile and that should take care of it.

Satisfied with this conclusion, he'd stood for the final prayer, had a short but friendly exchange with the man who'd sat next to him and exited the pew almost into the arms of the girl he'd vowed to avoid.

She'd looked totally different. Her eyes shone with a friendly smile and her color was back. She was stunning in a navy blue outfit that looked like it had been made for her.

She'd said she wanted them to meet some people and took them around as if they were celebrities. That's when he found out her name was Makima Gray, because people kept calling to her. The deacon was right, she was well-known.

Gabe finished with the dresser and found nothing out of the ordinary. Next was the closet. It didn't take too long to go through the pockets. His great-grandfather apparently had emptied his pockets as a habit.

Gabe handled each garment then took all the shoes out to see if there was something hidden in them. Shoes made good hiding places. He even examined the bottoms, remembering stories of hollow heels. He felt silly but he couldn't afford to pass up any possibility.

Makima had been wearing some nice shoes with three-inch heels and she'd walked confidently in them. He always noticed women's shoes; you could tell something about a woman by the shoes she wore.

That Alana. She certainly was different from Makima. Makima had a sort of dignity about her even under stress while Alana was all gaiety and sparkle. The deep red pants outfit she'd worn had clung to her slim body. She wasn't as tall as Makima and didn't have her sister's curves. Her shoes had been black sling backs and he'd bet she could have a date every night of the week if she wanted it.

He wondered how the sisters got along. Their brother, Bobby, seemed to be the quiet one of the siblings. He'd seemed to be all wrapped up in Valerie Wolf.

As Gabe searched through the rest of the room, even looking under the mattress, he speculated what Makima could possibly want to talk about with him that involved a business matter. She had seemed very serious about it.

By the time Drew came in he'd finished the room and had gone downstairs to have a bowl of chili and a salad.

"Have a good time?" Gabe asked.

"Yeah." Drew opened the refrigerator and pulled out a carton of ice cream. "Want some?"

"Sure."

Drew filled two bowls. "There was this guy in the movie who had to find out who was kidnapping little kids for ransom," he began. "And the cool thing was that it was a bunch of high school seniors who cracked the case."

Gabe was accustomed to listening to Drew's analysis of the movies he liked. When Drew finished, Gabe said, "How'd you and Jeff get along?"

"Fine. He's coming over tomorrow after school."

We're both having company tomorrow and we've only been here two days, Gabe mused as they went up to bed.

By the time Makima was ready to go to her appointment on Monday she'd tried on and discarded three different outfits. One was too dressy, the second was too informal and the third would do but that was all. She hadn't been this nervous getting ready for a presentation to a foundation, she thought as she selected a fourth outfit.

This would do, or maybe she was tired of her indecision. The deep violet wool jacket with a shawl collar had pants to match. With them she wore a silk georgette blouse in a geometric floral print. She found some earrings with a single violet stone and decided to wear her new suede sling backs with the covered buckle and a matching bag. Looking at her image in the full-length mirror she felt ready for a business appointment with Mr. Gabriel Bell.

As she walked up the familiar steps of Mr. Zeke's house, sadness overcame her. This was her first time back since he'd passed away. All her life she'd come up those steps and crossed the porch to ring this bell. As a little girl the porch had seemed so wide.

The door opened promptly just as it used to do but this time it was Gabe Bell who welcomed her in. He looks like he belongs here, she thought.

He wore dark pants with a striped pullover sweater and everything about him was well groomed.

"It's nice to see you again, Makima. Please come in."

"Thank you." She instinctively turned left into the living room. "Oh, you've opened the curtains. I'm so glad," she said involuntarily.

Gabe looked puzzled. "Great-Grandfather never opened them?"

"Not much as he grew older, and it was so dark in here. It's lovely to have the light again." She gazed around the room as if seeing old friends once more.

"Please have a seat and let me bring you something to drink," Gabe said. "Tea, coffee, soft drink?"

"Water will be fine, thanks."

He served the water on a small tray with a napkin and sat down opposite her with his own glass.

"I gather you've been here many times and are familiar with the house," he said.

"I've been coming here all my life," she said simply. "That's why it made me feel sad when I walked up the steps today. It's my first time here since Mr. Zeke passed."

"I understand," Gabe said and waited for her to continue.

"Miss Sarah used to call me her little girl. My father was principal of the school where she taught and they were great friends, which is one reason my parents allowed me to visit. Our house is on the street behind the church, so it was easy to walk or ride my bike over here." She took a sip of water and saw amusement in his eyes. What had she said that was funny?

"I suddenly had this picture of you with your hair in braids whizzing along on your bike." The openness of his smile invited her to smile with him at the picture and she smiled back before resuming her story.

"Miss Sarah had one daughter, Elizabeth, who died as an infant. But I guess you know all about that. Then she had two boys, but she'd always wanted a girl, so I was her make-believe daughter or granddaughter and we spent a lot of time together. Mr. Zeke was very kind to me, too. I used to follow him around to see what he was doing. After Miss Sarah died I came by often to keep him company. He'd explain to me how he fashioned parts of this house."

"You can tell he loved working with wood," Gabe said. "I'm finding out a lot about him little by little."

This was the opening Makima had been looking for.

"This may or may not be something you knew about, Gabe, but Mr. Zeke had promised to sell me some property." No, he hadn't known about that. She saw that instantly and girded herself for battle.

Gabe sat straight in his chair. "He promised to sell you some of this property where we are or did he have some more?"

"It was this property we always talked about," she said firmly.

"What was it for?"

"The Grayson Medical Clinic."

"I don't know anything about that."

"The need for it came about because of a tragedy, as is so often the case." Her tone softened and she relaxed in her chair.

"The youngest child in our family was my sister June. She was eighteen, getting ready to go to college. On a Saturday night she and three friends went to a football game at South Carolina State in Orangeburg. A drunk driver hit the car when they were almost home. June was sitting in the passenger seat in the front and that's what took the impact. Everybody in the car had some injuries but June died because we couldn't get her to the hospital in Swinton in time."

"I'm sorry," Gabe said "When did that happen?"

"Three years ago. Since then I've made the establishment of a medical clinic here in Grayson a priority."

"By yourself?" Gabe sounded a little disbelieving.

"No, everyone in Grayson is helping and there's a board."

"How have you progressed so far?"

"We have ten folders with details which I'll be happy to show you another time, but I can tell you that we've gone through most of the legal procedures. We've met with medical authorities and building contractors. We've written many grant proposals and met with quite a few foundations."

"Have you raised much money?"

"The first large sum was the insurance that was paid for June's wrongful death. Our family gave it as seed money. Since then we've added money from grants, foundations, organizations and frequent fund-raisers."

Gabe turned his glass in his hand. "Where does this property come in?" He fixed on her with a direct stare.

Makima knew this was the moment of truth. He had to believe as she did that Mr. Zeke had intended to sell her what she needed.

"I asked Mr. Zeke to sell us a part of his property for the clinic. I've never considered any other place because this location is perfect and there's something about it that draws me. I know that doesn't make much business sense but that's the way I feel."

"What exactly did he say, Makima?" Gabe asked.

"He said, 'We'll see.' I didn't have the down payment yet, so I didn't go beyond that, but each time I reminded him, he said, 'It'll still be here.' In other words, when I had the money ready he'd sell it to me. Then he died quite unexpectedly, so I'm coming to you." Makima took a deep breath and said a silent prayer as she waited for his response.

"How much property do you need?" he asked calmly.

"We can't afford more than five acres." Makima allowed herself to hope that this was going to work. It had to work for the sake of the whole community.

"It's a worthwhile project and I wish I could help you, Makima, but I can't." Gabe looked at her with sympathy.

Makima flinched as if she'd suffered a blow. She couldn't give up. The clinic had to be fought for.

"Why can't you?" she asked.

"The will doesn't permit it."

"Mr. Zeke's will?" Her eyes flashed. "That's hard to believe. You are his heir, aren't you?"

"Of course or I wouldn't be here," he said stiffly.

"You're his heir and you can't dispose of the property?" That didn't sound reasonable to her.

"As I said, I can't help you." His voice was now formal and cool.

"Can't or won't? I'd hoped for more understanding and coop- eration from Mr. Zeke's relative." She stood up. "I'm sorry to have wasted your time, Mr. Bell."

Gabe escorted her to the door in silence, opened it and said, "Thank you for coming, Miss Gray."

She felt him watching as she walked across the porch and down the steps, then got into her car.

What was she going to do now? She had to have that property.

Chapter 6

Gabe moved to the front window to watch Makima as she walked across the porch and down the steps. He could see the tension in her body and he knew he'd caused it.

He was sorry but there was nothing else he could have done. There was no way he could sell her any part of the property, not even one acre, much less five. He'd told her the will didn't permit it and she'd had the gall to imply that she didn't believe him, that he just didn't want to consider her offer. That had made him angry.

She didn't know him at all so where did she get off saying he was a liar?

He didn't know her either but he'd listened to all she had to say about the clinic and had actually been impressed by her story. Losing her sister in such a senseless accident must have been terrible and he could understand how the need for the clinic arose out of it. He could only vaguely imagine how he'd feel if it had been Drew in that car!

The clinic would surely cost hundreds of thousands of dollars and he wondered how Makima and her partners could raise that much money. He dealt with funding in the state agency he worked for and he knew it wasn't only the cost of getting a business up and running that one had to be concerned about. Keeping it running also cost money and that's why many enterprises folded after a year or two.

That would be a worse scenario for the clinic than if they didn't get it started in the first place. Had she thought about that?

He didn't see why she'd fixated on this property. There had to be other acres in Grayson on which the clinic could be built that would be just as convenient for the community as this was. But no, Miss Makima Gray had apparently made a unilateral decision for this spot and had bullied the people she was working with to accept it.

He could have told her the details of the will but he didn't see why he had to. That was his private business.

He needed to warn Drew not to talk about it, especially now that he'd met Jeff. It could slip out in a casual remark about them being here for only three months and Jeff could mention it to his sister, who would tell Makima's brother and the damage would be done.

The hardheaded woman would just have to deal with what he'd told her—that the will permitted no sale.

The next morning Gabe was beating eggs for an omelet while Drew made toast when there was a knock at the back door.

A gray-haired man wearing a sweater stuck his head in the door. "Can I come in?"

Gabe said, "You're just in time for breakfast. I'm Gabe Bell and this is my brother, Drew."

"Sam Williams is my name and I'm your neighbor directly across the street." They shook hands and Sam pulled out a chair at the table and made himself comfortable. "That omelet looks good but I'll have to pass it up. I'll join you for some coffee and toast. Zeke and I had coffee together most mornings, you know."

Sam had sharp eyes and a round face that sported a short gray beard, which Gabe noted was neatly trimmed. He appeared to be in his late seventies.

Gabe served the omelet, poured coffee for Sam and himself and milk for Drew. "How about some fruit to go with your toast, Mr. Williams?"

"Call me Sam. No fruit. I have it later in the day or it upsets my stomach." His eyes twinkled. "Digestive system isn't what it used to be."

He tasted his coffee. "You make a good cup of coffee, Gabe, I'm glad to say. Can't stand it weak. Heard the two of you caused quite a stir at church yesterday. Sorry I wasn't there to meet you but this is better. Always good to meet people across a table, you know." He twinkled at Drew. "You remember that, young Drew. Now, how old are you?"

"I'll be sixteen in a few months, Mr. Williams." Listening to this interesting neighbor, Drew had slowed his usual eating pace.

"Growing so fast you're going to be right up there with your brother in a few years. Bet you can't buy the groceries fast enough," he told Gabe.

His good humor made even Drew laugh, especially since he was pouring himself another tall glass of milk. "I'm thinking of putting him out to work to earn his keep," Gabe said just to see what Drew's reaction would be.

"Zeke was a smart man, you know," Sam said. "He grew most of the food him and Sarah ate. Had a garden every year and began one this year. Guess you've seen it. When we're through here I'll show it to you, young Drew, and tell you what you need to do to keep it going so you can put some food on this table."

The idea seemed to appeal to Drew. "Okay," he said.

I like this neighbor, Gabe thought, and waited to see what Sam would put him through. He took a bite of omelet and sipped his coffee.

Sam started in a roundabout way while enjoying his breakfast. "Zeke and I were alike in not having the pleasure of seeing our kids grown and having kids of their own. His daughter, Elizabeth, only lived a few months. Robert died at twenty when a horse threw him while Edward went up to New York and disappeared. It wasn't until years later that Zeke found out he'd died of tuberculosis and left two sons."

Gabe forgot to eat, immersed in this picture of his father's family of which he'd known nothing all these years.

"Since you and Drew are Bells, I take it that Edward Bell was your grandfather?"

"Apparently, but we never knew about him," Gabe said.

"Your father's name was?"

"Booker," Gabe and Drew said in unison.

An expression of satisfaction was clear on Sam's face and as Gabe poured more hot coffee, he warned himself to be vigilant because Sam appeared to be an expert at drawing information out of you. Therefore Gabe would offer only what he didn't mind everyone knowing about the conditions of the will. He'd no idea what Great-Grandfather might have confided to Sam. He only knew what he wasn't going to confide.

"Drew, I think I'd like another piece of toast to go with this good coffee," Sam said. Drew got up to replenish the toast supply and Sam asked Gabe, "You'd be about thirty-five or so?"

"You hit it on the head exactly."

"Single?"

"So far."

"Your parents?"

"Both deceased."

"I'm sorry to hear that, Gabe and Drew. I thought maybe they were since they weren't down here with you."

The sincerity in his voice was unmistakable and Gabe found no false note in it.

Drew put a plate of hot toast on the table and a jar of strawberry preserves. When everyone had eaten some, Gabe decided he would offer some facts.

"We were born and raised in Manhattan. The only relatives on our dad's side that we knew about was his brother, Jacob. Uncle Jake never married and had no children as far as we knew. Our mother, Virginia Riley, came from a large family and those were the aunts, uncles, cousins and grandparents we knew."

"What did Booker say when you asked about family on his side?"

"He'd say he didn't have any, or that he didn't want to talk about it, so early on we learned to leave that subject alone."

"Your uncle Jake never told you anything?"

"Nothing. We didn't see him on any regular basis. He'd breeze into town for a few days and we'd never know when he'd be back."

"Is he still living?"

"He died a year after Dad."

"I probably knew your great-grandfather as well as anyone in Grayson and better than most," Sam said thoughtfully. "For years we sat at this table together, especially after we were both widowed. He never said a word about what was to happen to this property. The one time I mentioned it he said it was taken care of. I expected that and never talked about it again."

He was silent and so were Gabe and Drew.

"He hadn't been ill, you know," he resumed. "He just died one day. The next thing I knew, there was a rumor flying around town that an heir from New York had been found. So naturally I was very concerned to meet that heir and see what he was like, you see." He raised an eyebrow, his sharp glance on Gabe.

"I understand. You wanted to see if the heir was worthy of your friend." Gabe looked at his inquisitor calmly. The two men measured each other and came to an agreeable conclusion.

"My great-grandfather apparently decided to make a search for Edward's son," Gabe said. "It must have been quite difficult because it was only a few weeks ago that Drew and I knew anything about this. We had a visit from an attorney who had worked for Great-Grandfather for some years. He established who he was and who we were. Then he read us the will. To say we were astonished doesn't begin to describe our feelings." He glanced at Drew.

"Blown away is what we were!" Drew said.

"It was very hard to believe. In New York inheritance scams are played on people every day, so it took some time to come to the conclusion that what the attorney told us was legitimate. I can't tell you all the details, but we are the heirs and we'll be here for a while as things work themselves out."

Sam was nodding his head. "Your great-grandfather was deep, so I'm not surprised that he worked it out that way. You know, he was quite a scholar in his own way, particularly about Africa. Read books about it all of the time and when something would come on television about that place, he'd tell me to come over and we'd watch it together."

"I have noticed a number of books about Africa in his office."

"Those are just the ones he kept. He used his library card for a lot of others." He drained his coffee cup. "Well, I guess I've taken up enough of your time for now. I'm real glad the two of you are here. Feel free to come over any time. It's the white house with the green shutters."

"What a character," Drew said, cleaning off the table as Gabe cleaned up the pans. "I like him."

"So do I, and I respect him. He's no dummy."

"He sure told us a lot about Pop's family. Seems like every day we find out a little more. Don't you think that's crazy?"

"In a way, but on the other hand, we're living where Pop's family began, so even though it was a long time ago, people here know bits and pieces that we couldn't hear about living in New York."

"He forgot to show me the garden," Drew remembered.

"I think he stayed longer than he'd planned but he won't forget. Watch for him tomorrow morning. What had you planned to do in the time before Jeff gets here?"

"Hadn't planned anything special. Why?"

"Do a little treasure hunt and see if anything at all looks unusual or that might be a clue for us."

"Okay."

"One other thing, Drew. Did you get the idea that Sam Williams wanted to know everything that was in the will?"

"Yeah. He was, like, champing at the bit but you didn't tell him."

"You and I both have to repeat to others what I told him because a lot of people are as curious as Sam is. Just say we can't talk about the details of the will and we'll be here for a while. The topic might come up when Jeff gets here because it's a natural question. Okay?"

"Sure, I can handle that."

Gabe was anxious to explore his great-grandfather's office. If there was something significant about the treasured destiny to be discovered, shouldn't it be in the place where he did most of his work and study?

He stood in the doorway, noting how it had been set up. A dark brown desk with three drawers on each side was on the wall to his right, flanked by a floor lamp and a two-drawer beige file. The rest of the wall was a closet.

Opposite the doorway where he stood was an eight-shelf bookcase. On one wall beside it was a large map of Africa while the map on the other side showed details of West Africa. A comfortable chair with a table lamp stood beside it. A curio cabinet, other maps of the world and several chairs completed the furnishings.

He created his own little library, Gabe observed, and probably spent most of his time here as he grew older. It was well lit, comfortable and warm. He could see himself spending evenings here dipping into the books.

He began his search at the desk. The drawers were filled with bills going back twenty years. Apparently, Great-Grandfather didn't believe in credit cards. All the receipts showed payment in cash. This even went for large items like the pickup truck Gabe had seen in the garage.

The house was paid for. The property tax statements represented the largest outgo of money. Gabe read the figure for the assessment of the property and whistled softly. He laid the paper down, stunned.

He couldn't fathom being the potential owner of such valuable property. It was like winning the lottery. He'd never thought of having a lot of money. The most he'd desired was enough for him and Drew to get by on comfortably.

Still a little dazed, he looked through the other drawers but discovered nothing out of the ordinary. The stacks of bank statements would have to wait for another time, when his head was clearer.

He stood before the map of Africa and studied it. The attorney, Mr. Moultrie, had told him that this destiny business had its origins with some African slaves, so Gabe could understand why Great-Grandfather had an interest in the continent. But it was so huge. Had one country been singled out?

He moved to the other map, which showed only the west coast of Africa and its countries. Most of the slave trade had embarked from the west coast, if he remembered his history. Maybe the ad been marked for easy identification as to the area the came from.

Gabe picked up the magnifying glass from the desk and looked closely but could see no mark of any kind.

He went around the walls, looking at the other maps and prints. He also looked behind them to satisfy himself that they contained no clues.

The bell rang downstairs and a minute later Drew yelled up, "Gabe, Jeff's here."

"I'm in the office. C'mon up."

Jeff didn't look anything like his sister, which was just as well, Gabe thought as he said hello. Jeff was broad across the shoulders and about five feet four inches. He had freckles and a broad nose.

"My mom reminded me to bring this book back since I was coming over here." He handed Gabe a hardcover volume.

"Whose is it?" Gabe wanted to know.

"Mr. Zeke's. He talked in our history class about Africa and said he had some books if anyone wanted to borrow one, so when I had to do a report I came and got that one."

"*Folktales of West Africa*," Gabe read aloud. "Is it a good book?"

"I liked what I read of it."

"What kind of grade did you get?" Drew asked.

"Ninety-one."

"Cool," Drew said. "Shows it was a good book for you. I didn't know our great-grandfather spoke in schools. Did he do it often?"

"Most every year for some grade. He was sort of an expert on Africa around here and he loved to talk about it."

Drew and Gabe exchanged a glance. One more piece of new information to add.

Later in the evening, Gabe went to sit on the bench in the field. *I learned some things about you today, Great-Grandfather,* he mused, *but there's more I need to know if I'm going to carry out your plans.*

What am I supposed to find and where are the clues you left in your house?

Chapter 7

Makima picked up the telephone on its first ring. "Makima Gray speaking."

"Good morning, Miss Gray."

She recognized the voice of the woman on the other end of the line. It was friendly but undergirded with the authority of a decision maker.

"This is Harriet Wetherell of Wetherell Associates. I hope you are well."

"I'm fine, Ms. Wetherell, and you?"

"Couldn't be better." With the social amenities out of the way, Harriet got down to business. "Did you receive the packet of material we sent you last week?"

"Yes, thank you. It was very informative."

"As I mentioned before when we talked, our company has a good reputation for living up to our motto, We Build For You. Whatever you have in mind we will provide in the highest quality and for a competitive price. I hope you read the comments from some of our clients. We urge you to talk to them and hear for yourself what they say about the structures we built for them."

"I know the little art gallery in Columbia you built. I've been there and admired the way the space was handled to give the maximum advantage for the artwork," Makima said. "Of course a medical clinic is totally different from an art gallery."

"Not really," Ms. Wetherell said thoughtfully. "Their functions aren't the same but each one has to be built to last, to be environmentally friendly, comfortable to inhabit, pleasing to the eye and highly specific for its activity."

"Those are all good points," Makima agreed. "I hadn't thought of it in that way."

"The last time you were here, you still hadn't made a decision about the exact location of your clinic, Miss Gray. May I ask how that's coming along?"

"Slowly, Ms. Wetherell. An obstacle has come up which may take some time to deal with." Makima had to work at keeping her voice pleasant and noncommittal as she thought of Gabriel Bell.

"I'm sorry to hear that, but these things happen in the real estate and construction business. I'll keep in touch, and meanwhile, if there's any matter we can help you with, please don't hesitate to call."

Wetherell Associates had been recommended to Makima and the board by a business in Rock Hill, South Carolina. "What they say they'll do, they do and on time. Not like most of these folk who work for you three days one week and don't come back until days later. You can't fire them because they have your money, but you only have a part of your construction."

That was a good recommendation, but the clinic group had to be thorough when there was so much of their precious money at stake. Was this corporation totally honest? Had there been any problem after the building had been standing a few years? How did they handle weather delays? How many crews did they have working at one time and were they all equally qualified?

Makima admired Harriet. She was CEO of the corporation and seemed to be straightforward and direct. Had always been courteous with the clinic group, but naturally she wanted to sign them to a contract. Makima could appreciate that, but no contract would be signed as far as Makima was concerned until all those questions had been answered to her satisfaction. And until she had figured out a way to negotiate a sale of property with Gabriel Bell.

He might think she'd given up. All that had happened was the first skirmish in the battle.

She knew beyond a doubt that the clinic was supposed to be built on Mr. Zeke's land. She'd prayed about the matter for years with all of the faith and earnestness she could muster and had never received a negative sign from God. Therefore she was following His will. That being the case, how could she fail?

This was just a test of her faith. Important things never came easily. You had to work hard and sometimes use strategy. She'd pray about it and think of something.

It was too bad troublesome things kept happening between them. First the catastrophe in the restaurant, which she might never live down, followed by the unexpected meeting at the church, and now his total refusal to consider Mr. Zeke's consent to sell her land for the clinic. He hadn't even taken the time to discuss it at length with her. A curt statement about the will not permitting it and that was all.

He was so attractive and she wished they could be friendly but obviously that wasn't going to be in the picture!

Makima straightened the papers on her desk and turned off the lamp. She might be able to head a project like the clinic, but she didn't seem to have much success with men. Reggie had walked away and now the first man she'd found interesting since him seemed to be nothing but bad news.

"You ready, young Drew?" Sam called at the back door the next morning, as Gabe had predicted.

"Come in for coffee," Gabe said.

"Already had some, thanks."

Drew clattered down the steps to join his garden instructor. Gabe watched them for a moment with a bemused expression. Who'd ever have thought Drew would be interested in gardening? As he went up to continue work in the office, it occurred to him that by living all his life in a Manhattan apartment the opportunity for gardening had never come up for Drew. What else might happen for the two of them in this new environment?

As he sifted through the bank statements, Makima came to mind as part of this new environment.

But she wasn't new. He'd met her kind before. Extremely attractive, intelligent, personable with people. The kind of skin you longed to touch. Hair you wanted to run your fingers through. Lips that were very kissable. And curves. Long legs. Beautiful shoes. And curves.

He had the feeling she could be snobbish at times if she found herself in circumstances where she was uncomfortable. Use it as a defense mechanism. She had the presence and the style to carry it off.

He knew the type well. In fact, he had been seriously involved with one called Olivia several years back. They'd dated for a year or so and he'd never been so in love. He'd been saving to get her a ring before popping the question. Then by pure accident he discovered that she'd been seeing a guy who lived in New Jersey, which explained why she'd been unavailable to go out with him sometimes, especially on weekends. He'd felt like a fool and a dupe and had promised himself to never get in such a situation again.

The few dates he'd had after that were casual and harmless. His social life had been curtailed anyway after his parents died. Leaving Drew alone in the apartment while he partied wasn't an option.

His boys would come over and sometimes bring girls along and that was it. This year Drew had complained that he didn't need Gabe babysitting him. He was going on sixteen and big enough to take care of himself. Gabe was touched, and just to stop Drew's bellyaching he went out a couple of Saturdays with Webster and Calvin.

Drew was always anxious to know the next day all about his evening out. Gabe obliged with an account of where they went and what music they heard. It had been a welcome change, but Gabe discovered that this was not how he wanted to spend his evenings. There'd been a time when he did but that time had passed.

He wondered if there were any clubs here in Grayson. What did Alana and her crowd do for entertainment other than go to the movies? As for Makima, she might not go out at all just for entertainment.

Getting the clinic up and working probably took all her time. Something like that could make you obsessive and she seemed the type. Immediately he had the image of her trying to get the salad off his jacket even when it was clear that the mayonnaise had already soaked into the fabric. He'd been so angry then but now when he thought of it, he was amused. One thing about the incident, she'd made an indelible impression on him. And on his jacket.

He was still smiling when the phone ran. It was the attorney, Jasper Moultrie.

"How are you and Drew settling in?" he asked.

Gabe filled him in on the trip, the church experience and Sam Williams.

"We've been learning about Great-Grandfather. Did you

know he's looked upon as an expert on Africa and even spoke to schools on the subject?"

"I believe he did mention that at one time," Moultrie said. "He never lost interest in the subject."

"You've seen this house, Mr. Moultrie?"

"Yes, I have."

"We were overwhelmed. Had no idea it was this grand. You know it's mostly his own work." Gabe heard the pride in his own voice and was surprised.

"Your great-grandfather was a man of many parts as they used to say of outstanding men."

"I see that. I've been going through his papers. Found his property tax assessment and my heart nearly stopped."

"I hope it gave you some motivation to observe the dictates of the will," Moultrie said calmly.

"Don't worry. I'm observing them. I've already searched his bedroom and now I'm working through his office. By the way, Mr. Moultrie, what did my great-grandfather look like? I haven't found any photographs of him yet."

"I'll do my best to describe him as I saw him. He stood about five-eight, had a powerful body and strong features. Deep-set eyes, broad nose and mouth. Wore his hair thick. Had a fine forehead. He was dark-skinned. Does that give you a picture?"

"Yes, it does."

"One more thing, he had a presence about him. He wasn't a loud-speaking man but he had your attention when he spoke."

"That I can imagine. I'm curious about another thing. Did you come to the funeral?"

"Yes, as quietly as possible. Someone had to lock up the house and see that all was in order."

"I wondered about that and how the rumor was started about an heir from New York. That was your doing?" Gabe asked. He didn't see how it could have been anyone else.

"I did it because the community had to have some idea about what was going to happen. I hoped it would prevent the kind of idle curiosity that occurs when houses are left unoccupied too long. You found everything was all right?"

"Yes. I expect Sam Williams across the street was watching it anyway."

"No doubt. Good man, Sam. Call me if you have any questions, Mr. Bell, and my regards to Drew."

Gabe went back to work with the image of his great-grandfather in his mind. He wished he had a photograph. It was strange that there weren't any in the house, but maybe they'd been put away in one of the numerous dressers. He'd keep an eye out for them. Meanwhile he was through with the desk so he started on the books.

They were organized by subject matter and since it was clear from the first glimpse that Africa was the predominant theme, he paid close attention to those books. Most of them showed signs of heavy usage but Gabe could find no clue in them. He did make a mental note that there were several on the small nation called the Gambia.

Downstairs he made tuna sandwiches with lettuce and tomato for lunch. He had to start getting more vegetables on Drew's plate any way he could.

"In a week or two I'm going with Mr. Williams to get stuff to put in the garden. He says we have to wait because it's too early now. You can't plant just any time," he proclaimed.

"That's good to know," Gabe replied. "What will you be planting?"

"Don't know yet. Some are already started in little pots and you have to look them over for the healthiest ones." He took another sandwich. "This is good. I never thought of putting tomato with tuna."

"Now that we're going to have our own vegetables we can experiment with our cooking instead of eating the same old things day after day." Gabe was serious but he was also giving Drew a new idea.

"Yeah, and you know what? The first time something comes up in the garden we can invite Mr. Williams over for dinner," he said with enthusiasm as he swallowed a large bite.

"Good idea," Gabe agreed. "By the way, Mr. Moultrie called to see how we're getting along."

"Did you tell him we haven't found anything yet?"

"He didn't even ask. He knows we just got here Saturday. I asked him how Great-Grandfather looked because I hadn't seen any pictures around here. Have you?"

"No. I was going to tell you the same thing because it's weird not to have a single picture of your family." Drew looked puzzled. "Don't you think so?"

"I guess they're all packed away."

"What'd he say Great-Grandfather looked like?"

Gabe repeated the description faithfully.

Drew listened, not eating. "Wish I could have seen him," he said.

"Me, too," Gabe echoed.

After lunch Gabe had great hopes of finding a clue when he returned to the office and opened the two-drawer file that stood beside the desk. What he found was that his great-grandfather had been a clipper. Folders labeled with many subjects were filled with clippings from newspapers and magazines.

He literally groaned. How in the world could he read all that stuff? But if he neglected to, would he be missing what he was supposed to discover? No wonder he was to be here three months.

He flipped through the folders: world history, U.S. history, black history, philosophy, religion, travel, South Carolina, North Carolina, weather, the environment, health, gardening, mechanics, carpentry, people in the news, the arts, food, and education.

Hadn't Moultrie said this man had to teach himself to read? Obviously he'd carried the love of it all through his life.

When he, Gabe, died, what would he leave behind that people could go through and be impressed by? If only Moultrie could have brought him here while Great-Grandfather was still in this house so he could have absorbed some of the richness of his life!

There were also folders containing the plans for this house. Some of them had been drawn by an architect and others by Ezekiel Bell Jr. To Gabe's untrained eye they looked equally professional.

He found statements and receipts for all of the lumber, the wiring, the nails and the hardware, everything that went into the building of the house. It was as if it had all been meticulously collected and saved for an accounting.

He scanned the folders again and made the decision that they would have to wait. If after he'd gone through the whole house and hadn't found the clues, then he'd come back and read every item in every folder.

He sighed with relief as he closed the folder drawer. He was halfway down the stairs when the phone rang. He hurried back to the office and picked it up with a breathless "Hello."

"Hello, Gabe, this is Makima. Were you running? You sound out of breath."

Gabe collapsed in a chair. "I was halfway downstairs and had to come back up. I guess Great-Grandfather never got around to cordless phones." Now, *this* call was a surprise. What did Miss Gray want this time? He noticed she'd called him Gabe instead of that haughty Mr. Bell she'd used before she stomped out the door yesterday.

"I want to apologize for the way I left your house. I lost my temper and said the wrong things to you. I'm sorry."

In his surprise Gabe didn't respond immediately, which seemed to make her hurry on.

"I was just so disappointed and I let that emotion take over. I hope you can forgive me," she said.

"It's all right, Makima. We all lose our tempers sometimes." Her apology sounded sincere and he was glad.

"How are the two of you settling in?"

"Pretty well."

"Have you met Sam Williams yet?"

"He came over and had breakfast with us. He's a very interesting man."

"He and Mr. Zeke were good buddies."

"So I understand. He didn't want the garden to die and today he showed Drew how to care for it and Drew seems to be interested."

She laughed. "That sounds just like him. It was good talking with you, Gabe, and I hope to see you around."

"Thanks for the call, Makima. I appreciate it."

She'd been wrong and had seen it after she'd calmed down. Not everyone, however, would have called to apologize. Especially a pretty woman. So he truly did appreciate it.

It was a big plus mark for her.

Even so, he wasn't going to let himself be drawn in by her good points or her physical attractiveness.

Been there, done that, and had been badly hurt.

Drew was his family now and that was all he needed.

Chapter 8

The sky was overcast and March winds had started to blow. Makima was glad she'd worn a pair of warm black pants and a long-sleeved red sweater.

"I'm going out for lunch, be back about one," she told Eugenia Palmer, the program director, who sat at the receptionist desk when Makima wasn't available.

"Have fun," Eugenia said as she opened her lunch bag. Her sprouts on low-carb bread, plus an apple and a thermos of green tea were guaranteed to bring down her weight if she persevered and she was determined to make it work.

Fun wasn't exactly what Makima anticipated, but she did enjoy her weekly lunch hour at her parents' home as long as she could avoid certain subjects.

Today, only her mother greeted her. "Dad's not going to be with us?" Makima was disappointed as it had been two weeks since she'd seen him.

"He had to go to Swinton to see someone. Said to tell you he's sorry to miss you."

Odessa Lines had been raised in the genteel home of a prominent minister. When the neighbor boy, Arthur Gray, had begun courting her, Reverend Lines had refused consent until Arthur had a steady job. Arthur and Odessa had both become teachers, but when Makima arrived, Odessa stayed home to raise her children. Arthur went into administration, rising steadily until he became principal of the high school.

Odessa closed the door behind Makima. "You warm enough, honey? It's turned chilly so I made your favorite—vegetable-beef soup."

Makima followed her mother into the spacious kitchen where the table was set for two.

"No wonder it smells so good in here," Makima said appreciatively.

Her mother set two steaming bowls of soup on the table where there were already thick chunks of crusty bread and butter.

"This is delicious, Mom," Makima said after the first taste. The broth was rich, the beef tender, the vegetables crisp. "I always tell you this soup could make you a lot of money if you sold it."

"I only cook for my family and my friends."

"Yes, I know, but this soup is special." A gleam came into Makima's eyes. "We could do a fund-raiser just with this soup."

Ignoring the expression of coolness in her mother's eyes, she plunged on. "We could sell it to stores and restaurants for church suppers and to homes. We haven't done that kind of event before. What do you think of that?"

"Who would do all the work, making that much soup?"

"You'd have to supervise the cooking because it's your creation, but we could get however many women you need in here to help."

"How would you collect the orders for it?"

"Assign our best salespeople to go around to stores and restaurants, put ads in the paper, send out flyers, make phone calls. The way we do most fund-raisers. The difference here would be selling to restaurants and some other businesses we selected."

"There're no preservatives in my soup, Makima."

"I know. That would be a great selling point. Having the sale on a Friday and Saturday would be the best time."

"What would you put it in?"

"We'd buy cases of sixteen- and thirty-two-ounce cartons."

"How much would you sell it for?"

"Don't know. We'd have to work out the cost of the ingredients, the cartons and any other expenses, then see what we could charge to make the effort worthwhile." She helped herself to more soup from the pot on the stove. "Ready for seconds?" she asked her mother, who shook her head no.

Makima continued with her description of what she was already thinking of as the Souperior Soup Sale.

"We'd have to do it while the weather is still cool. I know the quilting ladies would be glad to come and prepare the vegetables. If it's on the weekend we could borrow some large pots from the cafeteria or the churches. I'll have to think of who would be best to approach the businesses."

She stopped, realizing that she was speaking to silence. There was no response from her mother, who sat looking out the window. Makima felt her heart sink.

Her mother sighed. Her normally pleasant face was sad. "Everything with you now is the clinic. We can't even have a little lunch together and talk about ordinary things. It's always the clinic. It's taken over your life, Makima."

Makima laid her spoon on her plate and willed the tears from coming to her eyes.

"Do you ever think of anything else?" It was the tenderness

in her mother's expression that brought the tears despite Makima's best effort.

She reached across the table to touch her mother's hand. "Mom, I have to do this. I guess I can't think about much else until it's done. I know you don't see it that way and I'm sorry."

Her mother's hand clasped hers. "I know it's important. It was my baby that got killed. But can't other people take it over? Why must it be you carrying the load? Jim and Betty Forbes's two kids were hurt. Let them do some of the work."

"Jim is on the board, as you know and he does work hard. Most of the board members work hard, but to be honest, no one seems to care as much about it as I do."

"Have you ever thought that maybe they do, but because you take on the major load, they sit back and let you do it?" her mother said gently.

"I have sat back on some issues and waited for others to step forward," Makima said defensively.

"What happened, honey?"

"Nothing. Or people who said they'd take care of it, then dropped the ball or were late or it wasn't done right."

"I see."

They sat wordlessly, each looking out the window at the back patio where in warmer weather the luncheon would have taken place.

Her mother broke the silence. "I'm just a mother who wants to see her lovely thirty-two-year-old daughter have a life. I want to say just one more thing then we'll talk about something else."

Makima braced herself for what she knew was coming.

"I've always felt that you and Reggie would have been married by now. It was clear that he was in love with you, but after you became so involved with the clinic, I think you pushed him out of your life. I pray that won't happen again, honey. You deserve a loving husband and children." She patted her daughter's hand. "Now, what about some dessert?"

Makima didn't think she could swallow a bite, but she wasn't going to refuse her mother's peace offering.

"I'm ready for whatever you have."

The hot tea her mother served along with an apple turnover soothed Makima's throat and helped the light pastry go down.

"Tell me about church," her mother said. "If I'd known Mr. Zeke's heir was to be there I'd have let your dad go to Columbia by himself."

Makima described meeting the Bells, the warm welcome the minister had given them and how she'd introduced them around after the service.

"Alana told me the oldest brother is quite handsome and she was disappointed she couldn't get him to go to the movies with them."

"The young brother, Drew, went and I thought that was nice. He's almost the same age as Jeff, so he's already met a friend."

"Selina called me, she said he was very courteous."

"Drew?"

"No, the oldest one. What's his name?"

"Gabriel, but he said he goes by Gabe. He's anxious to visit Miss Selina because she was such good friends with Miss Sarah."

"Are they going to stay?"

"I've no idea." She looked at the clock. "Thanks for lunch, Mom. I have to go. Eugenia's sitting in for me."

At the door they hugged each other, a quiet gesture of deep familial love even where understanding was lacking.

Makima drove slowly to get her emotions under control before returning to work. This was the second time Mom had done this and it had cut Makima to the bone each time.

It was beyond her comprehension that her family couldn't give the dedication to the clinic that was required if it was to become a reality. This was a huge undertaking, so large that sometimes it scared her. When it did, she thought of June and she prayed, then asked for guidance as to what the next step should be.

In her darkest hours she thought that maybe her mom and dad lacked the degree of faith that she had. It was wrong to judge anyone else, but why couldn't they see that only faith could carry them through. After all, they were the ones who'd instilled in her and her siblings the value of religion in their lives, as well as a work ethic and a solid education. When her mother showed a failure to understand the motives that drove her to make the clinic a reality, Makima couldn't fight the despondency that came over her. It always took her several days to rise above it and to regain the conviction that what she was doing was right. No matter what others thought.

It took Gabe several hours to go through the books in the office. He was looking not only for slips of paper but the internal evidence from the books themselves.

The books on Africa were especially time-consuming as there were notes in the margins and cross-references his great-grandfather had made in his spiky script. Gabe scanned a number of these. If he stayed here and studied just these books, he'd know a lot more about Africa than he'd ever dreamt.

He could see himself spending evenings up here but that wasn't his mission. Somewhere in this house was his treasured destiny, and he had to find it. He put the last volume back on the shelf and glanced around to see what had yet to be searched. The closet and the curio cabinet.

The closet held odds and ends of clothing, hats on the shelf and several pairs of house shoes on the floor. All were innocent of clues.

The curio cabinet was a handsome piece of walnut furniture

that held six shallow drawers. The contents revealed another surprising aspect of his great-grandfather's character. The drawers were filled with seashells arranged from small to large. The patience it must have taken for such a task was hard to conceive. Gabe recalled seeing a book about seashells during his search.

The bottom drawer was deeper than the others. In it were the largest of the shells. Gabe's eye was immediately caught by a perfectly shaped ivory conch shell. He picked it up carefully. The back of his neck tingled.

There in its spiral was a piece of paper, tightly rolled to make it fit.

With great care he extracted it, put the shell back and closed the drawer.

His heart was beating fast.

He knew without a doubt that he held in his hand a clue his great-grandfather had placed there for him to find!

Chapter 9

Gabe took the piece of paper to the desk. He sat down and slowly unrolled it.

Great-Grandfather had made or had someone else make a scroll on parchment-like paper. It was the same length as an eight-and-a-half-by-eleven sheet of paper but half its width.

It was decorated around its borders by evenly spaced scrolls in black ink. In the center of the page were what appeared to be sentences because of their regular pattern.

Gabe couldn't understand a word of it. It might as well have been in Greek. In fact, he wished it had been because some of those words he would have recognized.

There were symbols at the top of the page, which he assumed to be the title, but the alphabet being used to relate the story was indecipherable.

He sat and looked at it a long time, trying to get some answers about it. One thing he did decide was that it had been written by

Great-Grandfather because although the characters were printed, there was enough of the spikiness to identify the writer.

He went to the window in the next room. Drew was looking at the garden, a hoe in his hand.

Gabe opened the window. "Drew, I found something."

Drew dropped the hoe. He had a huge grin on his face when he came into the office.

"Lemme see." He put out his hand.

Gabe gave the scroll to him and watched the grin turn to puzzlement.

"You can read this, right?" Drew asked hopefully.

"Wish I could, bro."

Drew plopped down in a chair. He turned the scroll upside down and then sideways. "It looks like a story," he finally said.

"I think so, too."

"Then why isn't it in English so you can read it? Maybe it's something else, a puzzle, or just a piece of paper Great-Grandfather picked up that he liked."

"I don't think it's an insignificant piece of paper," Gabe said thoughtfully.

"How do you know this is a real clue, Gabe? There wasn't an arrow pointing to it, was there?"

Gabe knew Drew wanted to be convinced this was valid, but all he could give him was his intuition.

"No arrow. I was looking in the drawers of that curio cabinet over there. It holds a collection of seashells and in the bottom drawer there's a conch shell. I knew when I saw it that it was special. I picked it up and the back of my neck tingled."

Drew gave him a wry glance and Gabe felt a little sheepish.

"I know, but I'm just telling you how I felt. I looked inside the spiral and found the scroll."

"Okay. I wish your neck would tingle again and let you know

what it says. What good is it if you can't read it?" He threw the scroll on the desk in frustration.

"Let's take it to the library in Swinton. Maybe we'll find some answers there," Gabe suggested.

When he got into the Lexus, Gabe checked the odometer. He wanted to see what the mileage into Swinton was. On the way he told Drew about the accident that had killed Makima Gray's youngest sister and how the freight train had delayed them from getting to the hospital in time to save her life. That was why they were trying to build a clinic in Grayson. It was seven miles to the railroad tracks, and another three put them in downtown Swinton. The library, according to the phone book, was on Liberty Street.

"Why don't we ask where Liberty Street is?" Drew said.

"It's more fun to drive up and down the streets until we find it. That's the way you learn a town and this one isn't very large. Isn't that where you went to the show?" He pointed to a building with a marquee advertising a movie.

"Yeah. I wonder if there's another one here."

"I doubt it. There're probably two or three different banks, but the population may not be large enough to support two movie houses. Down that street is the hospital. Let's swing by there."

The hospital consisted of two large buildings set in well-kept grounds, and three blocks down from it was the library.

The brick building was shaded by trees and had a large parking lot. The inside showed signs of recent renovations and Gabe felt hopeful that the staff here would be able to help him.

At the reference desk two people were taking care of the clients. When it was Gabe's turn, the lady with a little gray in her hair looked up. "May I help you?"

"I hope so." He handed her the scroll. "I have no idea what language this is and wondered if you could tell me."

"Well, now, this is certainly interesting," she said after giving it a thorough look. "I haven't seen anything like it. Helen, take a look at this."

After the two women conferred, the first one said, "Why don't you have a seat or look around while I work on this."

She disappeared into the reference stacks. Drew wandered away while Gabe sat on the bench and glanced around. There were work cubicles at the end of the room, most of which were occupied. He read a sign announcing The South Carolina Collection, for reference only. Young students were at the four computer stations, book bags on the floor beside them.

The librarian reappeared and he went back to the counter.

"I'm sorry to say that I could find nothing in our resources that would identify this language." She glanced again at the scroll. "Are you certain it is a genuine language, not one made up for a game?"

"It is a language," Gabe said and hoped he was right. He felt he was right.

"Then I would hazard a guess that it is in some African language," she said. "I wish I could be of more service to you. If you do identify it, I'd be pleased if you'd let me know."

He assured her he would and, finding Drew, went out to the car.

"What'd she say?" Drew asked.

"We're one step ahead," Gabe said, and on the way home related the entire conversation.

"As much as Great-Grandfather read about Africa, it makes sense, I guess. What's next?"

"Since she thought it was some African language, I'm going back over Great-Grandfather's collection and see if it tells me anything at all."

"What can I do?"

"All this brainpower I'm using keeps me in need of a nutritious meal," Gabe said with a sideways glance. "That give you an idea?"

"Yeah, gives me an idea of all the sneaky ways you try to get me to cook."

"You ever watch those guys on television that cook? Some of them even got me interested. Also there're some cookbooks in the kitchen but I guess you've seen them. If you need anything from the store just let me know."

The meal Drew called Gabe to several hours later was a surprise. Gabe had thought they'd have steak and potatoes, but instead Drew had put together a meat loaf. The mashed potatoes with a hint of garlic were different from the usual baked ones. There was even a mixed green salad. Drew shrugged off Gabe's compliments but said the next time they went to the store to get some stew meat and fish.

Gabe spent hours trying to find a clue to the scroll but nothing came to light. When he gave up the search at eleven and turned out the office lamp, he was too wired up to sleep.

He went out to the bench in the field. He felt comfortable in his heavy sweater as he listened to the small night sounds around him. He felt he was doing the same thing Great-Grandfather had done. Here he could feel close to this man who had gone to some extent to devise clues for Gabe.

I guess I have to prove my worth to be the recipient of this treasured destiny, whatever it is. Right, Great-Grandfather? I have to try to follow your subtle mind, be patient, and figure out the meaning of the clues as I find them.

I'm willing to try my best. I just hope I won't let you down.

His thoughts stopped whirring around. Calmness and contentment filled him and he left the field and went up to a night of dreamless sleep.

The next few days went by with Gabe going through other rooms and finding nothing of consequence. Occasionally he and Drew would go for a ride around Grayson.

In the back of his mind he noted some empty lots where Makima could put the clinic. The Grayson community was larger than he'd supposed. There was the central portion where the businesses were and the majority of the residences, but all around the outskirts he saw small farms and isolated houses.

He made it his business to be downtown in Grayson on Saturday to see if there would be a noticeable increase from the outlying people coming in to shop. There were, on the streets he saw, expanded numbers of people visiting and shopping. It gave the community a festive air.

The other characteristic he noticed in his wanderings was the number of churches everywhere, even on the country roads. They weren't large but there was a diversity, enough to suit every taste.

To give Makima credit, there didn't seem to be many available spaces of the size a clinic would require and they weren't in the central area of Grayson.

He didn't know what she and her group would do about it but he wished them well.

Sunday he decided to go to church and this time listen to the sermon. Drew saw Jeff and went to sit with him. Gabe sat at the end of the pew on the right side instead of in the central section.

Makima hadn't been one of the greeters this morning and he wondered if she was coming.

Maybe she was already here. He searched each row, and down in the front on his side he saw her in the third row.

Today she was wearing the turquoise jacket and earrings. She was talking to the woman beside her, who spoke with the man next to her. He bent forward to say something to Makima. He imagined they were her parents.

The choir marched in and the service began. There had been a disastrous fire in a nearby county during the week and the minister based his sermon on the need for compassion and an outpouring of help and service when such events happened. He noted what the media had reported of such giving and praised it.

"But that's not enough," he said. "It is in our daily lives that God commands us to be caring and sensitive to the needs of others. Sometimes the need isn't as obvious as hunger or pain, yet it's there. It may be that the person needs a good listener, a word of sincere encouragement, a prayer, someone to hold their hand."

That made sense to Gabe except for the prayer. He didn't know much about prayer personally.

He noticed that Makima and her parents seemed involved in the sermon. He glanced around to see how many other men were in the congregation. At least one-third, maybe more.

Not for the first time, he wondered why Pop had been so hostile to ministers. He'd always spoken of them with scorn and never stepped inside a church. According to his comments, they were all rogues and rascals. Ma disagreed with him, which had led to loud arguments once in a while.

"Go on to church if you want to. Just don't expect me to go," he'd explode.

"I'll go and pray for your soul," Ma would say, shaking her head sadly.

Gabe and Drew never went to Sunday school on a regular basis. Ma took them on Easter and Christmas. When Gabe got older he went with her on Mother's Day out of love and because it meant so much to her. She'd lived in Manhattan all of her married life. But she hadn't wanted to be buried there.

"Take me home to Virginia," she'd whispered to Gabe the day before she passed away. That was what her large family wanted, too, so the hearse took the body to a small town outside of Richmond.

The church hadn't even been as big as this one and there'd been standing room only on that sad day. Gabe's greatest concern had been for Drew and it had helped to have all his cousins around him.

Coming back to the quiet apartment had been heartrending

but people from the church Ma had attended did just what the minister preached about. They called on the phone, came to visit, invited them over and brought so much food Gabe hadn't had to cook for weeks.

Pop hadn't wanted to be buried at all. "Put me in the furnace and throw the ashes away," he'd said. But Ma refused to do anything that heathen, she'd said. She'd arranged a funeral at her church and was pleased at the number of his friends who attended.

Maybe on the trip back to New York when the three months were up, he and Drew would stop in Virginia and see all of Ma's folks. It was important for Drew to keep in touch with family.

An organ chord brought him out of his reverie and in another ten minutes the service was over. He walked outside and spoke with several people while he waited for Drew.

"Gabe, how are you this morning?" Makima appeared beside him. "I'd like you to meet my mother and father."

As they exchanged greetings, Gabe could see reflections of each in Makima.

It was from her mother that she got that dignity and pride that came to the surface at times and made her act snobbish. She hadn't yet acquired the life experience of cultivating the unaffected delight her mother displayed when she met someone she liked.

"I'm so glad to finally meet you, Mr. Bell," she said as she shook his hand. "My friend Selina has been telling me about you. Are you finding your way around all right?"

"I'm happy to meet you, too, Mrs. Gray, and please call me Gabe. Drew and I are beginning to feel very comfortable here."

"We're all going to have a bite to eat as we usually do after church, and you and your brother must come with us. Please say you will. It'll give us a chance to get acquainted. You didn't drive to church, did you?"

"No, we walked."

"That's good because you and your brother can ride with us and we'll meet the others at the restaurant. Isn't that a good idea, Arthur?" She beamed at her husband, who nodded.

Gabe saw Makima's glance just sliding away from him. If he consented, would she excuse herself?

"Hope you can come, Gabe, I'd like a chance to talk with you," Mr. Gray said.

"It sounds very nice and thanks." Gabe beckoned Drew over and introduced him.

"I'll round up the others and we'll see you at Rockwell's," Makima said.

Mr. Gray was tall and almost portly. He had a genial manner, direct gaze, firm mouth, and what he'd passed on to Makima was determination. He'd been a principal, according to Makima. Not surprising then to see the authority he still carried with him.

As he followed the Grays to their car, Gabe wondered if the insight into Makima's background that he got from meeting her parents would turn out to be good or bad.

Chapter 10

Rockwell's was on the corner of Wisteria and Sixth Streets in Grayson. It was decorated in tones of peach and yellow that shouldn't have worked yet it did. Pastoral prints were on the walls and the table linen carried out the soft color scheme. A slender vase with a yellow flower graced each table.

"This place just opened last year," Mrs. Gray confided. "The Rockwells had a restaurant in Maine but they got tired of the cold weather. They used to visit down here and decided to make the break for the sun. We're so thankful they did."

Alana breezed in, followed by Makima and Jeff. She wore a tailored black suit with a short skirt and a pink-and-white oxford shirt fastened at the neck with a pink bow tie. Dangling pink earrings and black heels with straps made her look anything but masculine.

"Gabe, hi. I missed you at church." She touched his arm and a waft of her perfume drifted by as she spoke to Drew.

"Bobby and Valerie couldn't make it but I brought Jeff," she announced.

The hostess came to seat them, and as Gabe followed the group, he saw that Makima was wearing black pumps that had a decorative strip of turquoise leather around it.

His mother had worked in the shoe department at Macy's for years and had said how you could tell a lot about women by the shoes they bought. At the dinner table she'd tell stories about the customers using the shoe ads in the paper to illustrate her point. She caught Gabe's imagination with her stories, and when he began going out with girls, he found himself noticing their footware.

How had Makima found such shoes that exactly matched her outfit? He couldn't imagine the hours of shopping it must have taken, but he certainly enjoyed the outcome.

At the round table there was a slight jockeying for position. He was amused to find that he was seated next to Makima and across from Alana. "You can't go wrong with anything on this menu, Gabe and Drew," Mr. Gray promised. "These people are good cooks."

"What are you having?" Gabe asked Makima.

She studied the menu a moment. "I promise not to have potato salad," she said quietly with a deadpan expression.

Gabe was taken by surprise. When he saw the smile in her eyes, he broke out laughing and she joined him.

"What's funny?" Alana asked.

Gabe left that to Makima, who merely said, "Nothing." She then asked her mother about the corn soufflé.

After much chatter around the table, people gave their orders and the waitress brought out hot bread with tiny jars of apple butter.

"This tastes like the apple butter we used to get in Virginia," Drew said.

"Virginia has some good apples. Is that where you lived?" Mrs. Gray asked.

"Ma's family lived there," Drew said.

"We were born and raised in Manhattan and always lived there except to visit Ma's family," Gabe explained.

He expected to have to answer many questions but he liked these people. He was relaxed and about to have a good meal. He'd already had a great moment with Makima. It was wonderful that she'd come to the point where she could laugh about the salad incident.

He had the wicked thought that maybe he would let her clean the jacket after all. It was still hanging in the closet. He didn't dare look at her because the laughter inside would burst out and then Alana would have a field day trying to make them tell her the joke.

"Manhattan. I love some parts of that city," Mrs. Gray said nostalgically. "We used to get up there now and then, didn't we, Arthur?"

"Anytime there was a conference nearby it gave us the excuse to go. Now that I'm retired—"

Alana interrupted her dad. "You don't need an excuse. What else is retirement for? Just pick up and go. See a Broadway musical. Go to the museums. That's what I'd do if I were in your shoes and didn't have to go to work every day."

"Using what for money?" her father asked.

"Your pension. That's what it's for."

Gabe could tell this was an ongoing conversation. Alana lived for the present moment and wanted her parents to do the same before it was too late.

The waitress and a helper came with the food, asked if there was anything else she could do, said, "Enjoy your lunch," and left.

Alana wasn't letting go of her point. "What about your parents, Gabe?"

"I tend to agree that you shouldn't wait and put that kind of thing off. Our mother always wanted to go on a cruise. So many of her friends went and would come back and tell her how great it was. Pop wouldn't go but he told her to go. Next time, she'd say. Then two years ago Pop caught the flu, which turned into pneumonia, and he died. Before the winter was out she got caught in the freezing rain and the same thing happened to her."

The Grays had all stopped eating. Alana looked stricken at her careless question. "I'm so sorry," she said.

"It's all right," Gabe said. "They married early and had a long life together. Drew and I are family to each other." He hurried on. "But we'd never been to South Carolina before, so this is an interesting trip for us."

"You didn't know Mr. Zeke?" Mr. Gray asked.

"We knew nothing about Pop's side of the family except for his brother, Uncle Jake, who visited once in a while."

"Maybe he didn't like to talk about his family. I know several people like that," Mrs. Gray said. "How long have we known Mr. Willis, Arthur? We have no idea where he came from or about his family. He just showed up here one day, got a job, and has been here about twenty years or more."

"I think something happened in Pop's life when he was little and he decided to cut himself off from family. We didn't even know he had a connection with South Carolina."

"I hope you don't mind my asking, Gabe, but how did you and Drew find out about Mr. Zeke?" Mr. Gray asked.

Gabe told him about Jasper Moultrie, adding little details about the visit. Drawing it out so he wouldn't have to go into specifics about the will.

He needn't have worried. This was an intelligent family and they knew where the line was drawn. That was emphasized when Mrs. Gray said, "We need to let you eat your lunch. This is good food, isn't it?"

Gabe was having lamb with vegetables and intended to have chocolate cake for dessert.

He turned to Makima who hadn't said a word, but he'd felt

her intense interest. "What do you do other than your clinic project, Makima? Do you have a nine-to-five job?"

"I work at the community center."

"Here in Grayson or in Swinton?"

"Grayson. It isn't much of a center yet but we're trying to expand it."

"Are you the director?" He couldn't imagine her being anything else.

She smiled. "At one time I thought I would be but now I'm glad that didn't work out. I'm the office manager."

"Who else do you have?"

"Program director and maintenance man, both part-time. We did have a part-time bookkeeper but he went to a full-time job in Orangeburg."

"Do you have any hobbies, Gabe?" Alana asked. She was looking at the dessert menu. "You don't cook by any chance, do you?"

"Drew and I are both trying to learn how. Why?"

"There's so little to do in Grayson, you have to make your own entertainment. I was just thinking, Makima, we ought to get the crowd together and have a cooking contest. Wouldn't that be fun?" She sparkled at Gabe.

"Sounds like fun to me. Is there anyplace to dance around here?"

"There're a couple of clubs but we don't usually go to them."

"I should hope not," Mrs. Gray said. "You always hear about trouble at those places."

"Someone has a house party on the weekend if we're lucky," Alana said.

"What about the community center?" he asked Makima.

"We have a big spring ball and a few other events."

Gabe looked at the dessert menu. "I'm going to have a piece of this luscious-looking chocolate cake, and maybe I'll get inspiration to make one for the cooking contest when you have it."

"I tasted it once and it was great but today I'm going to have the banana-cream pie," Alana told the waitress. "They use real whipped cream, Gabe."

"I'll try that next time."

"No dessert?" he asked Makima, noting she'd ordered only coffee.

"Alana can eat anything," she sighed, "and never gain an ounce. I'm not so lucky."

"I can't understand why women think they have to be skinny."

"Not skinny. Slender," she corrected him.

"Not slender. Thin." He liked getting a rise out of her.

"It makes our clothes fit better," she flashed back.

"Clothes look better when they fit around curves." Gabe let his appreciative glance at her make his point and was pleased when he saw the color rise in her face.

His cake came, two layers high with a deep fudge icing. It was absolutely delectable.

"Wouldn't you like a piece?" he teased her.

"Enjoy it, Gabe, and leave me to my coffee," she said dryly.

"Will you be home this coming weekend, Makima?" Alana asked.

"I have to go to Spartanburg on Saturday and I'll stay overnight. But I'm free the following weekend."

"We'll plan the cooking contest for that Saturday, then. Okay with you, Gabe?"

"You can count on me. Just let me know the details in time." He slid his glance over to Makima on whose saucer he'd placed a small piece of his cake while she was talking to Alana.

"You shouldn't have done that," she protested even as she was taking her last bite.

"Did you enjoy it?"

"It was delicious."

"I stand absolved." A piece or two of chocolate cake would

just add a little more definition to her curvy figure and he saw nothing wrong with that.

When Gabe pulled out his credit card at the end of the meal, Mr. Gray said, "Put that away, Gabe. We invited you and Drew and we never let guests pay."

Gabe protested and offered to at least leave the tip, but Mr. Gray was firm, so Gabe kept quiet. This might be a part of the southern hospitality he'd often heard of, for this family had certainly made him feel welcome.

He asked Drew about it when they arrived home after the Grays had dropped them off with an invitation to come visit them.

"I thought you were going to pay for us like usual. You should've given me a signal or something." He was reproachful as he hung up his navy sport coat. "That's why I ordered the fried chicken dinner and the cake for dessert."

"I did the same thing—ordered the expensive lamb, which I wouldn't have done had I'd known Mr. Gray would insist on paying."

"They're pretty generous," Drew said, "and real easy to talk to." He put on some jeans and a white T-shirt. "Jeff said Miss Makima used to be a teacher."

"Really? Wonder why she quit. She told me today that she works at the community center."

"Jeff goes over there to play basketball. You know what else he told me?" He followed Gabe into the office.

"What?"

"Most people think Great-Grandfather's trees are haunted."

Gabe was incredulous. "How can trees be haunted?"

"Jeff said the woods have been there so long and no one has ever been able to walk through them like you can through the other woods around here."

"That's why they're haunted? There has to be a better reason than that," Gabe scoffed.

"Jeff said there're stories of boys trying to climb the fence and every time they get scared and run away."

"They're scared of the barbed wire on top of it and rightly so."

"I'm just sayin' what he told me," Drew said, denying all responsibility.

Gabe looked at him speculatively. "When you're in the field near the woods, do you feel anything? Or hear anything?"

When Drew didn't answer right away, Gabe's interest sharpened.

"Maybe the first time we sat on the bench I kinda had a feeling that perhaps Great-Grandfather was around someplace," he said almost timidly, which was unlike Drew.

"I felt the same way," Gabe said quietly.

"You did?" There was relief in Drew's voice.

"We're his great-grandsons." Gabe was matter-of-fact. "That has nothing to do with the woods being haunted. Did Jeff say he ever tried to get in?"

"No. I don't think he would have tried that," Drew said positively.

"He doesn't strike me as a kid that'd get into that kind of mischief but you never know," Gabe agreed. "What about your schoolwork? Have you done any of it yet?"

"No. You said I could have a little vacation."

"Vacation's over. We've been here over a week so it's time to do something other than loaf around."

"I haven't been loafing. I'm cooking and learning to garden," Drew defended himself.

"Point made. Now begin the schoolwork and let me see it. Okay?"

"Okay."

Gabe wished he could assign himself something as simple as school lessons.

His homework was complex and discouraging yet imperative. For over a week he'd been searching for clues to his treasured destiny, and all he had to show was an indecipherable scroll.

Chapter 11

Makima was glad she'd gone to Rockwell's. Now she wouldn't have to bother with cooking. That meant she had a rare Sunday afternoon and evening with nothing to do, no meetings, no visits to be made to the shut-ins on the church list. She could spend the time however she desired.

She changed into some old woolen pants and a baggy sweater with USC on it. She looked out the window of her second-floor apartment at the flowers the owner had set into the ground last week. They were beginning to raise their lavender blossoms already. She wished she had talent for gardening or doing something outdoors. But she didn't. Her hobbies seemed to be indoor activities. Except for swimming. That she liked and when she'd been in college she'd found bicycling fun.

She surveyed the room with its sofa, chairs, tables and lamps. It was comfortable, but suddenly it didn't suit her. Wouldn't the sofa look better on the other side of the room?

She thought so but wasn't sure, so she put aside some chairs and tables and using her hip, pushed and nudged and pulled until the sofa was in its new position.

That meant that the chairs and tables and lamps had to be moved around as well. The one thing that didn't get moved was the compact entertainment center. She wasn't about to disconnect all those wires.

Several hours later the room looked quite different. For one thing, the entertainment center in its maple cabinet was no longer the focus of the room. She liked that. Some of her groupings had been quite inspired.

She liked the feel of the room. Perhaps she'd subconsciously used some feng shui concepts. Whatever it was, it had worked.

The restlessness that had been inside her was gone. She made a pot of tea, put it on a tray with her thinnest teacup and saucer. She set it on the table beside the chintz chair in its new corner facing the window.

With a sigh she settled in the chair and slowly enjoyed her tea. This was an indulgence she seldom had the time or the inclination for these days. There was always something urgent to do about the clinic after she got off from work.

When she'd stopped teaching to take on the clinic project, Mom and Dad had begged her to come back home so she wouldn't have the worry of an apartment to maintain. She'd tried it for six months.

The director's position at the community center had come up and she'd applied for it but had been passed over for a man. She swallowed her pride and took the position of office manager a few months later.

Her salary plus her savings from teaching had been enough to pay for this apartment and she'd made the break from her parents' house. They said they could understand since she'd been on her own since college, but she knew it had been difficult for her mother.

Occasionally the apartment seemed lonely but mostly she loved coming home to her own place. The tea was soothing and as she gazed out at the darkling sky she could see the stars beginning to appear.

What was Gabe doing? she wondered. The day had been full of surprises where he was concerned. She'd no idea her mother was going to invite him to lunch with them or that he'd go. Or that he would sit beside her. She thought for sure he'd sit beside Alana who certainly expected him to. But somehow he was standing behind Makima and pulled out a chair for her, so what was she to do except sit in it? The biggest surprise was to find herself feeling relaxed and confident enough to make a joke of the salad incident. She'd felt like a schoolgirl, almost giggling about it with him.

Alana had been dying of curiosity but there was no way she could tell her sister that embarrassing event. Alana would have handled it in her own unconcerned way and turned it into a laughing matter.

Her sister had no problem showing men she liked that she found them attractive. They usually returned the attention. She was sparkling all over Gabe and had certainly caught his interest as far as Makima could see.

But that was another surprising thing. He'd asked about her work and that was okay as it was impersonal. But that bit of back-and-forth wordplay he'd started about dessert and curves was personal.

And fun! She had to admit it. Not even Reggie had displayed that kind of wit. As she finished her tea she reflected on the differences between her and Alana. She was the oldest of the siblings and was already five when Alana was born.

It was Makima who accompanied her mother on her frequent rounds to visit the elderly and the sick, who learned how to sit attentively and listen to people, who went to church and helped her mother and the other ladies to take care of the flowers and the altar. She learned how to pray by observing her mother.

She also learned instinctively how to conduct herself as the eldest of the Gray children whose forbears had been so distinctive that the community had been named Grayson after them.

Decorum and dedication sat lightly on Alana from the beginning. She charmed people with her gay spirit, her laughter and her ceaseless energy.

Makima loved her younger sister with all her heart and knew she could never be as comfortable and natural with men as Alana was. She worried about her sometimes.

"I hope the right man comes along soon, I'm tired of waiting," she'd told Makima the last time they'd had a sister-to-sister conversation.

"Don't get too tired, honey. That can lead to mistakes," Makima had said affectionately. "Why don't you pray about it?"

Alana had shrugged that off. "I'm not like you, sis."

Makima got up from her chair, took the tray into the kitchen and washed out the teapot and the cup.

Maybe Alana had prayed after all, and Gabe Bell was the right man who'd finally come along.

She stood still, looking into space.

She'd see how things were between them in two weeks at the cooking-contest party. Meanwhile she'd tend to her own business and pray for assistance about land for the clinic.

Monday it started to rain. Tuesday it was still raining. The local television channels said the rain was welcome news to farmers. Rivers and creeks needed it also. It wasn't welcome news to Drew Bell, he didn't care what the TV said.

"Sam and I were s'posed to go get the stuff for the garden but now we have to wait until it gets dry," he grouched, kicking his toe against the back door at the water streaming down the window.

"It's not going to last forever so practice a little patience." Gabe set a plate of waffles and sausage on the table. He was feeling some frustration himself. "Do your homework this morning and if the rain hasn't stopped by this afternoon, there's something I want us both to do."

"What's that?" Drew showed a spark of interest as he forked half a sausage onto a square of waffle. Food always made Drew feel better.

"We need to go through everything in this house, looking for pictures. They must be hidden somewhere. It seems very strange to me that we haven't seen a single one."

"Didn't you look before?"

"A little, but my mind was on finding clues, not pictures."

Drew gave the matter his full attention as he drank a glass of milk. "Maybe they didn't believe in taking pictures. I saw a story on TV where some tribe didn't want their pictures taken because they thought the camera would steal their souls or something."

"Those tribes weren't familiar with cameras, but you can't say that about people now, especially Americans."

"I guess you're right. We'll probably find them someplace with both of us looking," Drew said.

The rain didn't stop and although the two of them searched the house, no photographs were found.

"That's really weird," Drew observed.

"It's more than that. There must be a reason for it and maybe it's a part of the whole business. I can't imagine what part but it has to mean something."

When they'd explored the garage on Saturday, Gabe had been hopeful that he'd find another rich source of material that would yield at least one clue. He should've known better.

The garage held a pickup truck and a Ford sedan. The floor was clean enough to eat on. Tools for the cars and for gardening hung on the wall in order. There were no boxes of odds and ends stacked up as Gabe had anticipated. The only items not on walls were fertilizers for the garden.

Great-Grandfather had built an addition to the garage that served as his workshop. Here again, all was in spotless order, no sawdust on the floor, nothing piled on the worktable. Drawers held neatly arranged tools. The tools were beautiful in themselves.

"Wish I knew what these were for," Drew said as he picked up first one and then the other.

"It's amazing how well he kept them, isn't it?" Gabe was thinking there's a lesson to be learned here.

As they went back through the garage, Drew asked, "Can I drive the pickup? I can get a learner's permit." He opened the door and hopped onto the driver's seat.

"You can't drive it and I can't either."

"Why not? You've got your license."

"Because it isn't insured in my name."

"Can't Mr. Moultrie do something about that?"

"I don't think so but I'll ask."

Gabe remembered this promise as Drew went back to his room on Tuesday after they'd come up without any photographs.

The attorney's answer was as he'd expected. "I'm sorry, Gabe, but the vehicles are a part of the total assets which will be released to you at the end of the three-month period or whenever you have been able to fulfill the terms of the will. You might be able to do that before the three months are up and I'm hoping you will."

"I have found something and even though I don't know what it means, I'm certain it's a part of the treasured-destiny business," Gabe said.

Moultrie's voice became more alert. "Please tell me about it."

Gabe described finding the scroll and taking it to the library "We still don't know what it means but the librarian calculated that it might be an African language."

"You'll be glad to know, Gabe, that the scroll is one of the items you're supposed to find." He sounded pleased now.

"It is? I knew it!" If he'd been a kid he'd have jumped up and down. Instead, Gabe let out a whoosh of relief. "That's great news. Can you tell me what it means?"

"No, I can't. But hold on to it and keep searching. Let me know the next time you find a clue."

As soon as he hung up, Gabe yelled for Drew.

"Yeah? What?" Drew said, appearing at the office door.

"I just talked with Mr. Moultrie. He said the scroll is one of the clues I was supposed to find!" The brothers high-fived each other.

"Did he tell you how to read it?"

"No. Just said be sure to keep it and let him know when we find the next one."

"Did you ask him about the pickup?"

"Sorry to disappoint you but the vehicles won't be released until the whole business is finished, so the sooner we find the other clues, the sooner this will be over and we can get on with our lives."

"What about the family pictures?"

"Forgot to ask him after we talked about the scroll. Right now I'm going to go through the third bedroom with a fine-tooth comb in case we missed something."

The rain continued through Wednesday, and on TV there were pictures of some creeks overflowing, but the weatherman thought that the system was moving to the west and Thursday would be drier.

The rain stopped Thursday afternoon. By Friday afternoon Gabe had searched the entire upstairs exhaustively.

The anticipation that had filled him after talking with Moultrie had dwindled as the empty hours went by. He didn't think he could stand one more hour of searching.

When the phone rang midafternoon he answered it eagerly.

"Gabe? This is Alana. Are you feeling like a fish with all this water?"

"Just about. How are you, Alana? It's good to hear your voice."

"Same to you. A bunch of us are going to Swinton to the movies tonight. Want to go with us?"

"Absolutely. I'm tired of being cooped up by the weather."

Her silvery laughter made him smile. "Aren't we all. We'll pick you up at six-thirty."

"Glad someone gets to go out," Drew mumbled when Gabe told him of the call. "What's showing?"

"No idea and don't care but I'll tell you when I get back."

"Hop in," Alana said when she drove up. She introduced the couple in the backseat as Carolyn Brown and Mark Watson.

"We all went to school together," she said.

Mark was fit and muscled, an athletic type, Gabe thought, which was borne out when Mark asked what sports he played.

"Shoot a few baskets now and then, do a little swimming and used to ride a bicycle. Like to watch Tiger Woods, he makes that game look so easy. Is there a golf course near here?"

"There're a couple. Did you bring some clubs with you?"

"No, but I can rent some, I guess."

"Great. We'll go out sometime."

"Carolyn and I play, too," Alana said.

"The more the merrier," Gabe said, smiling at her.

Carolyn was friendly and low-key. She asked Gabe about New York shows. "I visited a cousin there last summer and had a great time."

There was no lack of conversation on the way to Swinton. The movie was a riotous comedy and by the time they stopped at a restaurant afterward, Gabe felt comfortable and carefree.

The movie had been based on a hilarious mishap in the leading man's childhood. This led to shared stories, beginning with Carolyn, who recalled when she was in the third grade and Luther Adams kept pulling her hair.

"I remember," Alana said. "He wouldn't stop even when you told the teacher."

Her face lit up with mischief. "There was a friendly frog that lived near our backyard, so we put it in a bag with Luther's name on it. Right after recess we sneaked it onto the teacher's chair. It jumped out of the bag onto her desk. She screamed. The frog kept jumping around and the boys in the class had fun trying to catch it. When the teacher saw the bag with Luther's name on it, he had to stay after school all week."

"I can't beat that," Gabe said when they were through laughing. "The best I can do happened when I was in Virginia visiting my cousins. There were lots of them and I always wanted to tag along with the ones older than me. I was six, they were eight and nine. They wore boots because they went into the woods a lot. I filled the boots with water. I didn't know it would ruin them so I got it not only from them but from their parents. It was okay though because after a while I got to go with them."

"Poor little city boy," Alana teased.

"I sure was that," Gabe agreed.

"Not a bad thing to be. I'd love to live in a city." Alana sounded wistful. "So much to see and do all the time."

On the way home they talked about the cooking contest, the people to invite and Carolyn said to hold it at her place because she had a house, not an apartment. "We can squeeze more people in," she said, "and still have room to dance."

"What will you cook, Gabe?" Alana asked.

"It's a secret," he said.

"You can tell me," she cooed, and batted her eyelashes.

"Then it wouldn't be a secret." Gabe smiled back at her.

Alana was loads of fun, he thought as he said good-night. He'd enjoyed himself.

Too bad Makima had to work. The evening would have had a different flavor had she been there.

It was just as well. He couldn't afford to become interested in her.

With Alana, he was safe.

Chapter 12

"**M**orning, boys," Sam Williams called as he pushed the back door all the way open. "Beautiful day after all that rain."

"Hi, Mr. Sam. We going to the nursery today?" Drew asked, setting another place at the breakfast table.

"How about some bacon and home fries with your toast and coffee?" Gabe asked, setting the platter down.

"I shouldn't but it's mighty tempting. Maybe just a little."

As the meal progressed, Sam told them about his trip to Aiken. "I got tired of the rain so on Wednesday I called my friend Bert to tell him I'd be up. Bert and Jenny have a few horses and I like to spend some time with them every year. Aiken's just west of here, a pleasant drive."

"Do you ride, Sam?" Gabe asked.

"Used to when I was young. Now I watch others ride."

"We saw horses in fields around here. Are they just for work or do people ride them?" The thought of riding a horse was exciting to Drew and it shone in his eyes.

"Mostly they're for riding. Farmers use tractors and other equipment to work their fields."

When breakfast was over, Sam asked Gabe and Drew what vegetables they ate. "Collard greens are popular around here, but I don't know if you ate them in New York." The gleam in his eyes told Gabe he was being teased.

"No soul-food place at home could stay in business if it didn't have collard greens on its menu," Gabe said as he and Drew cleared up the kitchen.

"I like tomatoes, green beans and cabbage," Drew volunteered.

"We also eat carrots, green onions, lettuce, radishes and zucchini," Gabe added.

"You'd better come with us, Gabe, and we'll see what the nursery has." Sam added, "You know, some folks don't start planting until after Easter, but I always say put it in the ground and see what happens. You can always plant again."

"I go along with that," Gabe said.

"Me, too," Drew agreed.

The nursery in Grayson was colorful and fragrant. Apparently Sam wasn't the only person who intended to plant early. The aisles were filled with people and Gabe even recognized a couple he'd met at church. They passed the time of day and he thought how he'd only been in Grayson two weeks and already he knew folks to speak to. It made him feel good.

They came home with a little bit of everything. "Try it all," Sam insisted. "That's how you learn, young Drew."

Later that day Drew came to the office where Gabe was busy at the desk. "Can I talk to you about something?" He looked anxious.

Gabe stopped what he was doing. When Drew addressed him like that, it was serious. "Sure. Have a seat."

"Jeff wants to take me around tomorrow to meet some of his

friends and stuff. They all ride bikes and I need one. Could we go get me one? Today? Please?"

Drew had outgrown the one he'd had and hadn't replaced it, but Gabe could see that in a place like Grayson it was almost a necessity.

"Okay. Might not be a new one though."

"Just so it rides and doesn't look too funky," Drew said with a wide smile.

The phone book showed a bike shop only in Swinton, not Grayson. However, they saw when they got there that it had a good collection of new and used bikes. Drew looked at each one and finally chose a used one that looked almost new.

"Can I go over to Jeff's and show it to him?" he asked as soon as they got home.

"Call first."

Jeff was home and Drew went sailing off on the bike, pumping as fast as he could go. Gabe watched a moment, recalling how he'd first taught a Drew with short chubby legs to ride. Back in the office he worked on a packet of forwarded mail. Among the bills and junk mail was a note from his buddy, Calvin Peters.

> Gabe, Thought you were going to call me with your phone number. Did you go south and forget us already? Cal.

Trust Cal to make it short and sweet, Gabe mused, and leaned the note against the clock so he wouldn't forget it.

There were bills to be dealt with first: the car note, the credit cards, the gas cards and Macy's. He could have put any Macy's purchases on Visa but Ma had worked there for thirty years. It was the first credit card he'd applied for when he was twenty-one and he'd kept it as a souvenir of his mother.

There were a few odds and ends and by the time he'd written

all the checks he'd also come to the conclusion that he needed to go to work. He and Drew could scrape by on the money Moultrie gave him plus savings, but he didn't want to do that.

He knew he couldn't go through the weeks doing what had occupied him these first two weeks. It'd drive him crazy. They needed the money and he needed to take his mind off the search.

The bookkeeping position Makima had mentioned that was open at the community center sounded like a possibility. It was only part-time but it would help with the daily expenses. The other advantage was that it would get him out of the house. He would keep searching for clues, of course, but maybe coming at it fresh would give him better ideas for understanding Great-Grandfather's wily mind.

In church the next day Gabe thought how pleased Ma must be to know her sons had come three Sundays in a row. He'd never done that at home.

It wasn't that he didn't believe in God. When he thought about his religious views (which wasn't very often), he realized that at some early point in his life the idea of a God had been implanted in him, probably by his mother.

The problem was that as he grew up and matured he couldn't integrate the practice of a spiritual life with what he saw all around him, including in the church.

He didn't go as far as his father did. Undoubtedly there were good ministers who tried to lead a church in a truly spiritual way and who lived an honest life of goodness and humility themselves. He just hadn't met or heard of many.

What he'd come to believe in were those individuals who were good people, helping others, caring for others, serving the community. He didn't expect them to be perfect. He was far from that himself. But they were basically people trying to live a life according to what they understood of the fundamental principles of serving others even to the point of self-sacrifice.

Therefore Gabe saw no need to go to church except to escort his mother. She liked church; it comforted her. So he went.

Here in Grayson he attended church because it was two blocks from the house, it was a window into the community where he and Drew would be living for a while, the people had known Great-Grandfather, and Drew seemed to like going. Also it gave him something to do on Sunday.

Drew was sitting with Jeff and afterward, while Gabe was talking with Mr. and Mrs. Gray, he saw that several girls had been added to Jeff's group. Nothing like a new boy in town to get the girls fluttering.

"Makima's out of town and I don't know why Alana and Bobby didn't come to church," Mrs. Gray said. She looked at her husband as if he had the answer.

"Probably stayed in bed," he said with an amused glance at Gabe.

Reverend Givhans had made the rounds and now came to stand beside them. "Glad to see you, Mr. Bell."

"Call me Gabe, please." The two men shook hands.

"Arthur, Odessa, you won't mind if I take Gabe away for a minute, will you? I haven't had a chance to visit with him."

The Grays said goodbye and Gabe found himself following the pastor back into the church and entering a side door that led to his office.

Givhans reminded Gabe of his uncle Jake. He was a man of medium height, brown-skinned, a tidy mustache, round glasses, a large mouth and penetrating eyes. His voice was made for the platform, it was deep and resonant. When Gabe first heard him he'd been surprised at the volume this medium-size man produced.

His office was comfortable, with several chairs as well as a desk and plants. The walls were covered with pictures and it was to these that Givhans directed Gabe's attention.

"Here is the original church." The black-and-white photo of a small frame church was dated 1920 and stood on a bare lot. Subsequent photographs showed the growth and expansion of the building.

"The auditorium can hold five hundred people and below it on the basement level are all the classrooms, the dining hall and the choir room."

Gabe hoped that his intuition about what was coming next was wrong.

The pastor continued to speak about the numerous photos. Maybe he was mistaken, Gabe thought as he congratulated Givhans on the church activities and how pleased he and Drew had felt to be welcomed the first time they attended.

"There're a number of people in the congregation who love to give service," Givhans said. "You'd be amazed at how many youngsters of all ages come to our Sunday school. That's where our problem is, Gabe. We're in great need of more space and I'd been talking with Mr. Zeke about it for a few years." He leaned toward Gabe and fixed his eyes on him.

Gabe snatched at the first obstacle he could think of. "But you're too far away for a Sunday school class. The children can't walk two blocks there and back in all kinds of weather."

"We worked that out when the board first thought of it. The church buses, which we own would shuttle them there and back." He looked like a magician who had successfully pulled a live rabbit out of a hatbox.

"I understand that you haven't been here long, Gabe, and you haven't had time to deal with your inheritance yet."

"You're right, Reverend Givhans. I haven't."

"All I want to do is tell you about our situation and that we had conversations with Mr. Zeke about it, so that when you're ready you will keep the church in mind. Regardless of that, however, we hope that you and Drew will feel at home here and will participate in our activities." With another handshake, Reverend Givhans escorted Gabe to the door.

Gabe walked home feeling he'd escaped the worst of it. At least Givhans hadn't asked him outright to sell him some property and Gabe hadn't had to go through what he had with Makima.

Still, the pastor and his board had expectations and hopes, simply because Great-Grandfather had never told them an outright no.

He couldn't understand that. Why let these good people think there was a possibility of buying some of his land?

Naturally they came to him as soon as he showed up. It wasn't up to him to answer their prayers. All he could say was no and not even explain why. It made him seem like a Simon Legree.

As he turned into his yard he couldn't help but wonder how many other land-needy people were going to show up because Great-Grandfather had seemed to promise them something.

However many, the answer would still have to be no.

Chapter 13

Gabe found himself in an unexpected place Monday morning. Drew had returned yesterday from his long visit with Jeff, full of enthusiasm about enrolling in the school Jeff attended in Swinton.

"Jeff and I met some other kids today and they all go there. They say it's a pretty good high school. I'd like it a lot better than working here by myself. They have a swim team, too. Maybe I could get on it." He interrupted himself. "Probably too late in the year for that but at least I could go to the meets. I wouldn't have any trouble transferring to the school, would I?" He suddenly looked anxious and uncertain as he shifted in his chair opposite Gabe.

"Hold on a minute, Drew. I can see you're excited because you've made new friends. That's good. But Swinton High might not be as good academically as the one you've been attending at home."

"Maybe not. But I'll still be a sophomore here like I was at home and I promise to make good grades, which was more than I was doing. I just don't want to be stuck here studying by myself when I could be at school now that I know some people." He made his points with an earnestness that impressed Gabe.

It was true that if Drew would work hard he could accomplish more here than he had at home where his grades had gone down and he'd fallen in with the wrong crowd. Gabe could also understand his brother's desire to be involved in the social aspect of high school. Even he, Gabe, was getting bored staying at the house most of the time.

"Do you think I could be transferred, Gabe?"

"I don't see why not. We'll go first thing in the morning and see."

Drew broke out in a big smile, then he sobered. He stuck out his hand. "You won't be sorry, Gabe."

Now as Gabe stood to thank Mrs. Capers, the counselor with whom he and Drew had spent the past hour, he thought of what Drew's handshake had implied. If nothing else good came of this South Carolina adventure, his brother's reconciliation with school made it worthwhile.

He had his class assignments based on the material Gabe had shown the counselor from Drew's previous school. The books he'd need now filled his backpack and Gabe had promised to request his brother's transcripts.

"I'll be back to pick you up," he told Drew as they stood in the hallway.

"They have buses for everyone and I'll come home on that. Okay?"

"Sure." Gabe recalled seeing the yellow school bus as they first came into Grayson two weeks earlier but he hadn't realized it was a system-wide arrangement.

It was only nine-thirty when he got back to Grayson, a little late to apply for a job, but he didn't want to put it off until tomorrow. He found the community center on Park Street, four blocks from the center of town.

On one side of it was a car dealership, on the other a cleaner's and a barbershop. On the other side of the street was a small coffee shop, a dollar store and on the corner a storefront church.

The center looked as if it might have started out as a warehouse, but it had been spruced up on the outside with new windows and doors, and painted an ivory color. Its industrial edges had been softened by hedges which were green and healthy, while a ground cover with tiny blue blossoms greeted the eye as he walked up to the entrance over which hung a black-and-white sign, Grayson Community Center.

As Gabe opened the dark blue entrance door he noted with approval its heavy weight and solid construction. He stepped inside. Facing him was a large open space with a stage at one end. Several doors on each side indicated other rooms. On his immediate left was a door with Director on it. The door was open and Gabe walked in.

He was aware of two things at once. The office was vibrant with subtle yellow walls, blue-cushioned chairs and blue ceramic pieces on a table and the bookshelf behind the desk.

The person behind the desk shot his awareness sky-high.

"Makima! It seems a long time since I've seen you. How are you?"

The current of emotion he felt took him by surprise. She wore a lustrous violet blouse with matching necklace and earrings. The color did wonders for her complexion.

Apparently he wasn't the only one who felt surprise. "Gabe!" Makima smiled, her eyes warm and bright. "How nice to see you. Please sit down."

There were several chairs and Gabe chose the one directly across the desk. He couldn't take his eyes away from her. She had a faint curve at the corner of her mouth when she was relaxed, as she was now, and there were tiny crinkles around her eyes. Her hair was glossy, and the way the earrings dangled made him want to touch them to see what she would do.

Maybe she felt as he did, because she never stopped looking at him, and her close attention made Gabe almost forget what he'd come to the center for. He felt as if he and Makima could sit for hours communicating with or without words.

"I missed you at church yesterday," he said.

"I had some clinic work to do. Did you see Mom and Dad?" Her soft glance said she missed seeing him also.

"Yes, I did. Drew met some more of Jeff's friends and spent the afternoon with them."

"I know he enjoyed that. Jeff's a fine young man."

"You'll never guess what I did just before coming here."

"Tell me." I'm interested in whatever you have to say, her eyes promised.

Gabe told her all about Drew's sudden desire to attend the local high school. They discussed the likely advantages of this move and Gabe was delighted at how closely Makima's conclusions connected with his.

The time was going by and Gabe reluctantly decided to get down to business. He looked at his watch. "You probably have work to do, Makima, and I need to talk with someone about the bookkeeper position."

"You're applying for it?" she asked in surprise.

"Thought I'd give it a try. I've been working with figures for the state of New York for years so I think I can handle this. I need something to do that will take me out of the house at least part of the day, especially now that Drew will be in school."

"The salary can't compete with New York rates," she said as she opened a drawer and extracted a folder.

"I know, and I realize it's part-time, but that suits me fine."

She was suddenly all business as she laid forms on the desk. "Please fill these out and I'll let Dr. Cook, the director, know that you're here."

As she came from behind the desk and crossed the floor to go into the other office, Gabe admired the way her gray pants rounded her hips and fit her slim legs. Her gray suede pumps had a gold chain across the front. She never fails me, he thought.

It took him only a few minutes to fill out the application, then Makima ushered him into the director's office, introduced him and closed the door.

Dr. Thomas Cook stood, shook hands, gave Gabe a swift appraising glance and invited him to sit down. He appeared to be in his sixties, was nearly totally bald, wore glasses and had a round face decorated with a well-shaped mustache above a firm mouth. An aura of sharp intelligence was offset by laugh lines around his eyes. He had a presence of calm authority and Gabe thought it would be interesting to be around this man every day and work with him.

He scanned Gabe's application then laid it aside.

"It's good to have you with us in Grayson, Mr. Bell. I haven't been in New York recently. Is Dicky Wells still open for his Sunday-morning breakfast of crisp waffles and great fried chicken?"

"I haven't dropped in there for a while. Were you in New York long, Dr. Cook?"

"Long enough to put on some pounds eating at Sylvia's while in school at City College and doing graduate work at Columbia. Wonderful city," he said nostalgically. "I used to go back regularly, but not often now." He picked up the application, gave it a second glance then looked at Gabe. "I understand you're related to the late Ezekiel Bell."

Gabe was certain that Dr. Cook was in possession of all the generally known facts about him and Drew, but he obliged by relating to Dr. Cook what he'd told others here in Grayson.

As he spoke, Gabe had the feeling that it wasn't the facts Dr. Cook was listening for so much as the way Gabe presented them. What was the director looking for? The question was answered in Dr. Cook's next statement.

"Your great-grandfather was an extraordinary man, Mr. Bell, one for whom I had the greatest respect. He and I had a common interest in Africa. I taught African studies for some years in universities and I've done some traveling in African countries. Mr. Zeke had traveled to that continent through his years of study and research, so when I retired here we found we had a lot to talk about." His eyes met Gabe's and in them Gabe saw a restrained sadness.

He'd wanted to see how I'd respond to this important friendship he had with Great-Grandfather, Gabe thought. "I'm really glad to learn that Great-Grandfather had someone who could share his interest on his own level. I saw in some of his books a notation that said, TC. I wondered who or what the initials stood for. Now I know."

"We discussed many subjects in his books." Dr. Cook held the application unseeingly. He seemed to remember it was still in his hand and laid it down. "Do you know anything about our community center, Mr. Bell?"

"Only that from the outside it appears that it was once a warehouse."

"It was the only place Grayson could find three years ago when it decided it desperately needed a space here for community activities to serve our growing population, and to save them from having to go into Swinton. We did practically all of the rehabilitation work ourselves. It isn't the best but it will do until we can build a real center. As you might imagine, our funds are very limited. We have only five paid positions. The director, the office manager, maintenance, and the bookkeeper and program director share a full position."

"Do you have a lot of volunteers?"

"All of our activities depend on volunteers and we expect the staff to volunteer when possible. It's the only way we can afford to keep the center open." His penetrating glance required a response from Gabe.

"Makes sense to me. If hired, I'll be glad to volunteer," he said.

Dr. Cook discussed the function of the bookkeeper, told Gabe what his salary and hours would be, welcomed him to the staff and sent him back out to Makima for further details.

Makima had been sitting at her desk looking blindly at the work in front of her while Gabe was in Dr. Cook's office. Gabe's appearance at the center had taken her completely by surprise. He'd looked stylish and confident in his brown dress pants, white shirt, brown tie and brown tweed sport coat. She'd loved the way they'd simply taken up where they'd left off at Rockwell's restaurant.

His announcement of coming to apply for the bookkeeper position had jolted her into reality, for he'd certainly be hired. That meant they'd see each other every workday and how could she do that?

The problem was that Alana liked Gabe. She'd taken him to the movie along with Mark and Carolyn and had told Makima what a wonderful time they'd had. Alana was looking and hoping for a husband. She complained to Makima that she was tired of waiting for the right man to come along and Makima, wanting her sister's happiness, wondered if Gabe was that man.

She didn't want to stand in her sister's way. Gabe seemed to like Alana. He'd gone to the movie with her and had accepted her invitation to the cooking party.

The choice was his to make as to which sister he liked best.

Makima blinked. When she put it that way, she saw that she was making a mountain out of a molehill. Just because Alana was obviously smitten with Gabe, and just because she herself found him deeply attractive didn't mean that he felt anything other than enjoyment in the company of two single women he'd happened to meet.

She was relieved at that thought and when he came back to her desk, she was able to congratulate him and to fill him in on the day-to-day details at the center.

This was Monday and they would expect him to begin on Wednesday. She showed him around the center and answered his questions as any efficient office manager would do.

When she bid him goodbye, if there was a puzzled expression in his eyes she refused to acknowledge it but returned to her desk and settled to work.

Chapter 14

Dr. Cook was waiting when Gabe walked through the center door a few minutes to nine on a sunny but breezy Wednesday morning.

"Morning, Mr. Bell," Dr. Cook said.

"Good morning, Dr. Cook. Please call me Gabe, that's what I'm comfortable with."

Dr. Cook smiled. "I don't want you to think I'm checking your punctuality, Gabe. We're having a staff meeting and I want to show you where we meet. It isn't formal or fancy but it's convenient." He ushered Gabe into a room with a table big enough for eight or ten that was adjacent to the kitchen.

Makima was coming in from the kitchen with a plate of muffins to add to the coffee and plates already on the table. She was followed by the maintenance man, Jimmy Davis, whom Gabe had met Monday.

"Hi, Gabe," Jimmy said as he placed the cold beverages on

the table. Already seated was Eugenia Palmer, the program director, whose office was next to Gabe's. She smiled a greeting.

"We've found that eating while we work is the most productive use of our staff meeting time, Gabe. We hope you'll agree." Dr. Cook passed the muffins to Gabe.

"We take turns bringing the goodies," Makima said as she filled his coffee mug on which his name was already inscribed. "I'll put you on the list."

"The urgent matter on today's agenda is fund-raising. When was the last event, Makima?"

"The fall festival in early November," Makima replied after consulting her notes.

"How often do you have them?" Gabe asked.

"Whenever our funds are very low," Eugenia said.

"We've had bake sales, quilt sales, children's activities such as races where they get sponsors, flea markets, book sales, entertainment evenings, and anything else we could think of," Makima said.

"How about a golf tournament?" Gabe said.

"Haven't tried that yet," Dr. Cook said, "but it's a good idea to consider."

"I don't know how this would work," Gabe began slowly, "but I was wondering about combining two events."

"Which two?" Dr. Cook asked.

"A pancake breakfast to lure people in, followed by a flea market." He glanced around the table. Jimmy looked attentive for the first time. Eugenia and Makima were looking at each other with dawning alertness. Dr. Cook began making notes on his pad.

"Folks love flea markets," Jimmy observed.

"They like our pancake breakfasts, too, especially if Mama makes the batter," Makima said.

"We'd have to be sure it doesn't conflict with Easter," Eugenia pointed out, "since we want people to spend money here."

"Would it be possible to have the pancake breakfast inside and the flea market outside? I don't know what the weather is like here in April," Gabe said.

"In the event of rain the flea market could be moved indoors. It would be crowded but sometimes that's an advantage," Dr. Cook said.

More details were brought up, then Dr. Cook assigned Eugenia and Gabe to work on the costs, how much the tickets should be and how they should be sold. Makima was put in charge of the breakfast and Jimmy in charge of the tables, chairs and anything else needed for the event.

"I hope you will all work together as usual and call on your volunteers. I'm always available if you need me." Dr. Cook closed his notepad and stood up. "Good meeting and good to have you with us, Gabe."

"Thank you, sir," Gabe replied. "I can see this is going to be a great job." He'd been involved in a number of community services, especially the ones that helped young people. Through this center he'd be doing the same thing plus getting paid for four hours of bookkeeping which he could do standing on his head.

He liked Jimmy and Eugenia and looked forward to getting to know Makima better. Picking up the plates and glasses, he followed her into the kitchen where she began to wash the coffee mugs.

"Do you think this will work?" he asked, grabbing a towel from the rack and drying the dishes.

"A lot depends on the weather and how widely we can get the word out. We usually have good support but I'd like to see if we can top our record with this. The center needs the money." She emptied the sink and dried her hands. "When you get into the books, you'll soon see how close to the edge we always are. It doesn't permit us to carry out all the services we need to provide in Grayson."

"It seems to me you already do a lot," Gabe said as they walked back to her office.

"It's not enough. Youthful mothers and fathers need parenting classes, schoolchildren need homework help, seniors need activities they can't get anywhere else. The list goes on and on," she sighed.

At her office he opened her door and followed her inside. Gabe had thought Makima's energies were all focused on her clinic project. Now he knew he'd been wrong. Watching and listening intently to what she'd had to say this past hour he'd learned that some of the same compassionate instinct that drove her with the clinic spilled over into making the center a beacon of service to all who needed it.

"You're an unusual woman, Makima," he told her.

She looked up from the files she'd put on her desk and was caught in the warmth of his regard. Color rose in her face as they gazed at each other.

"Why do you say that?"

"You care so much for people and you try to do something for them instead of just paying lip service."

"I don't see myself that way."

Without thinking, Gabe leaned across the desk and tucked an errant lock of hair behind her ear. It felt like silk in his hand.

The color in her face deepened but she didn't pull away.

"How do you see yourself?" he asked softly, restraining himself from touching the satin smoothness of her cheek.

"For me life has to have purpose. I need to be doing something worthwhile."

Her voice was as quiet as his but he wondered if he'd heard a gentle challenge in her statement. Did she think he was a person who had no enduring concept of meaning in his life? This was another facet of Makima's personality he had to explore.

If that was what she wanted to think, he'd let her. For now.

He smiled at her. "You know what they say about all work and no play. So what are you bringing to the cooking party Saturday?"

She blinked at the change in his conversation, then rallied with a pert grin. "It's a surprise. How about you?"

"The same. I'm looking through my favorite recipes," he teased. "But now I'd better start looking at the center's books. See you later."

His office was small but held all he needed. There was a sizable wooden desk someone had donated. It was nicked here and there but had been well polished and the drawers were clean. A four-drawer file cabinet stood against the wall next to the desk. He had a large, comfortable swivel chair, two other chairs stood opposite the desk and a green plant decorated a lamp table. Someone had been caring for it, he thought, as the leaves were large and green. He'd have to remember to give it a drink now and then.

Examining the books, he knew he'd have to go through all of them since the inception of the center, but since that was only three years ago, it didn't present a problem. Just time-consuming, and he had plenty of that.

By the time he left work on Friday, Gabe was beginning to see a source of the center's financial problems. Some of the bookkeeping had not been up to his meticulous standards, but he'd found no evidence of embezzlement, just carelessness.

If any serious attempt at long-range planning had taken place it hadn't been successful enough to show up in the books. This was a matter he'd take up with Dr. Cook. But not just yet.

Get the books in perfect order first by a more sophisticated system than his predecessors had used. He'd enjoy doing that. It would make Makima happy, too. Which would make him happy.

He tapped on her office door before he went home and stuck his head in. "May I pick you up tomorrow for the cooking party?"

He saw her hesitate then she said, "I have a meeting in the early afternoon and I'm not sure when I'll be ready to go to Carolyn's. What time are we supposed to be there?"

"Alana said six o'clock. I can come get you any time you say."

She looked a little uncertain and he thought he'd persuaded her but she shook her head. "Thanks, Gabe, but I'll see you there."

With that he had to be satisfied but he had the feeling her refusal had to do with more than her meeting.

Drew had a great week. Each day he came home with something more to relate to Gabe about a new friend, a good teacher, the way a girl had looked at him. He even brought home a math test on which the teacher had written, "B, but I expect an A from you next time." Even riding on the school bus had been an adventure.

"Some of the juniors and seniors have cars and never ride the bus," he told Gabe wistfully.

"Is there any trouble on the bus?" Gabe asked.

"There're a couple of rowdies that the driver has to yell at but mostly everyone's okay."

Although Gabe suspected this wouldn't last, Drew was so glad to be in school with Jeff and other friends he'd made, he willingly followed the routine Gabe had set up with Drew's agreement. Do any garden work that was needed, then school assignments. Next was dinner, which they were taking turns preparing. After dinner he had to finish any schoolwork then he was free to ride his bike, talk on the phone and do anything else until bed, which on weeknights was a negotiated time between ten and eleven.

At first Drew had argued that since Gabe's new job was only part-time, why couldn't he do dinner every night?

"It doesn't work that way, Drew. I'm willing to do breakfast every weekday because you have to get out of the house before I do. But you have to get dinner every other night. That's not such a hardship and besides, you know you like to cook." They were cleaning up the kitchen after Gabe's dinner of fried chicken, cabbage the way he'd learned it from their mom and baked potatoes.

"Just because I like it doesn't mean I have to do it all the time," Drew grumbled.

"I have to do some cooking for a contest Saturday. Maybe you can help me think of something to take," Gabe said.

"You're going to be in a cooking contest? Man, that's wild!"

"It's just an idea Alana had for a different kind of party. She talked about it when we were at Rockwell's. Don't you remember?"

"Guess not. I was talking to Jeff most of the time."

"One thing I know I'll make is a triple-chocolate cake."

Drew's eyes got big and he made a slurping noise with his mouth, which made his brother frown. "Can I have a big piece? That's my absolute favorite."

"I'll try to save a piece to bring home."

"Gabe, you know there won't be any left from the party. You need to cut me a piece before you take it."

"No way, Drew. You've got a birthday coming up. I'll make you two. Okay?"

"I'm gonna remind you of that promise," he said as he started out of the kitchen. "Hey, I just remembered. What was that thing Ma made when we had company? She used those small chickens."

"Small chickens?"

"Yeah. They were almost like birds and she always made some good rice with them." He frowned in an effort to say something more that would make Gabe remember the dish.

"Small chickens like birds," Gabe thought aloud. Then he grinned. "You mean Cornish hens."

"Was that their real name? I never knew. The way she fixed them they were sure good, I remember that." Drew was positive.

"Great idea, bro. Thanks. I'll leave you some for your dinner."

"Can Jeff come over and have dinner with me tomorrow?" Drew knew when to press his advantage.

Gabe was already reaching for some cookbooks. "Okay," he said as he searched the index for Cornish hens. After finding a recipe that was almost like his mother's, he began a shopping list for the poultry and the cake. He was going to be busy Saturday morning, but it would be a welcome change from what he'd been doing and he was looking forward to the party. And Makima.

He was on his way upstairs when the phone rang. Now that Drew was in school most of the time the calls were for him, so Gabe didn't hurry.

"Gabe, it's Uncle Calvin for you," Drew yelled.

Gabe sank down in the office chair and picked up the phone. "Calvin! You won't believe me but I was going to call you later tonight," he said.

"You're right. I don't believe you." His friend's baritone voice was so familiar it filled Gabe with instant warmth.

"So when you coming to see us?" he asked.

"What do you mean? You haven't told me anything about Grayson or how you're getting along and the first thing you say is when am I coming down there!"

"You promised that as soon as Drew and I got settled in, you'd be down. Seriously, man, you've got to come see for yourself what we landed in. It's too much to try to tell you."

"That deep, huh? Maybe I should come while I'm waiting to hear from my editor about the latest manuscript."

"You finally sent it in? Great. Listen, this house is big, we've got plenty of space. Steer your 'Vette this way and come see what the South is like. How about next week?"

"I'll think about it and call you. Okay?"

"I'll be waiting." Gabe hung up the phone in a jubilant mood. His best friend, Calvin Peters, would soon be here. He couldn't wait to have his perspective on what was now Gabe's world.

Chapter 15

Makima hadn't exactly told Gabe the whole truth about a meeting today that would prevent her from letting him come by to take her to the cooking party at Carolyn's house.

His offer had caught her by surprise and she'd almost said yes when Alana popped into her mind. Alana knew how independent Makima was, that she preferred going places alone so she could leave when she wanted to get to her next appointment.

Even though Alana knew Gabe was working at the center, she also knew he didn't work on Saturday nor did Makima usually, therefore if they arrived together at Carolyn's, Alana would read something into it. That it was a date. That Gabe had asked and Makima had said yes and he'd take her home afterward.

Makima couldn't let that happen so she'd turned her overdue visit with Miss Eliza Bowen into a meeting. A Mother in the church, Miss Eliza was now in poor health. She was one of a dozen or so people Makima tried to keep up with through visits or by telephone.

She sat now in Miss Eliza's cozy kitchen, noticing how the morning sun illumined the blue-and-white-checked cloth on the round table where the thin china cups and saucers Miss Eliza used for company had been placed. Makima's hot-out-of-the-oven cherry coffee cake had been cut and served on delicate white dessert plates.

"Coffee's almost ready." Miss Eliza watched the coffee dripping into the glass pot.

"Your coffee always tastes so good," Makima said.

There was a *ping* and the red light went off. Miss Eliza filled the cups. "I don't stint on coffee. I buy the best and keep it fresh." She watched Makima take her first sip. "Now, don't that taste better than most?"

"It sure does." Makima had known her hostess a long time and the feisty old lady wasn't going to talk about her health until her coffee and cake were finished, so the conversation was about church and neighborhood affairs.

"That was mighty good and I appreciate that there's some left over for me to have some later," Miss Eliza said. "You're getting to be almost as good a cook as your mama," she said with a glint in her eyes.

Makima smiled but she wasn't going to be kept from the principal reason for her visit. "What does the doctor say about your arthritis?"

"He gave me something new to read about it but I haven't read it yet. Told me the health-food store in Swinton might have something that would help me."

"If you need a ride to Swinton, I can take you. How about one day next week?" Makima took her calendar out.

"Put your calendar away, Makima. My niece said she'd take me."

Makima looked up, surprised at the abrupt note in Miss Eliza's voice. Had she offended her by the offer?

The elderly woman gave Makima a penetrating look. "You

know I love you like my own, Makima, so I'm going to tell you what I'd say to my own. You spend too much time doing for others. Like getting up this morning to make that coffee cake and bringing it over here."

Makima had to blink to keep the tears away. She thought Miss Eliza liked her company and the way she never came empty-handed. Had she been wrong all this time?

"It isn't for me or for any of the other people in the community that you should be making coffee cake for breakfast just now." She leaned across the table and took Makima's hand. "Why aren't you doing that at your own breakfast table for your husband and children?"

The affection in her eyes and the clasp of her thin hand made the suppressed tears come up and trickle silently down Makima's cheeks. Miss Eliza's question on top of Makima's analysis as to why she had to reject Gabe's escort tonight connected painfully.

"Why, Makima?" Miss Eliza repeated gently.

"I don't know." She had to swallow to get the words out.

"What happened to that Reggie fellow that was around for a while?"'

"He left."

"You might not want to know what I think, but I'm going to tell you anyway so you won't make the same mistake twice. Reggie was personable and the two of you probably thought a lot of each other."

Makima's tears had dried and she was listening to Miss Eliza with all her heart. She'd always valued her insight about other people and the issues they'd discussed because of the wisdom and the directness the senior lady dispensed. But this would be the first time Makima was the subject, and Makima didn't know what to expect.

"Reggie wasn't strong enough for you, Makima. He saw that

part of you would always be involved with the clinic or some other project and where would that leave him as your husband? Would he always be second best? You need a man who won't feel threatened by what you do and is strong enough to win your love and loyalty. Reggie wasn't."

She patted Makima's hand and released it. "That's enough advice for today and knowing you, you probably have other things to do. Just think on what I've said."

That was a reminder Miss Eliza didn't need to give, Makima mused as she left her friend's house and went to the market to shop for the cooking party. What else could she think about? Fortunately she had a shopping list, so she didn't have to concentrate on what to buy.

At lunch several weeks ago her mother had raised the same question, which made Makima wonder if there was something about her that gave off a signal that she should be married. She hoped not. Always she'd felt sorry for women whose appearance and behavior indicated a hunger to be married.

In her case she hoped it was because she'd passed thirty and that her mother and Miss Eliza were thinking about the childbearing years. As she filled her cart she thought of the differences her two critics expressed about Reggie.

"You pushed him away," her mother had commented.

"He wasn't strong enough," Miss Eliza had said.

When she was back in her kitchen she put the smoked turkey wings, bouillon cubes, ginger and other seasonings in a deep pot with water to boil. Then as she began the long process of stripping the turnip greens from their central stems and washing them until the bottom of the sink was free of sand and grit, she let her mind probe the idea of Reggie.

Marriage had never been her primary goal. In her college years she'd thought of it vaguely as something that would naturally occur sometime in the future. After graduate school she'd begun teaching but found herself stymied by administrations opposed to her viewpoints.

June had been killed and she'd left teaching to work on the clinic project. She'd had neither time nor interest in a busy social life. Then Reggie Powell had appeared on the scene last fall and had made his interest in her clear from the beginning.

His persistence had been flattering and she'd begun to go to dinner and the movies with him when she could spare the time. His escort of her was frequent enough that people began to think of them as a couple. What people didn't know was that she couldn't force herself to participate in the intense lovemaking that Reggie desired.

"You never give us enough time so you can be comfortable with me and learn to feel for me what I feel for you," he'd complained.

Makima had taken herself to task and tried after that to show Reggie the affection she felt for him, but it hadn't been enough. He'd sent her a note a few weeks later:

> This isn't going to work for us, Makima, although I've been hoping it would, so I'm taking a job offer in Durham. I wish you well. Reggie.

Makima had blamed herself for not being able to hold Reggie. Her family had influenced her thinking as they'd practically set the wedding date and now she'd let the groom get away. But maybe that was only a part of the issue, if what Miss Eliza had said was true.

The greens were finally clean and she hadn't even noticed the passage of time. She cut them up and put them in the pot with the meat after taking out a cup of the broth for the dumplings.

In a small bowl she mixed cornmeal, salt, onion and an egg. She suddenly had an image of making a meal like this in a big kitchen with two or three children running around and her husband coming in to stand behind her, kiss her neck and say, "What smells so good, baby?"

Transported by the image and the thrill that ran up and down her back, she forgot what she was doing. Had Gabe ever had the dish she was making? She couldn't wait to see his reaction to her mother's recipe for greens with dumplings.

She steamed the dumplings carefully in the broth then covered the pot to transport it to Carolyn's.

The next big question was what to wear. She hadn't been to a party in a long time and she wanted this evening to be special. So maybe she'd wear that silky jumpsuit she'd bought on a whim the last time she'd gone shopping in Columbia.

On the other hand, that might be too showy. That's why she'd almost put it back on the rack but had succumbed to the sales-lady, who'd said it had been made for her coloring and her figure. Letting herself be flattered, she'd bought the jumpsuit but had never worn it.

She looked at several other outfits and laid an ankle-length rose sheath on the bed then went to take a shower. After putting on her underclothes, she ignored the sheath and went directly to the closet for the jumpsuit. It was almost the same color as her skin.

She chose glass earrings of three shades of brown. No necklace. Didn't want to break the flawless line of the jumpsuit. High-heeled brown sandals completed the outfit.

As she finished her makeup, drifted on some perfume and gave a final brush to her glossy hair, she winked at the woman in the mirror and turned out the light.

Chapter 16

Carolyn Brown's house already had cars in front of it and lights shone from every window when Gabe pulled up. He looked for Makima's car but didn't see it. He hoped she wouldn't be too late as he intended to spend most of the evening with her. To that end he'd dressed in a black silk turtleneck and pleated black pants. His sport coat was black with a small check and his tasseled loafers had a sheen.

He balanced his two boxes of food carefully and rang the bell. Alana opened the door.

"Gabe! I've been waiting for you." A big smile filled her face as she put her hand on his arm. She was dressed to allure in a flaming red outfit that had a fitted blouse and a flounced skirt that stopped at the knee. Her long legs were smooth in nude nylons and her shoes were silver with a high red heel.

Carolyn appeared beside Alana. "Welcome, Gabe. Let me

show you where to put the food. It's all in the kitchen for now in case you need the oven or the fridge."

"You made two things, Gabe? I can't wait to taste them." Alana sparkled at him. "Are you secretly a chef?"

"Not me. I just like to cook sometimes."

"Leave the food here and let me introduce you to the rest of the gang." Alana slid her arm through his and led him into the living and dining rooms.

He spoke to Bobby and Valerie and to Mark. The rest of the crowd were strangers to him. Music was going and drinks were being served. It was all friendly and like other house parties he was accustomed to except for the southern accents. And that each time the door opened the person who came in wasn't Makima.

He excused himself and went into the kitchen to check on his pan of Cornish hens. He'd just looked in the oven when the back door opened and Makima came in.

He was at her side instantly, taking hold of the box she was carrying. "I've been waiting for you. You should have let me bring you. I was beginning to think you weren't coming." His words ran together as he drank in the sight of her.

"It took me longer than I thought." Her smile held a trace of some emotion he hadn't seen before as they stood looking at each other.

He set her box on the table, thus seeing her fully for the first time. His reaction was what any woman would have wanted. Admiration filled his face as he pursed his mouth in a soundless whistle.

"You look absolutely spectacular, Makima." His voice caressed the words.

She blushed in acknowledgment. "You're looking very smart yourself," she murmured.

He took her hands and turned her around slowly. When she was facing him again, he said softly, "I know there'll be a lot of good food here tonight, but you're the feast for my eyes." He didn't want any other man basking in the womanly beauty she radiated. She was for him and him alone.

Makima was mesmerized. She hadn't let herself acknowledge that it was the thought of Gabe that had made her choose the jumpsuit. But now she gloried in how right her instinct had been even though it was unusual for her.

The hint of heat in his steady regard and the intimate quality in his voice had the same effect on her as when he'd leaned across her desk as if he couldn't help himself to touch her hair and tuck it behind her ear.

Her instinct told her that if they stood there a minute longer he was going to tighten his grip on her hands and pull her toward him.

She stepped back fractionally. "Where're Carolyn and Alana?"

Gabe let her go with the thought that they had the whole evening before them. "They're setting the table in the dining room." He lifted the cover of her pot. "Don't tell me you brought greens." He inhaled the fragrance of the food. "Not only is she beautiful, she can cook greens, too!"

"Who're you raving about?" Carolyn asked as she came in and stirred a pot on the back burner. "Oh, Makima. Time you got here, girl."

"Sorry to be late," Makima said.

"Actually you're just in time. Everyone else is here, so let's put it on."

Makima took her food to the dining room, where Alana was placing silverware. She looked at Makima critically. "I haven't seen that before. New?"

"No, just haven't worn it until now."

"Looks great on you," Alana said approvingly.

"Thanks. You're looking especially attractive in that red."

"Do you think Gabe'll like it?" she whispered.

"Any man would," Makima said.

Her own earlier moments with Gabe had been so unexpected and intense she'd forgotten for that magical time about Alana. But now it all returned, the idea that this might be the man her sister really wanted. And that she shouldn't be the one to stand in Alana's way. Alana was impatient to marry, Makima wasn't.

She went back into the kitchen to help bring out more food. Her life was already packed so full of obligations that she scarcely had time for social affairs like this. Regardless of what her mother and Miss Eliza thought, men came and went.

If and when it was her time, the right one would come along. Meanwhile, this one was for Alana. The knot in her stomach would go away as soon as she could eat something, even though her appetite had vanished.

The array of foods displayed on the long buffet brought excited comments from the crowd. The organizers had decided to award a prize to the best item in each category plus a grand prize for best of show. From hot ribs to baked chicken in sour-cream sauce to Gabe's Cornish hens with wild rice, and several other meats, plus Makima's turnip greens with cornmeal dumplings and candied yams with pecans leading the vegetable items and four kinds of salad as well as spoonbread, rolls that melted in your mouth and a baked-grits casserole, there was so much to tempt the appetite Gabe thought he'd never seen such a feast.

He'd taken his time filling his plate while keeping an eye on Makima. He'd picked out a table for them but she was making slow progress deciding what she wanted and was being followed by a few men whose attention to her was too close, as far as Gabe was concerned.

He mentally kicked himself for not making a definite comment to her about them eating together. His plate was finally full and he was holding up the line.

"Gabe, I've got a place for us over here," Alana said brightly, coming to stand beside him. She had two tall glasses in her hands. "I've got our drinks, iced tea and lemonade. You can have either one." Her eagerness to please was too apparent for him to do anything but follow her to the table for four where Valerie and Bobby were waiting.

He couldn't look back at the buffet to see who Makima left it with, but after a few minutes there was a little stir as Carolyn placed a small table for two near them.

A tall slim man who wore glasses and a long-sleeved burgundy polo shirt with khaki-colored Chinos brought up two chairs and seated Makima in the one facing Gabe.

Gabe remembered meeting the guy and liking him. What was his name? Greetings were exchanged across the tables before they all settled down to eat. Josh Dixon. That was it. Did he live in Grayson or was he from out of town? He tried to recall what he'd heard while keeping up with the conversation at his table.

Whoever he was, he certainly held Makima's attention. Their conversation was animated and continuous. So much so that he could never catch her eye.

He gave up trying and turned his attention to the conversation at his table when Alana asked about the Cornish hens he'd brought.

"That was Drew's idea." He entertained them with how his brother had made the suggestion and gently blackmailed him into Jeff's sharing some with him.

"Even as we speak," Gabe said, "they're having two each."

That led to anecdotes from Valerie, and the subject became serious as it turned to the education system, of which Jeff and Drew were a part.

Bobby, an independent insurance agent, said he had a fair number of clients who were paying on education policies so they could send their kids to a good college. "The problem is that tuition keeps going up every year."

"Still, it's better than nothing," Valerie said. "It's keeping them in school so they can graduate and qualify that's the problem now." She looked at her empty plate. "I wish I could eat more but I'm full."

"What did you bring, Bobby?" Gabe asked.

"The ribs."

"They were fork tender. How about you, Alana?"

"The shrimp salad. Our mom taught us all how to cook."

"She did a first-class job. What was your dish, Valerie?"

"The bacon-and-egg potato salad. We could open a restaurant with what we've cooked tonight."

"I hope we're not having dessert right away," Bobby said.

"That wouldn't be any fun," Alana said. She turned to Gabe, laying her hand on his. "First we clean up the plates, then games and dancing, then dessert, then voting and the awards. How does that sound?"

"Sounds like a plan to me," Gabe said. A plan that might get him some time with Makima after all.

Alana jumped to her feet, clapped her hands for attention and announced the plan. Gabe helped clean up the table while noticing that Makima and Josh were still talking. He deliberately stayed in the kitchen helping Valerie and Alana and joining in the talk going back and forth.

They were all laughing at a comment Alana had overheard, when Josh and Makima came in with their dishes. At the same time Mark asked Alana to come with him to choose some music.

Makima took Alana's place washing the silverware. "Loved the greens but I'd never had the dumplings before," Gabe said.

Josh leaned against the counter. "My grandmother used to make them but they weren't as light as yours."

"I just followed my mom's recipe," Makima said.

The last thing Gabe wanted to hear was another cooking discussion. "You live in Grayson?" he asked Josh.

"In Orangeburg. I'm in programming at the television station.

Carolyn's my cousin and she invited me over." He glanced at Makima. "I haven't been in South Carolina very long and I'm glad to meet some people."

Valerie came over from wiping off the stove and gathered up the clean silverware. "Where'd you come from, Josh?"

"Asheville, North Carolina."

The paper plates and garbage had been disposed of and now the silverware was ready for the dessert service. Makima had been silent throughout the conversation, but more than that it seemed to Gabe that she had distanced herself mentally and emotionally.

Where was the vibrant, responsive woman he'd talked to in this very kitchen several hours ago? Now he couldn't even make eye contact with her.

He heard the music begin in the other room with Luther's "Bad Boy, We're Having a Party." Seizing his opportunity, he took Makima's hand.

"Let's dance," he said, smiling at her surprise. Ignoring Josh and Valerie, he danced Makima out of the kitchen and into the living room where the small rugs had disappeared. They joined the other couples moving to the lively rhythm on the polished floor.

Makima seemed to pick up the energy of the music and he felt her relax as they danced in perfect harmony.

"Makima," he said, "don't go away again and leave me."

"I haven't been anywhere," she protested.

"Yeah, you have. Right after we said hello in the kitchen." He saw the faint color come into her face as she met his eyes. She knew exactly what he was talking about.

"I'm sorry you feel that way," she said softly.

"I was trying to wait for you so we could eat together."

She looked up at him swiftly. "Oh," she murmured.

Gabe didn't know if he should tell her that truth since it was her sister that had spiked his plan, but he needed her to know his preference.

He took her hands and swung her around then brought her close to him.

The dance ended and Josh and Alana appeared. "Time to change partners," Alana said gaily and whirled Gabe away to a hectic beat.

Makima was relieved to see them go. She hadn't anticipated how difficult the evening would be and the only way she could get through it was to pretend that Gabe wasn't there. It had helped to meet Josh and sit with him while he talked about his new position. Carolyn had told him about the clinic project and he thought he might be able to give her some exposure. That Gabe would immediately sense the remoteness she'd imposed upon herself surprised her. It made him much more dangerous.

For the rest of the evening she was careful to laugh and talk with him as long as it was with a group, and to be dancing with another man before he could get to her. That hadn't been hard to do. It must be this jumpsuit, she thought. She'd never been so popular.

She wasn't sure what Gabe would do when it came time to sit at tables again for dessert. Alana had made it clear throughout the evening that she and Gabe were a couple. Gabe wasn't the kind of man who would embarrass Alana by sitting with Makima, so Makima put it out of her mind.

When it was dessert time, Alana came to Makima. "I want you to see what Gabe brought before it gets cut," she said proudly.

The three-layer cake glistened with perfectly applied dark chocolate frosting. The top had deep curls of chocolate scattered over it and in each curl nestled a perfect strawberry.

"It's gorgeous," Makima murmured.

"He's really special, Makima," Alana whispered, her eyes shining.

"He certainly is." She looked around. "Where is he?"

"In the kitchen getting his serving ware for the cake. By the way, he wants you and Josh to sit at a table with us, so don't get caught up with anyone else."

Thankful for the warning, she told Josh and they got in line behind Alana and Gabe. Makima met Gabe's eyes now and then as she did her share of talking. There was an air of relaxation at the table as they slowly ate pie and cake and drank coffee.

She became aware that Josh and Gabe were vying with each other in witty entertainment. This was turning out to be the best part of her evening and she looked at Gabe appreciatively as she basked in the give-and-take of the two attractive men.

Carolyn stood and raised her hand. "Time to vote," she said. "Mark is passing around paper ballots and some pencils. Vote first for the best meat dish. Valerie and Alana will count the ballots."

Amid much laughter and joking comments the exercise was completed. Valerie announced there was a tie between the ribs and the Cornish hens. Both Bobby and Gabe received a paper rosette and a smacking kiss on the cheek from Carolyn.

Makima's turnip greens won in the vegetable category. "I'm sitting at the winners' table," Josh observed and gave Makima a quick kiss on the cheek.

Not to be outdone, Gabe kissed her other cheek. "Great going, Makima."

The other categories went by quickly. There were seven items as desserts. Gabe had sampled them all. He'd decided people here liked their sweets and didn't care if they were sinfully rich. There was banana-cream pie with real whipped cream, caramel apple pie, pound cake that melted in your mouth, peach cobbler, coconut pie, cheesecake and his own chocolate cake. He'd had to taste it to see if it was moist and light like it was supposed to be and deeply chocolate.

It must have been because it won in the dessert category. He felt a little disconcerted because he was a newcomer and he knew how people often were territorial about these things.

Carolyn said, "We're all good cooks, no doubt about it. We'll have to do this again." She waited for the applause to die. "This was Alana's bright idea, so as soon as you vote for best of show, she gets to present the award."

Gabe surreptitiously glanced at his watch. A little after midnight and he was ready to look in on Drew and Jeff just to be sure all was well. Drew had been right, there were only crumbs of the cake left although he'd hoped to take a slice home with him. Especially when he'd seen how many other desserts there were.

"The best of show winner is the triple-chocolate cake," Carolyn said.

Gabe's involuntary thought was, oh, no, not a third time. Then he saw Alana, smiling radiantly, coming toward him, and his heart dropped. He came to his feet to accept the third rosette and the wrapped package which had the shape of a book.

As everyone looked on applauding and whistling, Alana rose on her tiptoes and kissed him on the mouth.

More applause and whistles and he heard a woman say, "You go, girl." He hoped he wasn't flushing as he stole a quick glance at Makima then told the crowd thanks and he hoped he'd received a new cookbook so he could learn new dishes.

He sat down and asked Josh and Makima if the cake was really that good.

"Mom couldn't have done better," Makima assured him. "That's the highest compliment I can give you." She held his glance for a moment and he realized she was sending him a message. He couldn't read it but it seemed on the positive side.

Anxious now to get away, Gabe said his goodbyes as quickly as he could. "It was a great party and I enjoyed it very much," he told Alana, who walked him to the door.

"You're fabulous, Gabe. You're going home with three awards!"

"Not fabulous. Just lucky." He put his hand on the doorknob.

"See you at church tomorrow?" she asked.

"I don't think so. I've some work to do. Good night, Alana, and thanks again."

On the way home Gabe reviewed the evening. He didn't want to be conceited but he'd been around enough to know that Alana wanted his attention. She was the kind of confident woman who made no bones about men who attracted her. He liked her a lot, but not in that way. The problem was how to let her know without hurting her feelings or embarrassing her.

Or offending her sister.

He pulled into the driveway and went quietly upstairs. The light was on in Drew's room but both boys were sound asleep in front of the television. Popcorn bowls and soft drinks were on the floor beside them.

He turned the television off and got the boys to their beds.

By the time he got to his bed, he found the brief interlude with Drew and Jeff had been sufficient to take his mind from the problem he'd come home with.

He doused the light and went to sleep.

Chapter 17

The sun was playing hide-and-seek, at one moment casting light on the canopy of trees Gabe looked at from the upstairs window, and several minutes later hiding as a swiftly moving cloud covered it.

It looked like it might rain later on, but it didn't matter to him. He was in no mood to go to church today.

Jeff had gone home early to get ready to go to church, since he and Drew had talked to some girls named Angela and Penny last night, and arranged to meet them there. After service they were going with Penny, who'd promised to help her sister get ready for a party later that afternoon.

Gabe was glad to have the house to himself. The past week had been busy with the new job at the center. Then he'd found himself giving considerable time to Drew's awakened interest in school and his new friends. He hoped that would continue but he knew there was no guarantee.

Saturday there was laundry, shopping, cooking and the party.

He moved away from the window. Hands in the pockets of his jeans, he slowly circled the bedroom he was in. He looked at everything as if he were seeing it for the first time, while letting his mind float free.

This was what had been missing. He'd let himself become immersed in those other things and had lost his connection with his great-grandfather. Without it he might never discover the clue to the treasured destiny he'd been sent here to find.

He took his time, moving deliberately through each room in the house. When images of Makima entered his consciousness, he ruthlessly suppressed them. He'd think of her later. By the time he reached the kitchen he felt in tune once more with the man who'd built the house.

The wind had come up, blowing the clouds more swiftly across the sky. Taking a jacket from the hook by the door, Gabe went outside. He unlocked the gate that led to the grassy field and the wooden bench.

He settled himself on the hard seat, stretched out his legs and buttoned his jacket. He put his hands in the jacket's warm pockets.

In the next block a car started up. Music blared from the speakers then faded away as the car gathered speed. Two birds flew over the trees squawking at each other. Then all was silent.

Gabe surrendered himself to the solitude, the quiet and the breeze. He closed his eyes and relaxed his body. His mind now was crystal clear and he accepted into it any image, thought, memory, or fragment of idea.

The first image was Alana kissing him; it dissolved into a kiss from Makima after he won the third award. Then Reverend Givhans was looking for him with a lantern in his hand waving back and forth. A tall, noble, African man, walking with a cane, came into sight and looked steadily at Gabe before disappearing. Next, Mr. Moultrie told Gabe and Drew it had to be the sixth generation. Lastly, a light-skinned man gazed intently at something in his hand.

Gabe opened his eyes and meditated about what had come into his consciousness. He didn't know what most of it meant. Perhaps in the future understanding would come. But Great-Grandfather had been kind in leaving him with a specific message. Gabe couldn't have said how the transmittal had been made and at the moment he really didn't care. He was just grateful and went at once to test it.

In the living room he opened the doors of the massive bookcase. The shelves were deep enough to hold a double row of books. He removed all the volumes on the bottom row and stacked them carefully on the floor so he could replace them in order.

He hadn't stopped to get a flashlight. He laid on the floor and with closed eyes, began to run his fingers delicately over the wood. His heart racing, he probed every inch of it.

Nothing.

He sat up and breathed deeply. Rising to his feet, he stripped off the jacket and went to the kitchen for the flashlight that stayed in the bottom drawer under the counter.

Back in the living room he stretched out again on the floor. This time the mahogany wood was illumined by the focused light. Gabe moved its arch with agonizing slowness. Still it showed nothing.

He gritted his teeth. "I know you're here," he growled, "and if I have to, I'll take this whole thing apart."

Once more he went through the process, paying particular attention to the corners. He was moving the light from the bottom left-hand corner when he saw a reflection hit the light from above.

"There you are!" His voice was triumphant as he extracted a small key from the niche made for it in the corner. No wonder it had been so hard to find.

It looked like a key to a jewel box or a child's treasure chest. Drew was going to exclaim about jewels again when he saw it, Gabe thought with a smile. He turned it over and over in his hand, noting that it was sturdier than most small keys. He dropped it in his pocket and went to work replacing the books.

A key meant there was some item waiting to be unlocked. At first glance one would think the key was to the usual small chest, but Gabe wasn't convinced. Great-Grandfather had been a wily thinker, constructing a puzzle for Gabe to solve to prove he was worthy of his destiny. At least that was Gabe's conclusion.

The item for which the key had been made could be a drawer, a box or a hollowed-out book. Having read his share of mysteries, he knew the most unlikely detail could be fashioned as a locked hiding place. He groaned at the thought of searching every place in the large house for the lock to which this key belonged.

He ran his hands across the front row of books to be sure they were aligned. Returning to his office he looked up Moultrie's number. Probably he should wait to call him at his workplace tomorrow but he couldn't wait. He dialed the attorney's cell phone.

"Sorry to bother you on a Sunday," he said when Mr. Moultrie picked up.

"I'm always anxious to hear from you, Gabe. Did you find something?"

"A small key that was hidden in the big bookcase in the living room."

"Very good." The approval in his voice gave Gabe's mind ease.

"You and Drew are beginning your fourth week in Grayson. By the way, how is Drew getting along?"

"Better than I expected. He decided to transfer to the local high school and is doing well."

"Is that a fact? As I was saying, this is the beginning of your fourth week and you've already found the scroll and a key."

"Already? I feel like I'm going very slowly," Gabe protested.

"You still have two months and I predict that your pace will pick up." Mr. Moultrie sounded confident.

"I know what will help me, Mr. Moultrie, and I sincerely hope you can give me an answer to this question." The attorney hadn't revealed information to previous questions but maybe this time Gabe would be lucky.

"What's the question, Gabe?"

"The key I have, does it belong to something in this house?"

"No, it doesn't." Gabe expelled his breath in relief.

Moultrie went on. "You needn't worry about that part. Just put the key with the scroll because it's essential to the resolution of Mr. Bell's will. Do you have a safe-deposit box in Grayson?"

"No, I haven't."

"I suggest you get one. Put the key and the scroll in it. Incidentally, yours is key number one."

Gabe felt a jolt. "You mean there's another one for me to find?"

"No, you've found yours. The other one will appear in due time. Goodbye, Gabe, and say hello to Drew."

Gabe was certain he heard a faint chuckle as the attorney delivered the bombshell about the second key before he hung up.

As soon as Drew came home from Jeff's, Gabe showed him the key.

"That's a key for a chest of jewels, maybe diamonds, just like I said when Mr. Moultrie first told us about it," he said positively.

"You may be right but somehow I don't think so," Gabe said.

"Why not? That's what it looks like to me."

"Great-Grandfather wasn't a reckless man. I think if he had real jewels to pass on to us, he'd put them in a bank vault."

"Couldn't this be the key to a safe-deposit box somewhere? That's what you always see on television." His eyes lit up with a new idea. "Maybe somewhere in Charlotte where Mr. Moultrie lives. I bet he'd know."

Gabe told Drew about his conversation with the attorney.

"He said there was another key, that this was key number one and the other would appear in due time." He had to laugh at the comical expression on Drew's face. It reminded him of the first time his little brother had caught a firefly, held it tightly in his small palm while he ran to show it to Gabe. He'd opened his hand triumphantly only to find that the firefly was motionless. The light had disappeared.

"There're two different boxes?"

"I don't know, Drew. There might just be one but you have to have two different keys to open it. That sounds more like what Great-Grandfather would do." Anything to make it more complex.

Later that night Drew came into the office where Gabe was reading.

"I forgot to ask how you happened to find the key. Were you looking for a book downstairs?"

Gabe shook his head no. "I'd been thinking about Great-Grandfather and I went out to sit on his bench. That's when the idea came to look in the bookcase." He kept his answer as brief and ordinary as possible, knowing that Drew was already inclined to be uncomfortable at how frequently Gabe spent time on that bench.

"Don't get spooky on me, Gabe," Drew said seriously.

"There's nothing spooky about having ideas that you don't know exactly how you got. Everybody does that. Even you. What you need to worry about is me getting spooky if you didn't finish your homework for tomorrow." He crossed his eyes and made a scary face.

"I just have one more page to do." Drew turned to leave, then said, "I forgot to tell you I saw Miss Alana at church. She asked about you."

"Was her family there?"

"Yeah, but she was the only one who came over to talk to Jeff and me. She's really friendly."

Gabe thought about how dismayed Drew would have been to know Alana had been one of the people he'd seen while he was at the bench meditating.

Yet it wasn't Alana or even Makima who stayed in his mind as he drifted off to sleep later.

He wondered who the tall African with the penetrating gaze was, and what was the light-skinned man looking at in the palm of his hand?

Chapter 18

The doors to the sanctuary were closed and Makima could hear the choir singing. She pushed one of the doors quietly and the deacon standing inside turned his head in surprise. He held the door as she slipped in. They nodded to each other. An usher came toward her but Makima shook her head.

Instead of going to the front to her usual seat, she sat in the back row. She glanced at the other four people in the pew and was thankful she didn't know them. Being this late for church was unusual for her. Actually, she'd decided to stay home with the uncertain weather and the way she felt after last night.

But the years of habit were strong. Church was where you went for relief from pain and she was filled with pain. She hadn't come for the fellowship she usually enjoyed and she certainly hadn't come to see her family. That's why she was sitting in the back. She could leave as soon as the service was over and wouldn't have to talk to anyone.

Everything about the sanctuary and the service were well known to her. The familiar atmosphere they created helped her to relax. The pounding in her temples began to lessen.

Thank you, Lord, she thought gratefully.

Problems to be solved and work to be done. These she was accustomed to and went at them eagerly. But not headaches. Headaches meant emotions and they were much more difficult to handle. She had slipped away into her own private world, when she heard Reverend Givhans say, "Pain is hard for us to understand, and harder still for us to accept."

She hadn't looked at the program the deacon had put in her hand. Now she did. Today's sermon was on "The Meaning of Pain and Suffering." He was detailing the suffering visited upon humanity through natural disasters but then he came to the individual and the personal.

"It tests our faith," he said earnestly. "It helps to examine ourselves objectively. What did we do, or failed to do that has caused us such pain? Be honest and try to get to the root of it. Then decide what we can do about it. There's always something can we do if we pray with faith in our hearts, ask for insight and guidance, instead of whining or feeling sorry for ourselves. It is in overcoming our pain and suffering that we grow stronger. Stronger in faith, stronger in our ability to help others. Stronger in soul and in spirit."

Makima stored the words in her mind to think about later. All she knew now was that she had a dull ache not only in her head but also in her stomach that had nothing to do with food, and everything to do with Gabriel Bell.

She couldn't sit still any longer. The instant the pastor turned from the pulpit to sit down, she eased from her seat and left.

At home she changed into jeans and a sweater, replaced her heels and hose with warm socks and tennis shoes. She had to get out in the air. She didn't want to be cooped up in the car but she wanted to cover some ground.

Her bicycle! She hadn't been on it for months yet just the thought of riding it made her feel better. She took it from the storage space, dusted it off and rode it down the driveway. She stayed on the sidewalk until she came to Grayson Park.

The park had no official bike path but one had been made over the years by cyclists who didn't want to ride in the streets. There were a few children on the swings who waved to her. Two young women in colorful outfits were jogging, each with a dog on a leash. Makima had taught them both.

"Hi, Miss Gray," they said as she went by.

She left the park and rode through the streets until she came to Five Mile Road. On this country road she could avoid people who knew her, she hoped. Solitude was what she craved.

She picked her way carefully down the rural road. The sun went in and out of the clouds and she was glad she had on a warm sweater. The breeze on her face was refreshing and she could finally face the fact that her reaction to Gabe last night had not only been overwhelming but totally unexpected in its intensity.

Sure, she realized that she'd worn the jumpsuit because of him, but she'd thought that was more in the nature of a brief flirtation to make her feel good as an attractive woman.

The electricity between them when she'd walked in the back door could have illumined Carolyn's whole house. It had floored her. She'd never experienced such emotion. Her whole body hummed and when he'd taken her hands in his, her legs had felt weak.

She had no name for it because she didn't recognize it. What she did know was that she'd never encountered it with Reggie— or with anyone else.

Had she stayed an instant longer he would have kissed her. She could see the intent and the desire in his eyes. But she'd panicked and moved away.

How she'd wanted that kiss! She wanted it now more than

ever but Alana had taken it. The other prizewinners had been kissed on the cheek. Alana, brave and seeing her chance, had kissed Gabe on his mouth.

To Makima's dismay, she'd been jealous of her own dear sister who'd made it clear that she had feelings for Gabe. Makima'd been ashamed but that hadn't changed the nature of the sensation.

She yearned to know how Gabe's lips felt. She thought they'd be firm yet yielding, neither too dry nor too moist, and their pressure on hers would be tender yet exhilarating. Nothing like Reggie's, which hadn't moved her at all.

As her bicycle wheels turned, her eyes passed over the fields unseeingly. She was focused on the pain that was eating her because she now knew how important Gabe was to her, and because he felt the same way, if she could believe his actions last night. He'd immediately sensed her effort to break the bond between them and had called her on it when they were dancing.

She had no choice. She couldn't let the bond deepen. It had to be broken.

The blare of a horn from an oncoming car startled her. She saw she'd strayed toward the middle of the narrow road. She pulled back over to her side and when, a little farther along, she saw a small brick church, she rode over to it. She'd sit on the steps while she thought through her dilemma.

What was wrong with her? Why couldn't she ever win? She seemed to be losing out on all the significant issues in her life. She'd met the man who evoked a profound response in her, but it was the man her sister wanted. She was committed to the clinic project and had spent untold energy on it for many months but it was still far from a done deal or a contract. She'd been certain that the land needed for the clinic would be available from Mr. Zeke. But he was dead and there'd been nothing about it in his will.

She felt despondent, defeated and drained.

Maybe I need to move, she thought. She'd been offered a position with a public relations firm in Columbia. It would pay much more than the center could pay. As for the clinic, her mother had hinted that more people on the board would step up to their responsibilities if Makima would back off and let them. Was she that controlling? If so, that was another mark against her staying in Grayson.

Perhaps she'd be doing the board a favor if she moved. They might not do business her way, and it might take twice as long, but they wouldn't abandon the project. She was certain of that. It would be up to them to find another site. She wouldn't have to worry about it.

It was always in the back of her mind because it was connected with Gabe. If she moved to Columbia, Gabe and his land would no longer be an issue. She wouldn't have to see him at work every day. Nor would she have to endure the pain of seeing Alana win him over once she was out of the way.

Perhaps Columbia was too close. She visited many cities about the clinic project. She could make herself content in Chapel Hill, North Carolina. The temptation to run back and forth to Grayson wouldn't be as great as if she lived in Columbia.

There was no doubt that she'd find a good job, an attractive place to live, and make new friends.

The enormity of what she was proposing swept over her. How meaningless her life would be. She'd have to give up working on the memorial to her sister. She'd only see her family occasionally. The center would go on without her ideas and activity. She'd be without her church home and her special friends like Miss Eliza.

Most of all she'd give up the idea of a husband and children of her own! She wasn't a woman whose deepest feelings were easily engaged. She was beginning to see how the attraction between Gabe and her could progress if permitted. Miss Eliza had lit a spark and Makima's imagination had let it grow into a flame, fueled by a regard for Gabe she hadn't fully recognized.

She was already being scorched by the heat of the flame. She couldn't go through this misery and heartache another time. She doubted she'd find another Gabe. It had taken thirty-two years for them to meet. So the sensible idea was to content herself with being another Miss Eliza.

She didn't know how long she sat on the church steps. She contemplated the situation from every angle she could think of, including her possible future based on living someplace other than Grayson. Then she prayed.

Finally, with a deep sigh, she got on her bike and started back to town.

She could no longer tell what God wanted her to do.

Chapter 19

Monday morning Gabe woke up to heavy rain. After breakfast, he drove Drew to the school-bus stop. He invited the three other kids who were waiting there to get in the car with Drew until the bus came. Their chatter picked up his spirits and he was sorry when the bus arrived.

It was too early to go to the center. At home he resumed the cleaning up in the kitchen that had been interrupted when Drew had asked for a ride. The eggs went back into the fridge and the empty orange juice carton hit the trash. He didn't know what his brother had for lunch at the school cafeteria. What he could be sure of was the healthy breakfast and dinner Drew had at home each day.

Gabe took his time cleaning the stove. Usually he was eager to get to work to see Makima. Today, however, was different.

She had affected him in so many ways at the party. When he'd first seen her he'd been thunderstruck with an emotion that was primitive, intense and unexpected. He'd wanted to do what any male desired when he met his mate. Pick her up and take her to his lair away from anyone else.

Although she'd been responsive to him in those first thrilling moments, she'd escaped later by sitting with another male, while he'd been drawn away, unwillingly, by another female. He'd waited for his chance and when it came, he'd taken her onto the dance floor and made her aware that he'd sensed her withdrawal from their earlier connection.

Unfortunately they'd both been entangled by the social dictates of the event. Alana had attached herself to him in such a public way all evening that he'd felt unable to detach himself from her eager and constant attention. It would have been a humiliating rejection, and he couldn't bring himself to do it, even though his real interest had been focused on Makima. Makima had been in a similar situation with Josh Dixon, who'd made himself her escort for the evening.

The situation had been disturbing and for Gabe, unique. He had never before been deeply attracted to one sister while another sister had made obvious her attraction to him.

Another part of his dilemma was that he'd not declared his feelings to Makima. He'd barely begun to discern them himself. Nor did he know how she felt about him. Yet in those moments in the kitchen a current of vivid awareness had passed between them. He was certain she'd felt it, and it left him filled with yearning. How could he make clear his choice between the sisters without seeming presumptuous?

He found himself staring at the clock on the stove, which was shining like new from his prolonged cleaning. He was going to be late if he didn't hurry.

He needn't have worried. Eugenia Palmer, who covered the phone at the receptionist's desk when Makima was out, explained that Makima had gone to Charleston to interview a clinic specialist at the Medical University of South Carolina. She'd be back in the office tomorrow.

Feeling somewhat relieved, Gabe worked with Eugenia on the assignment they'd been given to calculate the costs of the pancake breakfast and flea-market fund-raiser.

On the way home he stopped at his bank and rented a safe-deposit box. In it he placed the scroll and the key. He should have more than that to show after weeks of searching, he thought as he drove home.

However, Mr. Moultrie had seemed pleased with his progress. Rather than sharing Gabe's disappointment, he'd predicted that the pace would go faster now. Did the attorney mean there was something special about the key that would have a bearing on the remainder of the quest for Gabe's treasured destiny?

After dinner that evening Gabe went up to the desk in the office. He'd found two unused ledgers in one of the drawers and had smiled inwardly at his great-grandfather thinking he'd need them even though he was one hundred.

Gabe had appropriated one. In it he'd made a list of every room, space, building, piece of furniture and item he'd examined. Also the date of the activity and the result. The list was extensive and many items had more than one check mark beside it.

He studied it carefully. What had he missed? Perhaps he hadn't paid enough careful attention to the piles of linen in the drawers, closets and on the beds. He and Drew hadn't actually unfolded each separate piece. To do so would take hours, but hours he had and he determined to begin after work tomorrow.

At work the next day Gabe went directly to his office. Usually he stopped for a few minutes to talk with Makima or Eugenia. But not today. He closed his door and continued working on the plan he intended to suggest to Director Cook for the next fiscal year.

He'd been working for some time when there was a knock

on the door. "Come in," he said, expecting to see Eugenia as he stood up.

"Am I disturbing you?"

"Not at all, Makima. Good morning." Why did she always have to look so devastatingly attractive no matter what she wore? Her crisp white blouse with cuffed sleeves was tucked into slim black pants. She'd tied a multicolored sash around her waist. It made him want to measure her waist with his hands to see if it could be as small as it seemed. Her low-heeled black shoes sported a red bow that matched the red in the sash.

Her glossy hair framed her face and her lips were set in a smile as she returned his greeting but there was a tug in his stomach as he saw that the smile didn't reach her eyes which were anxious and uncertain.

She held out a folder. "Dr. Cook wanted you to look through this at your convenience. It's the history of the center."

Gabe took it from her, his glance never leaving her face. "Thanks. Have a seat, Makima."

"I can't stay. My desk is piled with work," she said.

"Please, just for a minute," he urged. "I want to ask you something."

Makima slid into one of the chairs opposite his desk. Gabe sat also, hoping to put her at ease. He began with the one subject he knew she'd be willing to talk about. "Eugenia said you were in Charleston yesterday for a conference about your clinic. How did it go? Were you pleased?"

Her face brightened. "It went very well. I met several people who seem to know all there is about exactly the kind of clinic we have in mind for Grayson. One man has a relative here and plans to come up and said he'd be willing to meet with the board."

"That sounds good." What else could he say to keep her there a little longer? "How was your Sunday?"

He immediately regretted his phrasing. He meant it as a bland query to prolong the conversation, not in reference to the Saturday-night events. The tension that had begun to disappear began to rise again as she gave him a wary look.

"Mine was pretty lazy," he added quickly. "Drew went to church but I did chores most of the day and spent some time in the office. Did you do anything exciting?"

He thought she wasn't going to answer but then he saw her relax a fraction in her chair. "I got my bike out and went riding in the country," she said.

Gabe sat forward in his chair. "You're a bike rider?" His voice was enthusiastic and excited.

Makima responded to the animation in his voice and expression with a lifting of her own spirits. "I used to be but I'm too busy now. I can see you like it."

"Bike riding has always been my favorite outdoor sport. I play a little basketball and soccer but they can't compare to cycling for me. How long have you been riding?"

"I always liked it from childhood. When I was in college there was a group of us who formed a club and we took regular trips." She sat forward in her chair now and Gabe saw her genuine interest in the conversation was reflected in her eyes.

"There were four of us who took long trips," he said. "Once we even rode from Manhattan to Greenwich, Connecticut, and back."

"I don't think we ever went that far," she said. Then she smiled. "The longest and most exciting trip we made was to Hickory Knob State Park. We did it over a four-day weekend when several parents could chaperone us and be on hand to give us rides when the hills got too steep and long." She paused then said reminiscently, "I haven't been in such good physical shape since."

He was enchanted by the gaiety with which she not only answered his question but went on to relate several other incidents of that long-ago college activity. He countered with stories of his own and all self-consciousness between them vanished.

They were laughing about a spill he took which had resulted in his rolling down a hill when Makima looked at her watch. "I must get back to work," she exclaimed, getting up from her chair.

Gabe came from around his desk. "Thanks for the stories. I don't meet many people who enjoy bike riding. I wish I'd known you were going. We could have gone together. That would have been great!" He took a couple of steps to open the door for her.

He saw her face grow still and lose all its animation. "It was a spur-of-the-moment thing. I really must go now." She looked at his hand on the doorknob. "I really do have to get back to my desk, Gabe."

He couldn't let her leave like that. "Perhaps we could arrange another time, Makima." He knew it was unwise to press the issue but he needed to regain the positive response they'd just enjoyed in being together.

The tension built up again as they stood motionless. He should open the door but his hand wouldn't move.

"Makima?" His voice was a murmur.

She finally raised her eyes to his and all of the anxiety and uncertainty were back. "I don't think so, Gabe," she said.

The resignation in her voice pulled at him. For a wild instant he wanted to place himself against the door and hold her in his arms until she told him why. Then he'd change her mind.

But his fingers moved of their own accord to open the door and she left.

Instead of returning to her office, Makima went to the restroom, the only place she could lock the door and have privacy.

This was going to be so much more difficult than she'd anticipated. She'd meant to hand him the folder and leave. She hadn't counted on how just being in Gabe's presence would make her feel. This was unfamiliar territory and she realized now how cautious she was going to have to be where he was concerned. She had enjoyed being with Reggie but this was totally different.

She couldn't analyze it all yet, but what she'd just gone through alerted her defenses. Nothing about Gabe Bell could be taken lightly as far as her emotions were concerned.

Any of her friends could have talked to her about her trip yesterday, but the fact that Gabe had been interested was meaningful. Since his refusal to consider selling her a part of the land he'd inherited, the subject had disappeared from their conversation. She'd thought he had a subtle disapproval of the project. If he did, it hadn't been discernible half an hour ago.

How wonderful it had been to talk about bike riding even for the short time they had. It had been a passion of hers when she was younger and apparently one of his as well. They hadn't even scratched the surface of the joy the sport provided, and yet there'd been a meeting of the minds that had been exhilarating. She'd forgotten she was supposed to stay at a distance from him until he asked if they could they ride together.

All of the inner turmoil she'd suffered on her Sunday ride, with the resulting decision not to poach on the territory Alana had posted as hers, returned.

Gabe hadn't understood her refusal. She couldn't blame him, as she hadn't understood how hurt and frustrated she would feel telling him no without a reason.

Where before Makima had seen her path clearly about decisions she'd made in business and in other matters, and had been able with prayer and her own determined mind to carry them out, she realized that in matters where the heart was truly engaged, she couldn't see clearly from hour to hour. All she could do was feel.

Chapter 20

"Can I fix dinner tonight?" Drew asked as soon as he came in the door on Wednesday.

Gabe had planned to have fried catfish, some kind of rice, salad and corn bread but hadn't prepared anything yet. He wondered what Drew had in mind.

"Be my guest," he said. "What are we having?"

"Tacos, refried beans and Spanish rice." He threw his book bag on a chair, poured a glass of apple juice and took it with him to the shelf of cookbooks. "Any Mexican stuff in here?"

"I don't think so, but there might be some recipes in that *Encyclopedia of Cooking* over on the end of the shelf. What gave you the idea?"

"The chapter on Mexican culture we had in social studies today talked about some foods and it made me hungry for the tacos we used to get at that little place a couple of blocks from the apartment."

He brought the book to the table where Gabe was sitting and opened it.

"Do you miss home, Drew?" Gabe asked quietly as he watched his brother turn the pages of the cookbook.

"Yeah, a little." He kept turning the pages. Then he stopped and looked at Gabe. His round face took on thoughtful lines and his light brown eyes were unusually serious. "Not like I thought I would, though. After we were here, I was glad to get out of the school at home. Then I met Jeff right away and now I'm in a school where I get along with the teachers and the kids. I've got a cool bunch of people to hang out with and we always have something to do." He looked at the book again but didn't turn the page. "How about you?" He looked at Gabe. "You get homesick?"

"We've been here almost a month and I can count the times I've wished I could walk around to see Calvin and Webster. The puzzle Great-Grandfather left me has kept me busy. Then there's the job at the center and the church and the people we've met. I haven't had much time to be homesick." He thought for a moment then grinned at Drew. "We're pretty lucky, I'd say."

"Yeah, guess we are." He grinned then resumed his search, unsuccessfully. "Let's just go to the store and get stuff. I know they have taco shells and seasoning. There'll be recipes on the packages."

The market gave Drew everything he needed. Gabe left him to it and went to the office to look again at his lists. He hadn't examined all of the bank statements as thoroughly as possible and he had a feeling he might have missed an important clue.

He went to the drawers where the statements were neatly filed by the year. He decided to work backward, hoping to find a clue in at least the present decade.

"Gabe. Dinner!" Drew yelled.

Gabe was pleased to see that he'd gone through nine months, ticking off every expenditure. He'd made a good beginning.

The stove he'd cleaned so meticulously the day before yesterday was now spattered and spotted but Gabe didn't care. Drew was so proud of the crunchy tacos filled with meat, lettuce, tomatoes, cheese and a dollop of sour cream as well as the side dishes of Spanish rice and refried beans he served to Gabe.

"Are they okay?" he asked after Gabe had sampled them.

All Gabe could do was nod enthusiastically. Once his mouth was empty he told Drew, "You're getting to be a real cook."

When the meal was over Drew went to study for a math exam while Gabe cleaned the kitchen then returned to the bank statements. Here was a payment he hadn't noticed before made to Southern Tree Management Services. What was that about?

He reached for the phone book and found their listing in Orangeburg. He made a note of the number so he could call them tomorrow. By the time Drew came in to say good-night he was tired of looking at statements. He put a marker in the stack and decided to call it a night.

This was the week Calvin was supposed to drive down but Gabe hadn't heard from him yet so he dialed the familiar number.

"I was going to call you tomorrow," Calvin said.

"I've heard those promises before." Gabe settled back in the chair, a half smile on his face. "All I want to know is when are you leaving New York?"

"Actually, I'm leaving here tomorrow. That's what I was going to call you about. I've been as far south as Baltimore and from there I have the directions I got from the automobile travel agency. But I was wondering which way did you go?"

Their conversation ended with Calvin saying he'd probably arrive Friday afternoon as he wanted to take his time and enjoy the trip.

Gabe hung up the phone satisfied that Calvin would be here in this room with him by the day after tomorrow. He picked up the book on West Africa he'd been reading. Great-Grandfather's library would certainly interest his friend, he knew. No need to worry about how to entertain him for the few hours Gabe would be at the center.

He thought of how his own time there had taken on a different character. This morning at the staff meeting he'd done his best to act in his usual relaxed and friendly manner with everyone. Yet he couldn't help but wonder if people noticed that Makima rarely looked at him and addressed him only when necessary. They had been as formal with each other as if they'd been strangers.

Fortunately the meeting had been brief. Reports on arrangements for the fund-raiser had been given and the date set for the second Saturday in April.

He'd spent the rest of the morning making plans with Eugenia and then worked on the accounts. The job had turned dull now that he felt constrained about spending time with Makima on one pretext or another. No more casual cups of tea together or taking the amount disbursed for an activity to her for an explanation. He still wanted to do it but not at the cost of her becoming uncomfortable in his presence.

Calvin couldn't have come at a better time. He could count on his friend to keep his mind busy and away from being preoccupied with Makima. The two of them never ran out of conversation. There was so much to discuss about Great-Grandfather. Calvin would also be interested in Grayson and the surrounding area. He might even get new ideas for his writing since he'd never been this far south.

After work the next day Gabe called the Southern Tree Management Services, identified himself and asked to speak with the person who'd handled the account for Ezekiel Bell. "One moment, please," the operator said.

"May I help you?" The woman's voice was brisk but flavored with the accent Gabe's ear had grown pleasantly accustomed to this past month.

"My name is Gabriel Bell. Are you familiar with the trees on the property of Ezekiel Bell in the Grayson section of Swinton?"

"The person who was handling the Bell account has recently retired and I'll be taking care of it from now on. My name is Marie Frye. I see the last consultation was quite some time ago." There was a question in her voice which Gabe answered.

"My great-grandfather died recently," he explained.

"I'm sorry to hear that."

"I've inherited the property and I need to understand what my great-grandfather meant to do about the trees. Can you help me with that?"

"Yes, I can. We have records of when he first engaged our services some twenty years ago up to the present time. Will Monday afternoon at two o'clock be convenient for you?"

"Can you make it later? I'd like for my brother to be here and he doesn't get home until three."

"Three o'clock, then."

"You'll come here?" He needed to walk through the trees with her as she described what Great-Grandfather had envisioned.

"Of course, Mr. Bell."

"Thanks, Ms. Frye. I look forward to seeing you."

In the room next to his, Gabe stripped Calvin's bed. Remembering that the successful conversation he'd just had with Ms. Frye was the result of paying attention to his list of items that might have been overlooked in the search for clues to Great-Grandfather's puzzle, he shook out each piece of linen that he took from the bed. He looked under the mattress cover and then at each piece of the clean linen.

When he was finished with the bed, he went to the linen closet. He tried to think like his great-grandfather had thought. There were at least twenty sheets stacked up, plus thirty pillow slips in addition to odds and ends. Could a reasonable assumption be made that a clue would be found in such a heap of fabric?

He didn't think so but to be on the safe side, Gabe ran his hand carefully through every major fold. They were all smooth just as they should be.

He took the feather duster from the corner of the clothes closet and used it on the bedstead, the windowsills, the rocker, the lamp tables and the large dresser. The embroidered dresser scarf wasn't dirty but it didn't look fresh and he recalled seeing more somewhere.

They hadn't been in the linen closet because they were too long. Maybe they were downstairs with the table linen. The sideboard in the dining room had drawers for silverware and napkins, and a bottom drawer that was deep and long for tablecloths.

As Gabe sifted through them, he tried to envision the meals Great-Grandmother Sarah had prepared. His great-grandparents, their children and their guests had eaten her food at the table covered by this linen.

His father's father had been at this table. Gabe's hands stilled. He and Drew had missed so much of their heritage, but it wouldn't happen to him when he married. He'd make sure his children knew all of their relatives. Good, bad, indifferent, it didn't matter. They were all family and to be acknowledged as such. He'd probably never know why Pop had divorced himself from his family but more and more, Gabe realized how thankful he was that Great-Grandfather had persisted in finding him and Drew.

He got to the bottom of the tablecloths and came to a small pile of table scarves. The first two were too short for the upstairs dresser but the third one seemed like it would fit. He lifted it carefully from the ones beneath.

As he straightened out the remaining three or four, he heard the rustle of paper. Between the last two scarves, he saw the same kind of paper on which the scroll had been written.

Gabe pulled it out knowing he'd found another clue.

Chapter 21

Gabe closed the drawer. Each time he'd found a clue it hadn't led him to any greater understanding of what he was to discover in the end so this time he deliberately laid the dresser scarf over the paper so he couldn't see it.

Upstairs he changed the clean scarf for the one on the dresser, glanced around to be sure the room was ready for Calvin, then picked up the paper, took it to the office and laid it out on the desk. At his first glance at what looked like chicken scratches, Gabe had to restrain his urge to hit the desk or throw a book in his frustration. This was worse than the scroll!

The scroll had the appearance of a story from the beginning. The only problem was that it had unrecognizable language. What in the name of reason was this jumble of fat black toothpicks? It looked like child's play and made no sense whatsoever. After more moments of stewing about it, he decided if he calmed down enough to examine the paper objectively, he might be able to come to some conclusion.

With this thought, Gabe sat down at the desk, found a ruler, a pen and a sheet of blank paper. Measuring his find, he saw it was six inches long and nine inches wide. It had a white, black and brown decorative border that was one inch deep.

On this piece of parchment had been drawn six rows of the vertical black lines but they were not the same height. They seemed to have been randomly placed. When Gabe counted them, the majority were three quarters of an inch long, interspersed here and there with some that were a half inch and a few that were only a quarter inch in length. The six rows were uneven and they held a total of thirty-seven lines.

The picture, if you could call it that, was absurd. Gabe turned it around and looked at it from all angles but it suggested nothing to him. Great-Grandfather had outfoxed him this time.

Finally he concluded that it was a part of the story told on the original scroll which was now secure in the safe-deposit box. He'd put this one with it and find out the whole story when all of the clues had been uncovered. As he laid it aside it occurred to him that perhaps it had something to do with the trees which made him doubly anxious for Ms. Frye's visit on Monday.

Makima printed out the letter to the Chamber of Commerce that Dr. Cook had dictated this morning. She automatically glanced at it before adding it to the pile of letters awaiting his signature. It didn't sound right so she looked at the notes she'd taken in his office.

No wonder it sounded strange. She'd omitted two crucial sentences! She tore up the letter and hurriedly produced a corrected one then took them all in to him. Back in her office she prepared the signed letters for mailing while remembering this wasn't the only problem she'd had.

She'd misfiled several folders which made her waste time trying to find them. While putting together a report, she'd found herself sitting motionless, totally distracted from what she was supposed to be doing. It wasn't work that was on her mind. It was Gabe. She was still suffering from having to tell him at the end of their mutual enjoyment of talking about bike riding that she couldn't let him join her the next time she went. He'd looked baffled and disappointed. She knew he couldn't have interpreted her refusal as anything but a personal decision and he must have wondered what he'd done to deserve it.

She couldn't tell him it was because of Alana. On the other hand she couldn't see how to come to work each day knowing he was in the building and ignoring him. Or treating him impersonally. Her awareness of him was too strong. She didn't want him feeling he'd offended her, because he hadn't. What she needed to do was talk to him and find some way to let him know he wasn't to blame.

She was also in turmoil about the clinic. Should she and the board go ahead with the new agency that wanted to build it? They only required a five-thousand-dollar deposit which the board had in the bank. It would be a good business deal since the company had a good reputation.

Still, she had the lingering idea that the land should come from Mr. Zeke's property. Maybe she should go see Gabe and inquire one more time about this. He knew her better now and was more conversant with the clinic project than when she'd first approached him. He'd even expressed sympathy with her goal.

The more she thought about seeing him, the more it sounded like the right thing to do. She lifted the phone to call him, then replaced it. She'd just drop by on her way home from work.

She checked her makeup and hair before leaving work and was glad she was wearing her new hot pink plush corduroy jacket with her pink shirt and black pants. She'd seen how Gabe always looked at her shoes and hoped he'd notice the ruby suede flats that sported a big, sparkling rhinestone buckle.

By the time she turned onto Gabe's street her mouth was dry and her palms were damp. Maybe he wouldn't be home, but then she saw his Lexus, black and shiny in the driveway. She parked, got out, and walked to the door telling herself to be calm.

Gabe answered the bell. "Makima!" It was obvious that he was surprised, but before she could say anything, he smiled and opened the door. "Come on in."

Relaxed by his easy welcome, she reminded herself that she'd come to ask Gabe about the property, not anything personal. "I hope I'm not disturbing you, barging in this way." In the living room she sat on the couch. Gabe sat on the couch also, his glance studying her with open admiration.

"You could never disturb me, Makima. You're always welcome here." He didn't move but it seemed to her he had come so close that it took her breath away as his eyes locked with hers.

"I missed seeing you at work today." That wasn't what she was supposed to say but the words slipped out despite herself.

"I was there but I had the impression that you didn't want to see me so I didn't stop by."

"I never said that," she protested. Her hands twisted the handle of her bag nervously.

Now he did shift so that he was closer to her. The energy between them and the effort to explain herself filled her with confusion yet she couldn't look away from him. If she'd known it would be like this she would have gone straight home. Being in his presence and absorbing the intensity of his gaze was unlike anything in her experience. Unsure of what to do or say, she could only flounder around until she found the right words to help her out of her dilemma.

"I felt that was what you meant when you told me we couldn't go bike riding together. You seemed very clear on that," Gabe said quietly. Although there was no sense of accusation in his tone, Makima felt a flush rising in her face because he'd read her underlying decision correctly. That's what she'd meant that moment in her confusion.

What could she say now? She wanted to be honest with him but how could she bring Alana into this muddle? She couldn't. "I'm sorry I gave you that impression, Gabe." She bent her head as she searched for an explanation then looked at him again and saw no blame but the dawning of hope in his eyes. "It's hard for me to tell you all that's going on with me right now, but whatever it is, it doesn't mean that I want us to be strangers to each other." That was the best she could do and she waited anxiously for his reaction.

He reached over to cover her hand with his. "Does that mean I can hang out in your office for a few minutes when I feel the need to?" His pleased smile warmed her heart and instinctively she turned her hand to hold his.

"Gabe!" Drew called as he came down the stairs. By the time he appeared in the room Makima was sitting in her corner of the sofa, her hands on her bag.

"Oh, hi, Miss Makima," Drew said. "I didn't know you were here."

"Hi, Drew," she said. "I just stopped by for a minute. How's school going?"

"Good, except for chemistry." He gestured to the textbook in his hand. "I was going to ask you a question," he told Gabe. "It can wait until later."

"I don't know if I can help you. Chemistry was never my favorite subject," Gabe said.

"May I see the textbook?" Makima asked. Drew handed it to her and as she turned the pages, he looked at her hopefully.

"Was that what you taught?" he asked.

"Yes, and from an earlier edition of this same book." She

glanced from him to Gabe. "Would you like a little help some-time?"

"I sure would if it's all right with you," Drew said.

"That's very kind of you, Makima, but do you have the time?" Gabe asked.

After some discussion it was decided that tutoring sessions would be held at Makima's house as the need arose, with the first one being on Sunday evening. Drew thanked Makima and left the room.

"You sure this won't be an extra burden?" Gabe asked.

She shook her head. "It'll be interesting to see how much I remember. I tutored a number of students for a while after I stopped teaching."

"What is your fee?"

"No fee, Gabe, this is just friend to friend." She saw him open his mouth to protest. "If you paid me I'd have no excuse not to take on other students for a fee. I don't want to tie myself down that much." She walked over to the window. "What did you do about the garden Mr. Zeke planted every year?"

"Come outside and let me show you." On the way he told her how Sam Williams had come over and managed to get Drew interested in planting the vegetables and taking care of the plot.

"He's done a good job," Makima said, noting how straight the rows were. "I see a few green shoots already coming up."

"He looks after it as a part of his homework," Gabe said proudly.

"Mr. Zeke would like that. He never wanted anything on his property go to waste or be neglected," Makima said thoughtfully.

Gabe took her hand. "Let's go sit on his bench."

"This is nice," she sighed when they were seated. "I used to sit here with him. He would tell me stories about Africa. When I was a little girl I used to think he'd lived there, the stories were so real."

"Have you been there?"

"To Africa? No, but Daddy has mentioned some ancestor from there."

"I haven't been there, either. Shall I tell you a secret, Makima?" He stroked her hand.

"Please." Her eyes were wide with anticipation.

"Most of the time when I sit here I can feel Great-Grandfather's presence."

"I'm not surprised. Mr. Zeke had a powerful spirit, Gabe. Anyone who knew him spoke of it. Since he didn't have the chance to know you when he was alive, it makes sense to me that he would try to know you in some other way now that you're here."

"I knew you'd understand," he said appreciatively.

For a few moments they sat silently, hands entwined. Makima knew she had to ask Gabe again about the land for the clinic, but she didn't want to break this lovely spell. He might become angry again and she hesitated to risk a rupture in the closeness between them. Still the idea had come via prayer so she might as well get on with it and trust in the process.

"Makima," Gabe said before she could begin. "I want to tell you about Great-Grandfather so you'll understand about the land for the clinic. His will had very specific items. One was that no part of the property could be rented, leased, given away, or sold until I, his heir, had achieved certain goals. I can't tell you what they are, but you see my hands are tied regarding the property. It has to remain intact. I wasn't trying to be rude or disrespectful when you asked me about it before." He looked at her appealingly.

"Thank you for telling me, Gabe." Makima was so grateful that she hadn't had to ask him outright about the land. "You can be sure what you've told me will stay right here," she promised.

It wasn't until she was on the way home that she wondered if Mr. Zeke had set a time limit about the goals. Since Gabe had taken a job and Drew had entered school, it probably wasn't any time soon.

Gabe's offering of the information she needed was the answer to her prayer, even though the will prevented her from obtaining the land she'd dreamed of for the clinic. She might as well give serious thought to the Dakers and Sons Builders who had been recommended to her. Wetherell had been first in her mind but their rates were very high. Dakers only required a five-thousand-dollar deposit of earnest money. She would talk to the board and see if they'd agree to finally getting the project started.

Soon after Gabe had said goodbye to Makima he had a call from Carolyn Brown.

"Gabe, we're having a card party Saturday night at my house about eight. How about coming over?"

Gabe knew that if he went he'd be partnered with Alana. That was the last thing he wanted, especially on the heels of spending a wonderful hour with Makima. "Sorry, Carolyn. Can't make it but thanks for the invitation. Have fun and my regards to everyone."

Sooner or later he might have to let Alana know directly that it was her sister he was interested in. If he was lucky she'd get the message by his refusal of this invitation. He hoped so.

Chapter 22

The bag of fresh crullers Gabe had bought on his way to work gave out a tempting fragrance. He was trying to wait until ten-thirty which was the usual time people took a coffee break, but he couldn't contain himself. He had to see Makima now. Bag in hand, he knocked on her door and pushed it open when she said, "Come in."

"Good morning, Gabe," she said. Her face lit up in a smile. "What's in the bag?"

"Something I thought you'd enjoy with your coffee." He laid the bag on her desk.

"Crullers," she said as she peeked into the bag. "They smell heavenly. I like them better than doughnuts." She took one out of the bag and wrapped it in a napkin from her bottom desk drawer. "Thanks so much, Gabe." She extended the bag.

"They're all for you, Makima," he said.

"I can't eat three crullers, Gabe. Just think of all those

calories!" She sparkled at him as she tried to get him to take the bag.

"That's just what I'm thinking of," he replied. "How every one of those calories will look on you." He laid his hand against her cheek and whispered, "I love curves on you, Makima." Spell-bound, they gazed at each other.

Gabe suddenly remembered where he was and that Dr. Cook could walk in at any moment. He cleared his throat and moved toward the door. "By the way, are you going to the card party at Carolyn's tomorrow night?"

"I'll be at a board meeting. You going?"

"No, I'm not going. I don't want to give people the wrong impression, Makima." He looked at her steadily, hoping she would get the message. Something went swiftly across her face and he saw that she understood he was referring to her sister.

"Will I see you at church?" she asked.

"I'm not sure. My best friend, Calvin Peters, arrives today for a visit and I'll have to see what he wants to do."

"I'm glad for you, Gabe. Will he stay long enough for us to meet him?"

"Absolutely. He's a writer and he's interested in getting to know this part of the country."

"I wish I could get—" She was interrupted by a beep from Dr. Cook. "I'll be right there," she said.

"I'm gone." Gabe waved his hand and returned to his office. He'd meant only to say good-morning and hand her the crullers, but it seemed communication always blossomed between them even when they knew time was short.

Since he didn't know what time Calvin would arrive, he'd put a beef stew on in the Crock-Pot. Its aroma filled the house when he arrived home after running some errands when he left the center. As he emptied a bag of groceries, the phone rang.

"I've just turned off the interstate into Swinton. Now what do I do?" Calvin asked.

"You made good time, man. Now listen carefully because getting here is quite complex." Gabe grinned as he then gave Calvin the extremely simple directions.

"One of these days you'll tell a good joke," Calvin said drily and closed his cell phone.

Gabe was on the porch waiting when the black Corvette Calvin had inherited from his uncle Daniel rolled smoothly into the driveway. By the time he reached Calvin, his friend had emerged from the low door and stood looking at his surroundings in amazement. As they shook hands, Calvin said, "This mansion is what you've inherited? I am impressed!"

"You can appreciate how Drew and I felt when we first saw it," Gabe said. "Unlock your trunk so I can take your luggage in."

"Don't rush me, I'm still trying to take all this in." Calvin turned slowly around, viewing the entire property.

"You'll have all the time in the world to explore. Let's get you inside." Gabe took the keys from Calvin and opened the trunk. Left to himself Calvin would have leaned against the car for another half hour considering the house and grounds and expecting Gabe to stay with him.

"Come on, Calvin. Did you have a good trip?"

"Yes, it was quite instructive and I'm glad I made it. I must admit, however, I've had enough driving for a while." He carried a heavy black bag and followed Gabe into the house. Gabe was amused and pleased at Calvin's reaction to his great-grandfather's house and furnishings. He treated it like a museum. In fact, the respect he showed it made Gabe wonder if he had been remiss in his attitude. Of course, that was one of the differences between him and Calvin. Calvin was a profound observer who took his time about everything. He could not be rushed, a trait which Gabe and Webster, the other man in the group of three longtime friends, sometimes found inconvenient and downright annoying.

Yet in the end, Gabe had always found Calvin's judgments to be astute and correct. Drew came rushing in and submitted to a hug from his "Uncle Calvin" whom he'd known all his life, and who had promised that when he was old enough to drive, he could take the Corvette out for a short spin. With his uncle in the passenger seat, of course.

"What d'ya think of our place? I'll bet you never thought it'd look like this." Drew also had learned to respect Uncle Calvin's opinion.

"It's a wonderful property, Drew. Your great-grandfather was a true craftsman with an artistic bent. All the work in this house that I've seen so far shows he also had patience. That's a great quality. How're you doing in your schoolwork? You being patient and working hard?" Calvin had a penetrating gaze and Gabe watched Drew fidget under it.

"Gabe can tell you my grades are much better than they were at home. Chemistry is hard but a friend of ours who used to teach it is going to give me some tutoring." Drew was just a bit defensive.

"That's true. He's taking school seriously and doing his assignments every evening. He has a garden also. Why don't you show it to Calvin, Drew."

While they were outside, Gabe made a pan of corn bread, knowing Calvin had a fondness for it. Conversation at the dinner table was lively, covering the sights and sounds of travel from New York City to Grayson and the early experiences of Gabe and Drew in the town.

"People are so friendly," Drew said. "We got here on a Saturday, went to church the next day and I met this guy, Jeff, and we've been best friends ever since."

"That could happen to you because you're a friendly person

yourself. Not everyone is," Calvin said as he buttered a large piece of corn bread.

Drew, eager to prove his point, continued to give examples of how persons in the area had gone out of their way, as he saw it, to make him and his brother welcome. Calvin listened but didn't seem convinced. Gabe enjoyed the argument, understanding that Calvin was not only teaching Drew how to debate a point of view, he was also reflecting something of his personal experience, for he did not make friends easily. In New York's social life, one could have many acquaintances, but friends were hard to find.

He'd once told Gabe that Gabe was one of the two friends in his life. Gabe had cherished that confidence and resolved to never fail in loyalty to Calvin. At thirty-seven, Calvin was only two years Gabe's senior, but looked older. His skin had some red in it, his eyes were gray, his head was shaved and he wore a neat mustache. When they'd first met, Calvin was two grades ahead of Gabe, but they lived in the same neighborhood in Harlem. He'd helped his uncle in a clothing store and Gabe had worked there on weekends for a while. At City College they continued to hang out together.

Gabe and Webster were the ones who met people effortlessly. They called Calvin their silent partner. He genuinely liked people but his natural reserve and habit of observing rather than talking had led him into writing what he saw and felt. In college he'd produced a column for the school publication. After college he'd tried his hand at screenplays and then novels. Gabe and Webster had given him a rousing celebration when his first novel, *What's Next After Getting There,* had been published two years ago. The revised version of his second novel had just been sent out. Coming to Grayson would give him a breather, he'd told Gabe, while he waited to hear if he had to do anything else to please his editor before a publishing date was set.

"Aren't you going to say anything about our friends?" Drew appealed to Gabe.

"I thought you were doing pretty good by yourself. Since seeing is believing, why don't you and I have our friends over to meet Calvin. Then he can judge for himself."

Calvin immediately protested. "You don't need to go to any trouble for me. I'll accept that the two of you have made friends in Grayson."

"Sorry, Uncle Calvin, you're in for it now," Drew said gleefully.

"Think of it as giving you new material for a novel. After all, you've never been to the South before to experience firsthand the details of the culture," Gabe added.

"You're going to be here for a while, aren't you, Uncle Calvin, so you'd have to know people like Jeff, and the Gray family and Mr. Sam who lives across the street anyway."

"Okay, Drew. I give in. When are your friends coming over?" Calvin asked. He and Drew both looked at Gabe.

"Today is Friday, so how about a week from tomorrow?" He studied his brother across the table. Some of the softness had gone from his face and it occurred to Gabe that Drew rarely whined anymore. His younger brother's experience here had been good. There was no denying it. He'd been surprised and touched by Drew's strong defense of their Grayson friends. If he felt that way, would he be willing to return home when their time here came to a close? He stored the issue in the back of his mind to think about later.

After a late and leisurely breakfast the next day, Drew went off to Jeff's, and Gabe drove Calvin around the Swinton-Grayson area, pointing out the community center, the church, the high school and other places of interest. Calvin took it all in and when they returned home he said, "You've shown me this part of South Carolina that nurtured your great-grandfather. You've referred to his will but can you tell me more so I can understand him and how it uprooted your life so profoundly?"

"The place to tell you is sitting on his bench." Gabe unlocked the gate that led to the field where the bench stood, explaining to Calvin why he found the bench a special place for contemplation. He held nothing back as he related everything from Moultrie's initial visit to him in New York, to finding the second scroll with the odd lines. In fact, it was a relief to share it all with another adult he could trust and whose intelligence he respected. He spoke freely of his times of frustration and times of joy when he'd uncovered a clue.

He couldn't have asked for a better audience. Calvin's entire attention was focused on the story, his deep gray eyes reflecting feelings of surprise, consideration, apprehension, query and relief. "Your great-grandfather was an extraordinary man whom I wish I could have known," Calvin mused.

"I've said that more than once since I've been here." Gabe was pleased that Calvin had already formed that opinion.

"He fashioned this whole thing as if it were something out of mythology," Calvin said thoughtfully. There was a gleam in his eye as he scrutinized his friend. "Will you win or lose, O Mighty Hero?"

"I don't know what you're talking about, but I don't see myself as a Hercules," Gabe chuckled.

"I'll lay it out for you, because the more I think of it, the more it fits. You were living in your ordinary world when the attorney came to see you. Why did he come?" Calvin asked.

"To tell me about the will."

"Right. That was your call to adventure," Calvin explained.

"I didn't see it that way. Frankly, I thought the man was pulling a scam at first."

"So you were reluctant to see it as a call and accept it?"

"Sure. Wouldn't you?"

"This isn't about me, Gabe. The attorney encouraged you and persuaded you that this was genuine. Right?"

"I guess you could put it that way. After I looked at all the pros and cons, I thought I could take a few months and give it a try."

"Which is to say you crossed the threshold and entered the special world."

"Grayson is the special world?" Gabe asked unbelievingly.

"According to mythology, it's wherever the hero takes on the tasks and the goal the adventure calls for."

"You're putting me on, aren't you?" He was serious as he met Calvin's gaze.

"Would I do that to you?" Calvin's eyes crinkled.

"Yeah, you would if you thought I'd swallow it."

"Okay. I just thought you'd be interested to see how what's happening to you has a number of mythic elements." Calvin lapsed into silence. "It's so quiet and peaceful here," he said after a few moments.

It would be just like his great-grandfather to have done what Calvin was talking about, Gabe thought. He'd been a scholar with a fine mind and maybe when he designed his will he hadn't been able to resist making it a complex game instead of a straightforward transfer of property to his heir. Could this be why he used the phrase *treasured destiny?* Looking at it in this light made it more believable as a goal.

Calvin was relaxed with his eyes closed but he didn't fool Gabe. He'd seen that strategy before. It was one way to get the other person curious enough to ask a question that would resume the point Calvin had been making. Gabe didn't mind falling in with the strategy this time.

"Then what happens?" he asked.

Calvin opened his eyes. "The hero encounters allies and enemies as he goes through his tests, working up to the greatest ordeal, at the end of which he wins his reward."

"Good for me," Gabe said. "That doesn't sound too bad except I don't see any allies or enemies in Grayson. Unless Drew is an ally."

"But that isn't all," Calvin said smoothly.

"How can there be any more? He's got the reward, hasn't he?" Gabe was puzzled. This was getting to be too much.

"Yes, but he's pursued on the way back to the ordinary world and has a transforming experience."

"Tell me that's the end," Gabe pleaded with a smile.

"Almost. The end is that the hero returns with his reward or treasure and it is a benefit to the ordinary world."

"I can see how some of what you describe could possibly relate to carrying out the specifics of the will, such as having to find clues that will lead to whatever Great-Grandfather had in mind. But what if I don't find them all? I only have the two scrolls and the key."

"Do you seriously think that you won't find them all?" Calvin looked at Gabe unsmilingly.

"I haven't asked myself that question. It just seems very slow and frustrating, but I guess I'm confident about finding them."

"That's the hero speaking."

"What's the transformation about at the end?"

"As the hero deals with both enemies and allies in his quest, he begins to change. The ordeal brings on another one, but it's when he has to reenter the ordinary world with his treasure that the greatest change takes place because of all he's gone through and learned. He isn't the same person that he was before he began the adventure. Surely you can see that?"

Gabe nodded. Then he looked at his watch. "Time to start dinner."

On the way back to the house he said, "You've certainly put this little trip of mine to Grayson in a different perspective. I don't buy the whole premise but it is interesting to think about.

I know I'm not a mythic hero. I'm just your usual guy. And there's another thing about your story that doesn't fit," he said as he opened the kitchen door for Calvin.

"What's that?"

"I don't have any enemies."

"The adventure isn't over yet," Calvin said smugly.

Chapter 23

Ms. Marie Frye from the Southern Tree Management Service rang the bell precisely at three o'clock. She was a trim, wiry woman in her forties with thick brown hair under a bright yellow helmet. Her denim pants were tucked into brown boots and her light jacket had STMS embroidered over the picture of a tall tree.

Gabe invited her in and introduced Drew and Calvin, who were waiting in the living room. Ms. Frye opened a brown folder with the same logo on its cover as the one on her jacket.

"Mr. Bell first came to us twenty-two years ago because he wanted to sell some of his timber. He is listed as one of our private nonindustrial landowners."

She looked up from the folder. "I'm not sure how much you know about the timber industry, but people like Mr. Bell hold almost sixty percent of private forestland in the United States, some 1.4 million acres."

"You can safely assume that we know nothing about timber, Ms. Frye," Gabe said, "but we're willing to learn."

"In that case let's go right to the forest." She closed the folder and stood. "I can explain as we walk and you can ask questions about what you see."

As they went outside she asked Gabe, "Have you been in the forest, Mr. Bell?" He unlocked the gate as he thought about her question.

"Actually, I haven't. I've sat on the bench and looked at it but that's all." It hadn't held the appeal for him that the bench and field had from the first day. He noticed that she always described it as a forest while for him it had just been trees.

"What kind of trees are these?" Drew asked, walking beside Gabe.

"Mostly pine. Our company doesn't just purchase trees. After a stand has been harvested, as with Mr. Bell's twenty-two years ago, we work with the owner in a sustainable-forestry plan."

"To keep the trees healthy?" Gabe asked.

"That's a part of it, Mr. Bell."

"Please call me Gabe. I think of my great-grandfather as Mr. Bell."

The four of them were now walking abreast. The trees were not as thickly packed as they'd seemed from the bench and there were all kinds of grasses and unfamiliar plants on what Ms. Frye was calling the forest floor.

"I hear about forest fires," Gabe said. "Do you know if this one has ever burned?"

"Let me show you." She led them to a group of trees that had an accumulation of fallen branches, pine needles and two dead trees around them. "When this builds up over the years, it makes the forest susceptible to fire. This is why controlled burning is a part of the sustainable-forestry plan I mentioned earlier."

"So, did your company have a fire here?" Drew asked.

"According to our records there was one some years ago. It lessens the danger of a serious fire and keeps down disease. Also it thins out undesirable trees so new ones can be planted." They had been walking and learning about forestry for nearly an hour when Ms. Frye stopped.

"I hope I haven't worn you out." There was a twinkle in her eye. "You probably didn't expect to take such a long hike. This isn't even the end of Mr. Bell's forest, but I have a surprise for you." How could there be a surprise in the middle of all these trees? She'd already pointed out some of the occupants of the forest, like deer, rabbits and snakes. A large pond had been the biggest surprise to Gabe. He'd no idea the trees he'd looked at from the bench comprised what Ms. Frye called a living forest. Glancing at Drew, he saw the same dazed look on his face. Calvin, of course, wore his usual calm philosophical expression.

Ms. Frye veered left and led them for a few minutes to a section of denser growth than they had seen before. They followed silently as she pushed her way through it. Gabe began to have an eerie feeling. Suddenly they stepped into a clearing. In the middle of it was an ancient square building made of rough wooden planks.

"What is it?" Drew asked after a moment.

"A praise house," Calvin said quietly, "built by slaves as their own place of worship."

"That's what Mr. Bell told the first forester who walked through here with him. It's very old. I'm a born Southerner and I've heard about praise houses, but this is the first one I've ever seen," Ms. Frye said reverently.

Gabe was beyond speech. Somewhere in Africa, greedy men had rounded up people and caused them to be brought in chains to South Carolina where they were sold as slaves to people who owned the very land on which he and Drew were standing. Among them were black men whose African names he didn't know, but who had started his family line. They had endured a life of untold hardship as slaves, but out of that had come the determination to praise the Creator in their own way, in a place built by their own hands, from whatever materials they could find. The sight of the building, its purpose and the aura that surrounded it made such an impact on him that all he could do was try to take in its physical details. It was about the size of the garage, had square windows on its sides and a door with a single step. He could see places where Great-Grandfather had repaired and strengthened it while retaining its integrity as a venerable place of worship. Ms. Frye was saying it was a pity they couldn't go inside, but Mr. Bell had put a secure lock on the door to protect it from vandals. Gabe was certain that particular key was in Moultrie's possession and that the attorney would send it to him now.

On the way back to the house Gabe found his voice and asked how she knew where the praise house stood.

"One of our primary purposes is to protect special and unique places in the forests we manage, especially if they have historical value. In the case of this praise house it's well documented in the early 1800s and its precise location is on our map." When they got to her car and thanked her for the tour, she handed Gabe several brochures.

"We just touched the highlights, Gabe, so I'm giving you these to study at your leisure. When you've decided what you want to do about your forest, give me a call."

"It'll take a while," he said.

"There's no hurry. I'll be ready whenever you are."

"There's one thing I'm not clear on," Calvin said as they sat around the dinner table later. "Who built the praise house? If it dates back to the early 1800s, it couldn't have been your great-grandfather, who must have been born in 1906."

"I remember when Mr. Moultrie came to see us at home, he talked about Great-Grandfather's father. His name was Elijah, wasn't it, Gabe?" Drew asked. "Maybe he was the one."

"No, Great-Grandfather's father was the first Ezekiel Bell and he was born free. But *his* father, Elijah, was a slave, and Elijah's father, Moses, was a slave. I think it was probably Moses and the other slaves who lived on this land who built the praise house."

Calvin's face was thoughtful as he digested Gabe's genealogy. "I still don't understand how your great-grandfather knew about this property, because the praise house had been built so many years ago."

"Some of the details of the story Drew referred to that Moultrie told us makes more sense now." Gabe recalled what he could and relayed it to Drew and Calvin. "Apparently legends had come down from elderly Africans about a place they called 'De Land.' They said it was watched over by spirits because it held a treasure that was linked to the place in Africa where they'd come from. That same legend said men from the Bell line were its protectors."

Calvin raised his eyebrows. "That's the treasure you're to find?"

"I don't know yet until I get the key and we see what's inside, but somehow I don't think it's going to be that simple. Nothing my great-grandfather laid out for me has been simple or straightforward."

"We could've explored those trees, I mean, forest—the first week we arrived." Drew was thinking out loud. "If we had, maybe it'd all be over now." He picked up his knife and began drawing shapes on the table as he pondered that idea.

"But we'd still have had to find the two scrolls and the key, plus whatever else is hidden. At least now we have those clues," Gabe mused.

"Do you think the second key is in the praise house, Gabe?" This from Calvin.

"Even if it is, what do they unlock? Is it in the praise house also? I just don't know." He glanced at his watch. "Time to call Moultrie and see what he can tell us. He should be available by now according to his secretary."

The attorney answered on the first ring. "Sorry I missed you earlier, Gabe. I hope you and Drew are well and that you have news for me."

"We're well and hope you are also. Yes, there's great news. Today we found the praise house in the forest." Gabe couldn't help the echo of triumph in his voice. He needn't have worried. Moultrie had it, too.

"You finally found it? That's great, Gabe. Congratulations! How does it look?"

"I'm not sure how it's supposed to look because I've never seen one before but for something built in the early 1800s it seems remarkably sturdy."

"No vandalism?"

"None that I could see."

"That's what Mr. Bell worried about all of the time. I'd suggest that you and Drew say nothing about it for now." His voice took on a serious tone.

"I feel the same way. My best friend, a man I've known all my life, is visiting us, but he's totally trustworthy." Calvin raised a brow inquiringly. Drew looked at him and shrugged as if to say he didn't have a notion either of what his brother was talking about.

"I'll put the door key in express mail tomorrow. Be careful with it. You're making progress, Gabe, and I'm sure Mr. Bell would be very pleased with you, as I am. He always said intellect alone would not provide all the answers and he hoped his great-grandson would come to understand that." A shiver went over Gabe as he recalled how knowledge of the key had come to him while he'd been meditating on the bench. Perhaps the spirits were still watching over De Land and its Bell inhabitants.

When Moultrie hung up, Gabe recounted the conversation.

"Will you wait till I'm home to open the door?" Drew asked.

"Of course." He turned to Calvin. "What's generally in a praise house?"

"Usually benches for the congregation. Probably not a pulpit, not back then. I think that's all. Perhaps a hook or two to hang a light on."

"When he said you needed more than intellect, Gabe, I bet he was talking about those times when you were acting kinda weird." Gabe rolled his eyes but Drew addressed himself to Calvin. "You should've seen him. So many evenings he'd go out there and just sit."

"I guess he felt near your great-grandfather there," Calvin explained.

"That's what I told him," Gabe said.

"Yeah, I know, but it made me—" he searched for the right word "—worried." He was defensive as he glanced at the adults opposite him.

Gabe knuckled his brother's head affectionately. "I understand. After all, you didn't want a crazy dude for a brother."

As they got up from the table Calvin winked at Drew. "You keep on looking after him, he needs to be kept in line."

The board meeting had been unexpectedly brief, Makima thought, to end in such a momentous decision. The attorney and the other six members had said they'd gone over and over the contract offered by Dakers and Sons. They'd taken it apart and discussed it all. So there was nothing more to do but sign the paper and enclose the five-thousand-dollar bank draft, put it in the envelope and be finally through with this phase. Someone had brought a bottle of sparkling grape juice to pour into the champagne flutes and with much laughter and congratulations the deed was done. Makima took the envelope to the post office on the way home. She prayed fervently that they had done God's will and that the clinic would profit from tonight's work.

Chapter 24

The smooth buzz of sewing machines interrupted the speculation about the praise house that had been with Gabe all the way to work. The calendar on the bulletin board in the center reminded him that a beginner's sewing class was starting today and would meet every Tuesday until noon. Gabe counted nine ladies testing their machines and chattering amongst themselves as the instructor assembled her supplies. The center was steadily attracting more such activities. Dr. Cook said it was getting to be the first place people in Grayson thought of when they needed a place outside of their homes or church. For a nominal fee they could fit their needs into the posted schedule. The center was clean, lighted, had a stage and a kitchen, as well as a reputation for being safe and well run.

Gabe felt fortunate to be involved with the community in this way and soon would be ready to show Dr. Cook how the center could be more financially secure. He'd been working on the plan as well as the upcoming fund-raiser, when there was a light knock and Makima opened the door. Gabe jumped to his feet and came around the desk.

"Hey," he said softly, smiling into her eyes and holding her hands. He closed the door and held a chair for her. She shook her head, her eyes locked with his.

"Hey, yourself," she murmured. "I won't sit because if I do, I'll stay too long."

"You can't stay too long, Makima?" Gabe didn't know what he was saying but he knew he was asking her a question and her eyes were saying yes. The air crackled as he pulled her to him. He was still looking at her when his lips brushed hers once and again. She made a tiny sound and he dropped her hands and enfolded her in his arms as he kissed her again. He felt her arms come around him and he forgot where he was. He took her face in his hands and moved his mouth on hers with long deep kisses. His phone rang and they both jumped. Eyes dazed, Gabe held Makima with one hand and picked up the phone with the other.

"This is Gabe," he said huskily. He listened for a moment. "I'll bring the figures over in about ten minutes, Eugenia." He turned back to Makima. "Now, where were we?"

She stepped back and dropped her arms. "We were about to say goodbye and get back to work. I only stopped by to say hello." She was flushed as she patted her hair in place. He watched her gravely.

"Your hair's all right. I've been wanting to kiss you almost from the moment we met, Makima. Now I want to even more."

Without touching her, he leaned his face toward her just enough for his mouth to caress hers. "So sweet," he breathed. "This will have to hold me until next time."

Makima didn't remember walking from Gabe's office to hers. She remembered being thankful that Dr. Cook was in Columbia today and aside from a few phone calls, the rest of the day was hers. She'd meant to tell Gabe good-morning and what the board had done. The board's action had dovetailed nicely with his decision to explain how Mr. Zeke's land was tied up in his will. Even so, she'd thought he'd be relieved to know the matter of clinic land had now been resolved. But as soon as she'd seen Gabe all her senses had started to hum. Nothing could have stopped her from moving toward him and responding to his kiss. Each one had been better than the one before and had awakened in her a hunger she couldn't describe. It was a blessing the phone had rung and yet she was sorry it had.

She daydreamed through the rest of the day and often found herself smiling into space, the work she was supposed to be doing untouched. She told herself she was being as silly as a schoolgirl but she didn't care. This kind of euphoria was what she'd read about but had never experienced. It was liberating, exhilarating and joyous and she was going to bask in it as long as she could. She knew enough about life to understand this level of emotion couldn't be sustained indefinitely, but if this was a part of the divine plan for her, it would become a deep foundation for something permanent. That future was in God's hands. Meanwhile she was happy in the present as she relived once more those golden moments in Gabe's arms when his eyes cherished her and his mouth caressed her.

Drew arrived home almost on a run from the corner where the school bus dropped him off each day. "Did the key come?" he asked, excitement in his voice and eyes.

Gabe pulled a key from his pocket to show Drew. "Calvin and I were just waiting for you."

The three of them made the trip through the forest much faster than when they'd walked with Ms. Frye. "You sure you know the way?" Drew asked twice. "The trees look all the same to me."

"I made notes so we wouldn't get lost," Gabe assured him. "You might want to come by yourself, Drew, so pay attention to all that's around the trees and you'll begin to see different things." Calvin walked beside Drew and began to point out the varieties of vegetation. Gabe was thankful he didn't have to pay attention to them. Between Makima and the praise house he had more than enough on his mind. Both filled him with profound sensations, both had an intense impact upon him and would, he knew, change some part of his life forever. Makima drew him in a way no other woman had. He'd spent much more time with Olivia Eagles, had almost married her, yet she hadn't called to his inmost being as Makima did. Their first embrace this morning had confirmed what his intuition had told him, that she was the woman for him. She had met him more than halfway with a sweetness that instantly ignited his senses to a flare-up point. It was strange, what Drew would call weird, to think of Makima and the praise house together. He couldn't explain it, but each one would bring something special into his life. His eager footsteps brought him to the place where Ms. Frye had announced the surprise.

"We're almost there," he told Drew.

They pushed through the dense undergrowth and into the clearing. Taking the key from his pocket, he inserted it into the heavy lock, wondering what he'd do if it didn't work. But the tumblers moved smoothly and the door opened. Light came in from the windows and the open door to reveal a plain room constructed with unadorned wood. Gabe counted eight long benches, four on each side, leaving a narrow middle aisle. Rough planks made up the floor. The air was musty and there were a few cobwebs hanging from the ceiling, but otherwise the place was clean.

"There's something carved on the front wall," he said.

"I was just noticing that." Calvin followed Gabe, with Drew behind him.

"It's a man. I wonder who he is." Drew peered at the image carved into the wood. The carver's talent was remarkable in his depiction of a tall, noble, African man walking with a cane. Around his neck, wrists and waist he wore leather strips from which hung an assortment of small leather pouches.

"He certainly was someone special," Calvin remarked. "Just looking at the carving you can feel his power and spirituality." Gabe was stunned. This was a lifelike carving of the very man he'd seen the day he'd meditated and afterward knew where to find the key.

"Look at this one, Gabe. It's a cross." Drew had moved along and was pointing to another carving about four feet from the man. The cross had the same dimensions as the man and everything about it was perfect.

"The carver was a true artist," Gabe said reverently.

"I agree. He's managed to make you feel from those two simple pieces of crossed wood the same spiritual power the African man displays."

"But why are they both up there?" asked Drew.

"Let's take the easy one first," Calvin answered, sensing that Gabe wasn't in a communicative mood. "The cross symbolizes Christianity, right?"

"Yeah."

"Slaves brought from Africa often weren't permitted to practice the religion they brought with them. They were taught Christianity and became Christians. They built praise houses like this to practice that religion. I think that's why you see the cross."

"The man that's there, maybe he had something to do with the religion they had in Africa."

"Could be, or he was an important person in the history of their tribe. What do you think, Gabe?"

"All I know is he had a special meaning, otherwise he

wouldn't be on this wall, in the middle of this forest in an obscure place like Grayson," Gabe said. They searched the other walls but they were bare. They looked under every bench but found nothing. Outside they could see how the ground had been kept free of tall grasses and broken branches. The vines which normally would have totally enveloped the praise house if left to nature hadn't been allowed to flourish.

"As one of the Bell line, your great-grandfather certainly kept this place protected," Calvin told Gabe. Now it was up to him, Gabriel Riley Bell, to be the protector.

At work the next day, Dr. Cook said at the staff meeting that he'd seen the flyers about the fund-raiser in several places and he congratulated Makima. Eugenia and Gabe reported the sale of tickets thus far to organizations and church groups. After the meeting Gabe stopped in Eugenia's office to invite her and her husband to the party for Calvin.

"Sounds like fun. I'll talk with Tony and let you know tomorrow," she said.

He'd also invited Carolyn and Mark. Mrs. Gray had called to say she and her husband would have to decline. They'd forgotten a meeting her husband had to attend in Columbia and she was going with him so they could see a show later. From Eugenia's office Gabe strolled over to Makima's. He promised himself he'd leave the door ajar so he wouldn't succumb to the temptation to kiss her.

"Gabe! Come in." Makima's smile lit up her face. "Good meeting, wasn't it?"

"Very good, and I think the attendance at the fund-raiser is going to be outstanding."

"I hope so." She searched his face. "I'm glad you're here because I wanted to say something to you as soon as I saw you but not in front of the others."

"What is it?" Was it about the kiss? Maybe she was going to warn him away. He wasn't going to go no matter what she said.

"Something's happened to you since I saw you last." She hesitated. "I can sense it in you and I know it's good." She paused a moment. "You may not want to talk about it, but I needed you to know I'm happy for you."

Gabe had to touch this woman who was so attuned to him that she could subconsciously perceive his emotions. He reached out for her hand and held it against his cheek. He pressed a kiss into her palm before releasing her. "How do you know me so well?" he murmured.

She blushed. "I don't know."

"I can't tell you what happened yet, but one day soon I'll show you." It wouldn't be fair to let her see the praise house when the three of them had agreed not to speak of it to anyone. He changed the conversation to restrain himself from telling her of his discovery.

"Your mother called to say she and your dad have to go to Columbia Saturday."

"Will that upset your seating arrangement?" she said teasingly.

"It's not that formal. Eugenia, Tony, Carolyn and Mark are coming. How about Alana?"

"We haven't talked about it but I can't see her staying away. All her crowd will be there. I don't know what was going on with her Sunday but she'll show up out of curiosity if nothing else."

"Good. Jeff and Drew plus Penny and Angela makes fourteen in all."

"That's a good number. Is there anything I can do to help?"

"Yes. Just be there. For me. Come early and stay late." They gazed at each other in silence, a swirl of enchantment holding them until Gabe cleared his throat.

"See you later," he said and closed her door soundlessly behind him.

Chapter 25

Gabe sat at the head of Great-Grandfather's table Saturday night. Now it was his table with his guests and he was filled with celebration. This was his first time as a true host. Great-Grandmother Sarah had been his guide. He'd had the house cleaned then filled it with fresh flowers. With great care he'd made a selection from the table linen, the silverware, the crystal and the dishes. He'd ordered a centerpiece of spring blossoms that wouldn't interfere with people seeing each other, and a number of small candles, which now illumined the table with a festive flair. He'd even found dainty holders for place cards. The long table had been extended to seat all fourteen people and it was with a gleam of amusement that he had assigned places.

"Calvin, I'm placing you at the other end of the table opposite me since you're the guest of honor. I'm thinking of putting Alana on your right since you tend to be rather quiet on these occasions and she's lively."

"I'll have to take your word about her. She certainly ignored me when we met," Calvin said drily.

"I apologize on her behalf. That wasn't the Alana I know. So, will you take a chance on her tonight?"

Calvin shrugged. "Okay."

Gabe had dismissed the idea of cooking except for making his cake for dessert, depending instead on the catering service from Rockwell's Restaurant. Released from kitchen duties, he and Drew had visited the barber, shined their shoes and dressed up. Gabe wore his new navy sport coat with the faint gray stripe, gray slacks, powder-blue shirt and silk tie. Drew wore new khakis and a new blue-and-ivory-striped shirt with a solid blue tie.

"You're growing too fast," Gabe had grumbled. He'd bought shirts for Drew six weeks ago and now they were too short.

"I can't help it," Drew had beamed.

"Thank goodness you can still wear your blazer." Gabe looked at his young brother who would be taller than him if this growth spurt continued. "About tonight. This is the first time you and I are having a dinner party. I expect you to be a good host to Angela, Penny and Jeff. See that they have food and something to drink when they first come in and that the girls meet everyone. Okay?"

Drew grinned. "Penny's already called me twice today. She's so excited. It's going to be fun."

Calvin looked very cosmopolitan in dark slacks with a sport coat that was fitted at his slim waist. He wore a collarless ivory shirt and half boots made of kid. The three of them had met their guests at the door, had taken them on a tour of the house, and urged them to enjoy the beverages and hors d'oeuvres the Rockwell's waiters were serving. Alana was late, but she had arrived wearing a fitted silver gown that was on the edge of daring. With her four-inch-heeled sandals and the diamond studs in her ears, she affected the entrance that Gabe was sure had been her intention.

"I'm so glad to see you, Alana," he said as he and Calvin met her at the door. "You remember my friend, Calvin Peters, don't you?"

"Of course." The smile she gave Calvin did not reach her eyes.

"Miss Gray. It was kind of you to fit us into your busy schedule," Calvin said gravely.

Touché, Gabe thought as Alana blinked in surprise, but her recovery was swift.

"Let us all hope it will be worthwhile." Her eyes met and challenged Calvin's for a moment. She linked arms with the two men, flashed her flirtatious smile and entered the party.

Gabe's effort at making the table presentable was rewarded when his guests took their places for dinner.

"How beautiful!" Makima said and touched his hand.

"Did you have professional help?" Eugenia asked as she looked for her place card.

"No, I just tried to make the best use of what Great-Grandmother Sarah had." He was watching Alana. She was looking everywhere for her place card except near Calvin, who stood at his chair waiting to seat her.

A hint of color rose in her face as the chairs filled up and Carolyn said, "You're here, Alana."

When Calvin held the chair for her, she gave him a tight smile and a muttered, "Thanks."

"Not at all," he replied. When all were in place, Gabe rose to his feet, goblet in hand.

"To new friends who have welcomed Drew and me, and to my oldest friend, Calvin, welcome to Grayson."

The clink of crystal was mixed with jovial comments all up and down the table as people welcomed Calvin. Alana had looked at Gabe as he made the toast and touched her goblet to Carolyn's on her right and to Mark's across from her.

Enough was enough, Calvin decided. "What have I done to

offend you, Miss Gray?" He ignored the salad the waiter placed before him. His voice was low, his gaze penetrating.

Startled, Alana looked up from her salad. "Nothing, I don't even know you," she said crisply.

"Exactly. That makes me wonder why you've chosen to be so rude to me." His voice held a mild inquiry. Alana's eyes widened with shock and color heated her face. She glanced around to see if anyone was noticing her and Calvin.

"I'm sorry if I've hurt your feelings," she said quickly.

Calvin raised an eyebrow. "My feelings aren't so easily hurt, Miss Gray. I was just curious about your behavior."

Gabe couldn't hear the conversation between Calvin and Alana but he'd watched the byplay. He saw Calvin turn away and engage Mark in a lively conversation while Alana kept her head down and picked at her salad.

"You're giving us a great meal," Makima told Gabe as the entrée of medallions of beef with herbed red potatoes, asparagus spears and onion green beans was served.

Seated at Gabe's right, she graced his table and it made his heart sing each time he looked at her. Tonight she wore her hair up in a style that enhanced the contours of her face, the beautiful line of her neck and the elegance of earrings that complemented her silk emerald gown with its mandarin collar.

"Rockwell's had a surprising variety to choose from. I was trying to get something everyone could enjoy." Their attention to the food was accompanied by a hum of conversation and laughter that told Gabe his dinner party was a success. Drew and his group were blending in. If Mom and Pop could see him now they'd be proud of their youngest son. They might even think that Gabe was doing a decent job of parenting. What would it be like to have Thanksgiving dinner here at this table? Or Christmas with the house decorated with festive greens, candles at the windows and a tall tree decorated with Mom's ornaments dominating the living room? There probably wouldn't be any snow for those winter holidays but what did that matter? Hadn't Drew mentioned just the other day about being on the school swim team next year? He seemed to be completely contented with his present life. Jeff and the girls and the other friends in their crowd were wholesome kids who weren't rebellious about going to school and already talked about college as a natural outcome after graduation. That was a far cry from what had been happening at home.

But what about himself? he wondered as he answered a question from Eugenia and gave Makima a smile. Was he ready to seriously consider moving from New York to Grayson? They were worlds apart as far as economics and culture were concerned. He'd never known anything but that lifestyle for his thirty-five years except for brief visits to his mother's family in Virginia. A burst of laughter at Calvin's end of the table brought him out of his meditative state. Alana had become the Alana Gabe knew, holding the people around her in gaiety as she finished an anecdote, her eyes flashing and her laugh husky. She cut her eyes at Calvin, who responded with an involuntary curving of his lips. It was true, Gabe thought, that Grayson wouldn't give him old school friends like Calvin and Webster, but they could visit each other. However, Grayson would give him something he found himself increasingly hungry for, a lifeline to his family. The constancy of blood ties with Great-Grandfather emanating from this house. The carrying on of the life lived as a Bell on this property. Neither New York nor anyplace else could give him that, and he was beginning to feel that this was more important than his job in New York or any other connection he had to the city.

How would he be received here if he made this drastic move? Visiting was one thing, permanency was another. They would have to work hard at being integrated into the community. They'd made a beginning by going to the Grayson Community Church, Drew was making friends at school, and he was meeting people through the center.

"Gabe, I loved the beef. You'll have to tell me how it's done," Tony called up the table from his place between Valerie and Mark.

"I wish I knew but I didn't prepare it. Glad you liked it," Gabe said.

Other compliments on the meal were followed by Calvin who said, "Gabe might not have prepared the earlier courses but the dessert is his specialty."

The waiter placed the triple-chocolate cake in the center of the table. It sat, tall and splendid on a lacy white doily, surrounded by glistening red raspberries and an outer row of luscious strawberries. The guests applauded as the waiter now set the cake in front of Gabe, who sliced it and lifted each piece onto one of Sarah's finest dessert plates. French-vanilla ice cream went to those who desired it and steaming coffee was poured from a silver pot into thin china cups. The level of conversation became muted as people concentrated on the rich dessert and the coffee.

Gabe wondered if his guests should now be tactfully encouraged to return to the living room, and when the dessert plates were empty, he suggested adjourning to the more comfortable seats in the living room. Personally he preferred lingering around the table, but the catering service would have to be paid by the hour and they needed to clean up the dining room. There was another full coffee service there, thanks to the fact that the china closet held three separate sets of fine china. Carolyn and Valerie met at the coffee table.

"I don't know where I'm going to put this but it's such good coffee," Carolyn said.

"The table was gorgeous, wasn't it? I hadn't eaten here before." Valerie sipped her coffee appreciatively.

"My aunt used to come here for dinner and she said how Miss

Sarah set the prettiest table around," Carolyn recalled. Gabe had deliberately placed a copy of Calvin's book on the top of a lamp table as a way of letting his guests discover it without Gabe making an announcement. Eugenia was the first to pick it up. She showed it to others and Calvin soon had a circle of interested people around him.

"I didn't know he's a published writer," Makima told Gabe.

"This is his first novel to reach publication. He's just submitted a second one to his editor."

"Somehow that isn't surprising to me, he's an observant man," she said.

"What with one thing and another I haven't talked to you lately about the clinic project. How's it coming?" he asked, wishing the party was over so he and Makima could be alone. They'd been next to each other all evening but never alone. Just looking at her lit a spark inside him and he wanted to hold her and touch her. He saw suppressed excitement in her eyes.

"We signed the contract and put it in the mail Monday night after the board meeting."

"That's wonderful! I'm so glad for you, Makima." His eyes gleamed with joy for her. "Does everyone know or can we tell the people here?"

"No official announcement has been made yet but it's public business and everyone here has given money to it," she said.

Gabe stood and pulled Makima to her feet. "Listen, people. Makima has good news to announce." Then he sat down. His heart felt like it would burst with pride as Makima, the epitome of elegant dignity and poise, spoke.

"The board has signed a contract with Dakers and Sons to break ground and begin the construction of the Grayson Community Health Clinic."

He joined others in cheering. Alana was one of the first to reach her with an embrace. The sisters looked at each other with affection. Alana whispered to Makima, then stepped away for Calvin, who congratulated Makima. Gabe was watching Makima's face, but when he glanced away, he noticed that Calvin was standing silently and unobtrusively near Alana, who had a slightly fragile air about her despite a quiet smile for her sister. He wasn't surprised when she told him goodbye a little later.

"It was a lovely party," she said. He started to escort her out but stopped when he saw Calvin waiting. Others began taking their leave and within fifteen minutes the room was empty except for Makima.

She'd said, "I should go," but he'd held her arm and ignored her words. Calvin and Drew had disappeared and the caterers had gone. Gabe went around the room dousing all the lights except one. He closed the doors then turned to where Makima stood watching him. The smile in her eyes was a touch wary.

"Why do I feel like Little Red Riding Hood?" she said as he came toward her.

"Because I'm the Big Bad Wolf? Or because I've been wanting to hold you in my arms since you walked through my door hours and hours ago?"

Surely no other woman could fit so wonderfully in his arms. She was so exquisitely formed, matching him in all the right places. Her skin was like the smoothest velvet, her fragrance like the loveliest spring breeze. With the first kiss, the spark he'd had turned into a flame. Her mouth was sweet and welcoming, murmuring his name as she put her arm around his neck and touched his hair with soft strokes. Their kisses were long and deep. Makima's legs weakened and she clutched Gabe around the waist. He sat on the couch and pulled her down with him. She leaned against him and yielded when he surrounded her with his strong arms and took her mouth with such fierce hunger that all she could do was surrender, letting her own hunger have sway. Breathless and unnerved, she put her hands against his chest.

"I have to breathe," she murmured.

"I know, sweetheart. I'm sorry." He was breathing hard, his voice raspy as he apologized. "I got carried away." He held her face tenderly between his hands. "You light a flame in me, Makima, that burns and burns."

She blushed but kept her eyes on his.

"I've never had a flame, but you've lit a spark that seems to grow stronger each time I'm near you. Promise me you won't do anything to extinguish it." He covered her face with soft kisses. "Promise?"

"I promise." Makima floated home dazed with happiness and joy.

Chapter 26

"I could get used to this weather," Calvin remarked as he walked to church the next day with Gabe and Drew. A few puffy clouds sailed in the blue sky. A balmy breeze stirred the tendrils of Spanish moss on Mr. Darby's oak trees while spring flowers bloomed in most of the yards they passed.

"TV showed cold rain for New York," Gabe said.

"Jeff said you can do stuff outside all year in Grayson, which reminds me, Gabe, why aren't there basketball hoops at the center?"

"We talked about it at staff meetings and we're going to get two as soon as we have the money. We know we need them."

The stream of people going into the church was larger than usual. As they took their places in the line, Gabe wondered if they'd be able to find seats. It was Easter and they should have come earlier. For the first time they were asked to sit in the balcony.

"I like this, you can see everyone," Drew said. Gabe looked

toward the front pews for Makima. There she was in a rich yellow suit, sitting next to her parents. But who was that man engaging her in conversation? Alana was on his other side and a second stranger was talking to her.

"Who do you suppose they are?" Calvin asked Gabe.

"Don't know, but we'll find out after service." As it happened, they only had to wait until the secretary announced the visitors. The man talking to Makima was Lawrence Stoddard, the other was Dr. Youssou Hakim, here to do research on his Senegalese ancestors.

Gabe got a clear look at them later when Mrs. Gray introduced Lawrence as her second cousin by marriage. He was of medium height, light-skinned, and had a friendly face. There was nothing that made him stand out except his eyes. They were brown, but what caught Gabe's notice was their watchfulness. He stored that away and decided to be vigilant, especially since the man kept glancing at Makima with appreciation. He couldn't blame him, but Gabe casually placed his hand on her arm as they talked so this man would know she was taken.

Makima was radiant this morning, with smiles for everyone in their group. "You look beautiful, Makima," he murmured. "And happy."

"I'm very happy," she replied, looking into his eyes.

"For the same reason I am?" he whispered.

"Yes." He loved how they could speak so intimately there in the churchyard, surrounded by people. His heart had a steady deep rhythm and as he felt its beat, he wondered if he and Makima would be standing in this place years from now, surrounded by their children and grandchildren.

Dr. Youssou Hakim was somewhat familiar to Gabe because in New York there were so many Africans from the countries of that huge continent. He was dark with a round face, full lips and a broad nose. The language of his Senegalese homeland had been overlaid by the excellent English he'd learned at an American university.

"Lawrence and I met last year when we were both working on a project for a university in Massachusetts," he explained in answer to a question from Alana. "When it came to an end, Lawrence invited me to travel to South Carolina with him, and since it was on my list of places where some of my ancestors were brought as slaves, I agreed."

"Will you be going to Charleston also?" Alana asked, giving him her full attention.

"Yes, I expect to."

"Your name is familiar," Calvin interjected. "Might I have read a publication of yours?"

"Perhaps. There was a book and some articles a few years ago, after I left university," he said modestly.

Alana seemed impressed, Gabe thought as he watched the three of them. Had she reacted that way when Calvin's book was brought out last night? He questioned Calvin as they walked home from church. Drew had joined Jeff for the afternoon.

"Did Alana see your book last night?"

"Yes, I saw her look at it while Carolyn and a couple of the others were asking me about it." Gabe waited to see if Calvin would volunteer any more observations. "She acted as if she wasn't interested, but I noticed she didn't move out of hearing range of the conversation."

"Did she mention it to you?"

Calvin chuckled. "'Nice book,' she said."

Gabe grinned. "So that business with Dr. Hakim was mainly for your benefit, not his, even though he thought it was."

"Alana hasn't learned yet that there are games one doesn't need to play."

"That's so true." As they came to the house he asked his friend, "Are you thinking of taking on the role of her instructor?"

"She's a very interesting young woman," Calvin said as he went into the house.

* * *

Lawrence was at the center working in Makima's office when Gabe knocked on her door the next morning. He blinked in surprise as Lawrence continued stuffing envelopes at a side table as if he'd worked there for months.

"Morning, Gabe," he said cheerfully.

"Good morning," Gabe said. He greeted Makima then gave in to his curiosity. "You seem to be very busy," he told Lawrence. Had Mrs. Gray asked Makima to find him a job at the center?

"He's our newest volunteer," Makima said, "and since I had this mailing to go out I put him right to work on it."

"I've done this kind of community work before and I'll be glad to help out while I'm here." His fingers moved efficiently folding the letter, placing it in the envelope and sealing it. He'd make a good pickpocket, Gabe thought, and was glad the man couldn't read his mind.

"I hope you don't mind my saying you're a lucky man, Gabe," Lawrence said.

"Why do you say that?"

"To have had someone in your family who was a hundred years old."

How had he learned about Great-Grandfather? Gabe slid a glance at Makima.

"Lawrence hasn't been here since he was a child and we were talking about Grayson, how it's grown. Naturally Mr. Zeke's name came up as one of our most outstanding citizens," she said in answer to his unspoken query.

"I've never known a centenarian before," Lawrence said almost wistfully.

"Unfortunately I didn't get to know my great-grandfather in person, but I'm finding out about him from living in the house he built. He was a fine craftsman." There was such an eager expression on Lawrence's face that Gabe involuntarily said, "Would you like to see it?"

"Yes, if it isn't a bother," Lawrence replied.

"I'll bring him by after work if that's convenient," Makima offered. Gabe would rather have seen Makima by herself. Still, if he was clever, he should be able to steal a moment alone with her. Calvin or Drew could show Lawrence around. Anyway, he wasn't sure Lawrence would really appreciate the quality of Great-Grandfather's work.

He found he was wrong.

Later, at the house, Lawrence said, "I've dabbled in real estate off and on for years and this is one of the best pieces of property I've seen crafted by a single man." He spoke knowingly about the types of wood used and how they functioned in unique ways.

"Did you ever sell real estate in New York?" Gabe asked.

"Not in the city. But in the north, south, east and west of the country. Texas is the best. It's so big and it's easy to make a deal there." He laid his hand on the stair. "This house is a treasure. You used to come here as a little girl, Makima?"

"I spent a lot of time with Mr. Zeke and his wife."

"He knew a lot about Africa." Lawrence made it a statement.

"It was his great interest and he used to lecture on it in the local schools," she said. Neither Drew nor Calvin were home so Gabe had to stay with Lawrence as they went outside to see the field and the trees.

Lawrence whistled as he surveyed the trees. "All these belong to the property?" he asked Gabe. When Gabe nodded yes, his next question was one that Gabe felt was intrusive. "How many acres?"

"I'm not sure." As a real estate person, that was a reasonable thing to ask, but Gabe wasn't required to answer it.

* * *

Makima didn't know what to make of Lawrence Stoddard. He continued to come to the center every day and was willing to do whatever was necessary. His cheerful personality made him welcome in any group. She already had him lined up for the fund-raiser on Saturday to help with the pancake breakfast. He and his friend were staying at the only motel in Grayson. It was none of her business, but she wondered what they were using for money. Apparently they'd just come from a job in Massachusetts but what happened when that money ran out? She didn't want Lawrence sponging off her parents. She had a mistrust of adults who weren't working. That was the way she'd been raised. She, Bobby and Alana had worked since they were in high school, beginning with small jobs and small money, but it had instilled in them responsibility and accountability.

She needed to talk with Alana and see what she thought about Lawrence. And about Gabe. And about Calvin. Makima made them a simple supper of a western omelet, a bowl of fresh fruit and toasted bagels with cream cheese.

"Next time, add home fries," Alana said, preparing a pot of tea.

"We don't need any kind of fries." Makima put the dishes in the dishwasher.

"We didn't need those delicious bagels with cream cheese, either, but I didn't notice you refusing them."

"That's different." Makima grinned. "They're a favorite of mine and I cooked. You cook next time and you can have whatever you want." Makima took the cranberry scalloped teapot into the living room. Alana brought the dainty cups decorated with cranberry insets and gold leaves. Makima poured the tea, then plunged into the most important issue.

"Alana, are you mad at me because of Gabe?"

"I was at first, to be honest. I was hurt, too, because you knew how I felt about him." Their eyes met over their teacups.

"I did and that's what made me feel I had to suppress my own feelings for him. I tried to pay no attention when he began to show his attraction to me. I want you to know I wasn't trying to get between you." Makima's eyes were bright with moisture as she gazed at her sister.

"I know you wouldn't do that," Alana said affectionately. "You probably wouldn't even know how," she added teasingly.

She sipped her tea and when she spoke again her face was sober. "I liked Gabe and made no bones about it, but he made it clear that you're the one he cares about. I had to face that fact. You're a good match, better than we would have been so it's all right. You believe me?" She looked at her sister until Makima nodded her understanding.

They finished their tea in the harmony Makima had hoped for. She hated being at odds with Alana. Alana set her empty cup and saucer on the table beside her chair.

"Calvin Peters is another matter," she declared. "He's different from Gabe. Do you know what he said to me at the dinner when we all sat down?"

"I've no idea." She couldn't wait to find out. "Gabe made the toast and I happened to touch my goblet with Carolyn's next to me and Mark's across from me and that was all. Then—"

"Wait a minute," Makima interrupted. "Not with Calvin who was the one being toasted and who sat on your left?"

Alana shifted in her chair. "No, I didn't."

"What did he say?"

Alana repeated word for word what Calvin had said, the tone of his voice and the look in his eyes. "Gabe would never have said that to me, nor Mark, nor any of the men I know," she said indignantly.

"But, honey, you were rude just like he said. What got into you to act that way? You said you weren't mad at me or Gabe."

Alana pushed her bottom lip out. Just like she did as a child when she misbehaved, then she looked at Makima sheepishly. "I really don't know. Maybe I was mad at myself. Something about Calvin Peters struck me the wrong way the minute I saw him. He was trouble and I knew it."

"Did you say anything back to him?"

"I said I was sorry if I hurt his feelings and he had the nerve to say his feelings weren't that easily hurt. Then he turned his back on me and talked to Mark for the longest time."

"Poor baby," Makima said.

"It did sit me back on my heels. I felt embarrassed and I hoped no one had heard us. I couldn't get over that he had told me that truth so calmly to my face." She poured more tea. "The funny thing was that I felt him watching me all evening. Not obviously but like he was always there. It gave me the oddest feeling. When I was ready to leave he was there to walk me to my car."

"Did he say anything?" This was fascinating.

"He held my arm, said he hoped I'd had a good time and thanked me for coming. Said, 'Good night, Alana. I hope to see you soon.' What do you make of that?"

"What do you think?"

"I'm not sure," Alana said slowly. "First he's rude to me then he acts almost like he's protecting me. I've never met a man like him."

"Perhaps he sees something in you no one else has seen. He's not a shallow person, you know, Alana."

"I know. I can't read him at all," she confessed.

"That makes a good challenge for you, doesn't it?"

She flashed an Alana smile at Makima. "I'll admit it keeps me interested."

"I haven't had a chance to tell you that Lawrence has been coming to the center every day volunteering his services," Makima said.

"He has? What does Gabe think about him?"

"We both can see that he's a good worker and gets along with people. Gabe invited him to see his place and I took him over."

"Why?" Alana seemed puzzled.

"Lawrence seemed so interested in Mr. Zeke because of the things we told him about him being a centenarian. He told Gabe that he's been involved in real estate and he was quite impressed by Mr. Zeke's house."

"He bothers you, doesn't he?"

"A little. What's your take on him and Dr. Hakim?"

"To be honest, I hadn't paid them any attention."

"You seemed to on Sunday."

"That was just to get a reaction from Calvin, I'm sorry to say, because it didn't work."

"It isn't anything I can put my finger on so it may be just my imagination."

"Perhaps, but if he's at the center, you and Gabe need to keep an eye on him."

Chapter 27

"**I**'m taking Alana to Columbia tonight," Calvin said when Gabe came home from the center and proposed going out later for dinner. He was at the desk in the office, busy at his laptop, and he looked up for a moment to make the announcement.

"Really?" Gabe walked over to stand where he could see Calvin's face. "Where in Columbia?"

"I left the choice of restaurant up to her since I don't know the city."

"Why are you going all the way to Columbia? There are good restaurants closer than that."

Calvin stopped typing. "To make a point."

"What point?"

"You're not going to let me alone, are you?" He looked up at Gabe.

"It's your business." Gabe shrugged. "I just hope you know what you're getting into with a woman like Alana."

"Alana has a vitality and fire that I like, but I know there's more to her than that. I want to get beyond that surface, which means spending a lot of time together. That's why I chose Columbia. By the time I get back tonight I hope to have a better idea of who Alana Gray is."

Gabe considered that, but knowing how reserved his friend was, he asked, "Will you also open up enough to let her see more of you than she has?"

"I guess I'll have to, won't I," Calvin said.

Gabe left the office to Calvin and went outside. He felt restless and went to sit on the bench. Usually he could get his mind settled here but not today. His thoughts were like bees buzzing around and around in his head. Calvin had intrigued him with his decision to spend a long evening with Alana. Whatever the outcome, he envied their time together. That's what he wanted, too. Time with Makima. But not out anywhere. He wanted to bring her to the praise house. That's what he really wanted.

As soon as he phrased that thought, the restlessness and uncertainty disappeared. He'd told Drew and Calvin the place should be kept a secret for now. But Makima wasn't just anybody, she could be trusted. He hurried to the house.

"I want to show Makima the praise house. Is that all right with the two of you?"

"Sure. You didn't need to ask," Drew said and Calvin agreed. Gabe called her at the center.

"This is Gabe. Are you alone?"

"Yes. Why?" Makima said curiously.

"Remember the other day when you said something good had happened for me?"

"And you said one day you'd tell me about it."

"This is the day. Are you free after work?"

"Yes."

"Come over and wear some flats."

"That sounds really interesting. I'll be there."

Gabe was waiting for her on the porch. He ran down the steps to her car and opened her door. "It seems so long since I've seen you," he said.

"I feel the same way—" she smiled "—although it's been only five hours."

"We'll get started right away and come back to the house later," he said, taking her hand and walking through the gate to the trees.

"I'm so excited, Gabe. I kept trying to guess what it is and I can't," she said.

"You'll see." They stepped into the forest where the sun was still strong enough to cast light through the canopy of tall pines.

"Did Great-Grandfather ever bring you in here, Makima?" It had occurred to him that she might be one of the few persons who had seen inside this forest.

"Yes. I'd forgotten all about it until now."

"How old were you?"

"Around seven or eight."

"Did you go far?"

"Not too far because my legs got tired." She was looking around as she tried to keep up with him. He slowed down. In his excitement he'd walked fast, eager to get to the praise house with her. He began pointing out the features Marie Frye had shown him and as they walked and talked together, they seemed to arrive at the dense shrubbery that held the praise house in half the time. He pulled aside the vegetation veil so she could step into the clearing. He watched her face, for he had the intuition that she'd recognize the building for what it was. He was right.

Makima gazed at the structure in awe. "It's a praise house!" She looked around at the sheltering trees. "All this time Mr. Zeke had a praise house hidden in his trees!"

Gabe unlocked the door. He went back for Makima who was

still standing a few feet away. "Let's go in," he said and hand in hand they walked through the door. Immediately Gabe felt immersed in an ephemeral swirl of emotion and heard, as if coming through the atmosphere, an echo of drums. Makima's hand tightened in his. Her eyes were wide as she turned to him questioningly. He nodded, letting her know they'd shared the experience. They moved slowly down the aisle to the front wall where he showed her the carvings of the African man on the left side and the cross on the right.

"Their holy man," she said of the African. "Then they became Christian and carved in the cross." They sat side by side on the front bench and spoke in hushed tones.

"I know Mr. Zeke spent a lot of time here," she said.

"Communing with his ancestors," Gabe replied. "I can feel it. That's why I love to come here."

"The spirit still lingers."

"It does for me."

"You can pray here?" she asked.

"I think a person can pray anywhere." He looked around at the rough wooden walls and the planks on the floor. "Here I can feel the sadness and the joy of the Africans enslaved on this land. Their spirit calls out to me." He was silent, thinking it out. He wanted Makima to understand even though she might not agree. "Church is more social. It doesn't make me feel the way this praise house does."

"I think Mr. Zeke was able to do both," she said, "but he lived one hundred years and you've only lived thirty-five." There was a silence, which Makima broke. "Sitting here I'm remembering words Mr. Zeke spoke that I'd forgotten all these years. Once he said, 'I see your face long ago.' I didn't understand it then and I don't understand it now."

"Do you know anything about your lineage?" Gabe asked.

"Only that we all came from Africa at one time or another."

"Have you seen other praise houses?" he asked.

"I've seen two, one in Beaufort County and one in Georgia. But this one is special probably because I'm close to the slaves who built it. The spirit is forceful."

"I thought you'd feel the same as I do. That's why I wanted you to see it, but it's still a confidential matter."

"Of course. You can trust me, Gabe."

As they went out and Gabe locked the door he thanked her for coming with him.

"I'm the one who's thankful," she said. The sun was less bright as they hurried back through the forest. When they came to the bench he asked her to stay for supper.

"I wish I could but I have a meeting in another hour."

"Let's sit here for a little while before you go," he urged. He gently took her in his arms and kissed her. "I wanted to do this before but it didn't seem appropriate in the praise house."

"We're not in the praise house now," she whispered, her eyes soft and tender. Putting her arms around his neck she returned his kiss and added several more of her own. "May I ask you a very personal question, Gabe?"

She was still in his arms and he wasn't sure what to expect as she gazed down at his arm around her. "You may ask me anything at all, Makima."

"Did you have a lot of girls in New York?"

He laid her head against his chest and stroked her hair. "I dated a lot but they were just fun, nothing serious until I met Olivia. We got along well and I thought I was in love with her. In fact, I was thinking of asking her to marry me when I found out she'd been cheating on me with a guy in New Jersey. It turned out for the best because Mom got sick and died. Pop had died not long before, so that left me in charge of Drew. Olivia was not the kind of woman who'd have welcomed Drew into our home had we been married."

"You were lucky," Makima said. "So was Drew, although he probably doesn't know it."

"How about you? As attractive as you are it surprises me that you're not married." He'd wanted to know this from the beginning.

"When I was in school I went out a little but not much. Once I finished school the men I met didn't attract me until Reggie Powell moved here a few years ago. He seemed to be everything I wanted in a man and we saw a lot of each other. My family was practically planning the wedding when he wrote me a farewell note and took a job in another city."

He dumped this elegant, dignified, intelligent woman! How she must have suffered in a town like this where she was so well known and respected. Gabe caressed her cheek and cuddled her. "I'm so sorry, honey. That must have hurt."

It had hurt because it had assured Makima that she couldn't hold a man. She wasn't feminine enough. Attract, yes. Hold, no. Yet here was Gabe, a man she'd dropped potato salad on in a public place, who'd refused to sell her land for the clinic, who'd been the target of the oh-so-feminine Alana, who was a New Yorker down to his fingertips, holding her in his arms in a most possessive way. She turned around so she could face him. She had to make him understand how she felt.

"It did hurt, but you've made it all go away. Reggie said he was leaving because I wasn't doing my part in the relationship. I truly didn't understand what he meant because I was doing the best I could. Then I saw you in that restaurant and something happened. Each time I saw you the awareness grew until you were like a tingle in me all of the time." She pulled his head down and kissed him fiercely. She strained to get closer to him, forgetting where she was. Forgetting everything except this man who awakened emotions in her she'd never experienced. Finally she made herself let go and move back from Gabe. "Now I know what Reggie meant," she said, holding his gaze.

Gabe had to clear his throat before he could speak. "Lawrence said it best the other day. I'm a lucky man!"

Chapter 28

By seven o'clock Saturday morning the center was buzzing with the staff and their volunteers making their preparations for the fund-raiser.

"It looks like rain," people said to each other as they set up breakfast tables, wrapped plasticware in napkins, filled pitchers with syrup and assembled paper plates and cups. The butter pats were in the refrigerator and the coffee urns were ready to turn on.

"We'll just have to hope it doesn't," others said.

"Everyone, remember we planned what to do if it does rain," Dr. Cook said, "so we don't need to get upset. Just follow the plan."

"Good administrator," Calvin told Gabe.

"Yes, he is. If it rains, Jimmy and the crew will move the flea-market tables inside. It'll be a little crowded but that adds to the fun if all is going well."

At seven-thirty, Dr. Cook told Mrs. Gray to serve breakfast to her volunteers. He, Eugenia and Tony collected the money or tickets since even volunteers were expected to pay.

The breakfast of three large pancakes, two sausages, orange juice and coffee were served to Gabe, Makima, Alana, Calvin, Lawrence and several of Mrs. Gray's friends from church.

"This is wonderful food," Gabe said.

"You rarely get pancakes like this in New York," Calvin agreed.

"Mama's one of the best cooks in the area," Alana said. "But we'd better hurry so we'll be ready for the eight-o'clockers. They're the ones who're at the door right at eight."

Gabe thought Alana might be exaggerating but sure enough, when the doors opened officially at eight, there were some twenty people in line. He and his group were kept busy serving the individual plates with pancakes hot off the griddle.

He heard a woman say to her neighbor, "I always come to this pancake breakfast 'cause I know Mrs. Gray doesn't make 'em ahead of time and let them get all soggy. I don't mind waiting a while."

Gabe put this evaluation in the back of his mind as he went back into the kitchen. Mrs. Gray in a chef's hat, which her daughters had put on her with much ceremony, commandeered the large grill that produced twelve pancakes at a time. Two electric grills had been set up with Mrs. Henderson at one and Mrs. Greely at the other. Next year, Gabe thought, he'd propose the purchase of another large grill.

By ten o'clock Gabe worried that Mrs. Gray might run out of batter.

"What do we do if that happens?" he asked Makima.

"It won't happen. Don't worry. She always makes more than enough."

Soon after, two potential disasters occurred. The rain came and Jimmy and his crew ran to bring the tables inside. Confusion occurred until the customers got into the action and within minutes all was safe.

Then Calvin came up to Gabe. "Alana just saw a busload of people pull in. Do we have enough food?"

This time Gabe, worried about the food, went directly to Mrs. Gray with the message.

"How many people in the bus?" she asked calmly.

"Probably around sixty."

"There's plenty of batter. You might check for butter and sausages."

He called Makima to help him. She teased him with a sassy grin after they found there was enough of everything. "I told you we don't believe in running out of food when we're feeding people."

By eleven, the sixty people in the bus had been fed as well as local latecomers, the kitchen was closed, and Gabe breathed a sigh of relief. On the flea-market side so many items had been donated that Jimmy appealed to Gabe for help.

"We need any tables you can spare," he said, "and more people to price what keeps coming in." He looked a little harried. "I didn't expect such a crowd."

"You can take Alana and Calvin and I'll be over as soon as we get the kitchen cleaned up."

"The flyer said from eight to twelve but I don't see folks leaving," Calvin remarked. He and Alana made their way through groups of ladies showing garments to each other, children of all ages playing on the floor, and knots of men talking together.

"Why should they leave? They're full of good food and now they're shopping without having to go out in the rain, and they're visiting, catching up with people they haven't seen in a while," she pointed out. They stood side by side sorting through a garbage bag filled with clothing that Jimmy had said needed to be priced.

He'd given them a guide sheet and said, "Use your own judgment," then hurried away.

As they worked together, Alana asked, "Have you ever done this before?" Somehow she couldn't see this man setting up a flea market.

"No, never." Calvin looked at a pair of brown pants that were slightly worn, priced them at one dollar and put them in the men's-clothing pile. "This is a new experience for me," he said. As he reached into the bag, he saw Lawrence approaching.

"Need some help with that?" Lawrence asked Alana.

Alana, conscious of sudden tension from Calvin, shook her head. "We've got this under control, but Jimmy was looking for more help down at the other end," she said. She watched him as he went down the tables talking to people, surprised at how she'd sent him to Jimmy instead of keeping him beside her to flirt in her usual manner.

She felt Calvin's gaze but she didn't let herself look at him. The evening they'd spent together flashed through her mind, revealing a sudden insight. Without ever saying the words, Calvin had let her know by the way he treated her that she was a woman worthy of deference and respect. She didn't need to put herself on display just because she was physically attractive. Not that she'd ever thought of herself in those terms, yet now she could acknowledge that her coquettish behavior was her way of making up for the fact that she wasn't like Makima, could never compete with her sister whom she loved but also secretly envied.

She put her hand in the bag to get another garment and felt Calvin stroking her arm.

"Thank you," he said. He brought out a woman's jacket and smoothed it on the table. "You asked had I worked at a flea market before. I told you this was a new experience for me."

She was spellbound by his tender gaze. They might have

been alone in a space where only the two of them existed communicating heart to heart.

"You are a new experience to me, Alana. No other woman has intrigued me as you do."

"It's the same with me," she murmured. "I don't know what to make of you, Calvin." Her voice caressed his name and he shivered.

"Uncle Calvin," Drew said. "Jimmy sent me to get the clothes you've priced." Calvin privately wondered how long Drew had been standing there and what he'd heard. It didn't matter. When he'd seen Alana act against her usual self in sending Lawrence away, he'd had to tell her how he felt. He was jubilant inside as he joked with Drew and piled his arms with clothing.

"I've been hearing the cash registers ringing nonstop," Alana said. "How much money has the flea market made?"

"I'm not sure but Jimmy said it's the most they've ever taken in so he's pretty happy."

The center staff meeting on Wednesday was a triumph. Mutual congratulations were exchanged for the work the staffers did at the fund-raiser as well as all the volunteers they'd recruited. A big cheer went up when Dr. Cook announced the total amount of money the center would have after all expenses had been paid.

"Combining the pancake breakfast with the flea market was a brilliant idea that Gabe had, but it wouldn't have been this successful if all of you hadn't put your best effort behind it."

"It seems to me in looking over the books that the best way to keep the center in healthy funds each year is to do something like this on a regular basis," Gabe said, directing his comment to Dr. Cook. He'd meant to bring this plan to Dr. Cook in his office, but this was too good an opportunity to miss.

"Could you be more specific?" Dr. Cook asked.

"We could plan three or four major events a year. They would be the kind that no other organization could do in the way the center could. They'd be highly publicized and be of a quality that would permit us to charge a good fee, and also the kind that would keep people coming back year after year."

"I've always wanted to put on a community fashion show involving the men, women, youth and children of this community. I know it would be a lot of work to do it right but it would also bring in money because everyone would want to see their relatives and friends on the stage," Makima said.

"I think we should do the flea-market-and-breakfast combo again. I heard so many people say good things about it," Jimmy offered.

"That reminds me that I heard one woman say she always comes to this one because she knows Mrs. Gray doesn't serve any soggy pancakes," Gabe said.

That brought on more anecdotes until Eugenia said, "Wasn't it too crowded in here? Maybe if we do it again we should get a bigger place."

Dr. Cook said, "It was crowded, but I heard no complaints. That was part of the success, I think."

Others agreed with him and Gabe put in the final reason. "Holding it somewhere else defeats our purpose since we'd have to pay a rental fee and insurance. All we need to do for any of these events is to be as creative as possible in how we use the space."

"We already have the spring dance and the winter ball, so we could keep them or schedule an event for children and youth instead," Eugenia said.

"Something for our young people is very important and I think that should be one of the major events of the year. Let's begin to think about this idea. Put our thoughts on paper and in the coming months we'll refine them so we'll be ready when next year comes." Dr. Cook thanked the staff again and adjourned the meeting.

"How's your mother?" Gabe asked Makima as they walked back to their offices.

"She stayed home from church Sunday and laid around Monday until the swelling in her feet went down. She's fine and anxious to hear how much money we made. She said to tell you thanks for the roses. That was so thoughtful."

"She's an amazing woman. I tried to figure out how she made all that batter."

"She begins days ahead. Measures out the dry ingredients for fifty pancakes and packages it. The day before, she does the same with the eggs, the milk and the oil. The day of the breakfast, she mixes fifty at a time. It's simple. The sausages go in the oven the day before on sheet pans, a hundred at a time. They're drained and packaged, so all they need is heating."

They came to her office. He didn't go in but stood a moment more since no one else was around. He always hated leaving her. Despite the excellent staff meeting, he saw her eyes were shadowed. "Are you not rested yet or is there something bothering you? I don't like to see your eyes like this." He touched her lids with a tender gesture.

"I think I'm a worrywart," she said. "We haven't heard from Dakers and Sons yet."

"It's only been a few days, hasn't it?"

"Actually, it's been two full weeks."

"Has it been that long?" He did a rapid calculation. "It has, hasn't it? Has your attorney been in touch with them?"

"He's left a couple of messages, he said, and they say they'll get back to him."

"Where are they located?"

"Rock Hill, South Carolina."

"I'm sure they'll be in touch soon, honey. They're just involved with someone else's project. Go to bed early tonight and get some rest. You worked so hard getting the fund-raiser together."

"No harder than anyone else but I do feel a little down. Tomorrow when you see me, the shadows will be gone." She glanced around to be sure they were alone, gave him a swift kiss and went into her office.

Gabe was not at all as sanguine about Dakers as he'd told Makima and he called Mr. Moultrie in Charlotte as soon as he got home.

"You're close to Rock Hill, South Carolina, aren't you?" he asked when the attorney came on the phone.

"Yes. It's just across the state line."

Gabe explained the situation about Dakers and Sons. "Can you check them out for me? Are they aboveboard and just slow with a new client or is it another scenario? I'd appreciate knowing as soon as possible and thanks."

Mr. Moultrie called later that day. "Gabe, I have a colleague in Rock Hill and he investigated the firm. I'm sorry to have to tell you, it was a scam from start to finish, with fraudulent brochures, references, price schedules, detailed pictures and analyses of previous projects they'd done. They set up shop in a town, lure a few people in, ask for a deposit that they know most people will give them because they're lower than legitimate builders, then they take the money and run."

"Aren't they in the Rock Hill phone book?"

"They are, with a modest advertisement. But the phone has been disconnected and the building is empty and locked. I'm sorry for your friend, Gabe."

Gabe felt sick to his stomach. All he could think of was how Makima was going to feel. "Can they be traced?" he asked.

"My colleague and I are going to see what can be done. It might be possible since it's just happened. I'll let you know."

Gabe put the phone down and slumped in his chair. How could he give Makima this news? She would be devastated. Maybe he shouldn't, because their attorney would find it out, wouldn't he? But how soon? Wouldn't she want to know as soon as possible?

"Calvin!" he called. "Come in here, please." He needed some help.

When Calvin appeared he told him the whole story. "I don't know what I should do. Go to the center and tell her? Call her and tell her? Don't say anything and let their attorney find out?"

"Are you her friend?" Calvin asked.

"Of course I am."

"You have to tell her. But not by yourself. I'll get Alana and meet you there in thirty minutes," he said as he began calling Alana on his cell phone.

Chapter 29

"Gabe! What are you doing back here?" Makima asked in surprise. "I'm just getting ready to close up." As Alana and Calvin followed Gabe in, she smiled. "Hi, you two. What is this, are we all going somewhere?"

"I wish we were, honey," Gabe said soberly, "but I'm afraid it isn't that pleasant."

"What's happened? Is it Mom?" Her face turned ashen and she looked at Alana.

Alana went to her. "Mom and Dad are both fine. Bobby, too." She put her arm around Makima who was standing behind her desk.

"Tell her what you found out, Gabe," Alana said.

"It's about Dakers and Sons. They've disappeared from Rock Hill. Their office is closed and their phone is disconnected." Gabe saw that every word he spoke was a physical blow to Makima. At first her face showed utter disbelief, then shock as what he was saying began to sink in. Her eyes rolled back in her head and her body crumpled into a dead faint. He dashed behind the desk to take her weight from Alana.

"Get some water," he said as he eased Makima into her chair with Calvin's help. Alana came back with a damp washcloth and laid it on Makima's forehead. She poured a little water from the glass she had into Gabe's hand.

"Rub her wrist." Tears ran down Alana's face as she begged her sister to wake up and gently rubbed her face with the wet washcloth. Gabe's stomach muscles were clenched so tight they hurt. With one hand he rubbed Makima's wrist, with the other he stroked her hair.

Her eyelids fluttered and she opened her eyes. They were blank, then puzzled as she saw the washcloth.

"What happened?" she asked.

"You fainted," Alana said. "Are you all right now?"

"Yes," Makima said as she sat up straight in her chair. She took a tissue from the box and patted the moisture from her face and wrist.

Gabe stepped away, knowing she was trying to overcome her moment of weakness. He appreciated her effort, but nothing could hide the horror of what had happened from showing in her eyes.

"How did you know?" she asked him.

"This morning when you mentioned it had been two weeks and you were worried because Dakers and Sons hadn't been in touch, it sounded ominous to me so I called attorney Moultrie in Charlotte and asked him to check it out since he was so close to Rock Hill. He called me several hours later. A colleague of his who lives in Rock Hill went to their office. It was empty and the phone had been disconnected. People around them said they'd left in the night."

"But they have our five thousand dollars," she said.

"I know, Makima," Gabe said gently. "It's a classic scam

where a company moves in, lures customers through brochures, advertisements, pictures of completed projects, references from satisfied customers and schedules of payments which are just enough lower than legitimate companies' to make doing business with them attractive. The minute they've made their quota of clients who've paid the deposit, they leave in the night, go to another small town, change their name and do it again."

"Can they be tracked down?"

"Moultrie said he and his friend are going to try. Because it's been so recent they might have a chance."

She dropped her head as if unable to meet his eyes. "What am I going to do?" she murmured in despair.

Gabe yearned to take her in his arms and fight her battles for her, but she wasn't the kind of woman who would allow that. Her independence and pride made her stand up to whatever happened.

"Tell your attorney exactly what happened and let him take it from there. You're not the only one responsible, Makima. It was a board decision, wasn't it?" Gabe asked.

"Yes. However, I was the one who found Dakers and Sons," she said.

"Nevertheless, you didn't act alone. That's what you must remember." Gabe felt he was talking to a brick wall, the wall of perseverance and pride that made Makima who she was, but could also be a hindrance. She wasn't listening to him at all.

"Come on, Makima, let's go home. I'll drive you," Alana said.

When she stood, Gabe saw her sway a little from dizziness and he moved to steady her. She turned sharply away from him to take Alana's arm.

She was shutting him out.

When they were outside, Calvin said, "It won't last. She's in shock and confusing the message with the messenger."

"I hope you're right," Gabe said as the sisters got in Makima's car. Alana was at the wheel and she waved goodbye. Makima looked straight ahead.

"Maybe I didn't do the right thing after all, even though it was from friendship and caring. The board's attorney would have found it out eventually."

"He should have found it out sooner than this," Calvin said.

"She said he called and left messages so I guess he thought that was all that was necessary."

"He's not much of a lawyer. After the first week he should have been on their doorstep."

"You're right." Gabe sighed. "It would have saved so much heartbreak." He got in his car. "See you at home."

Gabe wasn't surprised to see Eugenia at Makima's desk the next day. "She's sick and won't be in for the rest of the week," Eugenia said. "I could see it coming on, you know, because she didn't look well yesterday."

In his office as he worked on the plans for next year's fund-raisers, Gabe wondered how long it would take for the news to leak out. It was a shame. Grayson people had been giving money to build the clinic for three years. Of course that five thousand wasn't all they had for the project, but still, it represented a lot of community effort.

Some people were going to be sympathetic and some were going to be angry and critical of the board. This was going to make it harder to continue to raise money.

The worst thing for Makima was that she was the public face of the clinic project. That was fine when matters were going well. But now she was going to get the brunt of the blame from the public. That, on top of her strong feeling of responsibility, translates into guilt. *It's no wonder she's ill,* he thought.

He wanted to call her but knew he'd have to wait until she was ready to talk to him. He ached for her and wished he had the right to be with her, support her, find those thieves and get the money back for her.

That night he took a chance and dialed her number. No answer, no "please leave your number and I'll call you back" message.

When Calvin came in he said, "I just talked to Alana. She said Makima isn't at her apartment. She is really sick and her mother came and took her home."

"What's wrong with her?"

"It's the flu. She has a fever and feels miserable on top of all the other."

"What about the board?"

"As soon as Alana took her home, Makima called the attorney to tell him what happened. Then she began crying and was so upset Alana called their mother, who came and took Makima home. Mrs. Gray won't let her talk to anyone just yet, Alana said." He looked at Gabe with concern. "I'm sorry, Gabe."

"At least she's getting good care and that's the important thing." That was vital and he found himself praying that she would soon be well.

He sent her a big bouquet of spring flowers the next day and refrained from calling her.

Drew called Gabe and Calvin in the evening to turn on the television. "That African guy we met is on," he yelled. Dr. Hakim was being interviewed on a local channel. He spoke of being from Dakar in Senegal, how he'd come to America to study history and had taught a few years at a university in Washington, D.C.

"What brings you to South Carolina?" the interviewer asked.

"I am seeking signs of my ancestors who were brought here as slaves. When I find them I will be ready to return home. I have been away too long."

The program ended and Gabe turned off the set. "What kind of signs is he looking for?" he asked Calvin.

"I don't know. Would he think of your praise house as a sign?"

"Maybe it would be if the Africans on this land were from Senegal, but in all of Great-Grandfather's books and notes, I've seen nothing that says so. I'm certainly not going to invite Hakim here to see it."

Sam Williams came to breakfast Saturday to enjoy a long visit with Calvin. After he'd satisfied his curiosity about him, he asked Gabe, "I don't know if you've heard anything about the clinic but there's talk that they got gypped out of the deposit they sent to the construction company they signed a contract with."

"That'd be a real shame if it's true," Gabe said. "You don't always know who you can trust these days."

"It was an upstate company, from what I heard. Probably best to stay with someone close by that you can keep an eye on."

"Maybe they can get a lawyer to get the money back," Calvin said.

"I sure hope so," Gabe said.

"So do I," echoed Sam.

Makima felt like a ghost, frail, insubstantial, disconnected from what she'd known as real life. When she'd come to her old bedroom in her parents' house she'd been thankful to slip under the covers and let the world go away.

Feverish and nauseous, she'd let her mother nurse her. Even when she tried to sleep, the cloud of the lost money hung over her. Her dreams were troubled and her agitation prevented her from getting any better. Mrs. Gray called the family doctor and begged him to make a house call.

Dr. Parker examined Makima. "Listen to me, young woman," he said sternly. "You're not doing yourself any good and you're worrying your mother. Once you're well and out of this bed, you can take care of your clinic business." She blinked in surprise.

"Yes, I've heard that the board had a bit of bad luck but I don't want you thinking about it now. I'm giving you some medicine for the flu symptoms plus a strong sedative because I want your body and mind at ease. You need to rest so you can recover more quickly. Do you understand me?"

She nodded yes. "Thank you," she said in a weak voice.

She slept that night, most of Saturday and most of Sunday. When she went to the bathroom Sunday evening, she was as weak as a kitten but her mind was clear for the first time. It took her forty minutes to shower and put on a clean gown. She didn't have the strength yet to wash her hair. That would have to wait.

Her mother had changed the bed linens in her absence and it felt so good to be clean again that she found herself smiling. "Ready for some food?" Her mother placed a steaming bowl of vegetable soup on her bed tray.

"Do you think I can keep it down?" Makima looked at it hungrily.

"Try a little at a time. You must have some nourishment, you know."

The first spoonful tasted delicious and little by little she managed to eat all of it. She snuggled down in the bed again.

"That was good. Thanks, Mom."

"Now that you're feeling a little better, would you like to talk to Gabe? He's called so many times," her mother said lingering at the door.

"Not yet," Makima said.

When she was alone again, Makima laid on her back, her eyes wide open, and thought about Gabe. During the fog of her illness, Alana had remarked about the lovely flowers he'd sent. That was very nice of him.

Dr. Parker had told her that when she was well she could take care of her clinic business. She was on her way to being well and she was ready to deal with the clinic.

She was angry! More angry than she'd ever been in her life. Not at her parents who'd taken such loving care of her, but at almost everyone else.

She was afraid to say she was angry at God so she wouldn't put it that way. But how could He let this happen when all she was trying to do was provide a service to the community? A service that was much needed, for without it people like her baby sister could be put at risk and die?

How could He ignore the hours of work so many people had given to make that money those thieves stole? They had put on fund-raisers in good faith to help raise the clinic money. These were not rich people. Mrs. Wilkins had six children yet she'd managed to give fifty dollars to the fund. Pressed it into Makima's hand with a smile. "I know you all need money to build that clinic and you'll take good care of it," she'd said.

What was she thinking now of her hard-earned fifty dollars? That Makima and the board hadn't been careful enough with it.

She could read off a whole list of people like Mrs. Wilkins who'd contributed to the clinic project. Each name just made her heart ache more and increased her anger.

She was angry at the board. They should have done more research. Rock Hill wasn't that far away. A few of them could have easily driven there and back, seen the people face-to-face. Asked around about them. That's what smart people do. She and the board weren't smart.

She was raging with anger at Dakers and Sons or whoever they were. She was determined to do everything in her power to find them, get the money back and have them thrown in jail!

She was angry at Gabe. No, she shouldn't be, but she was. This whole mess wouldn't have happened if the board had known they would be able to get the land they needed from Mr. Zeke. She didn't care what the will said. Gabe could have done something about it! Negotiated something and then the board could have accepted the Wetherell contract and all would have been well. So really, in a sense, this debacle stemmed from Gabe's stubbornness about the land. It was all his fault!

Then to make matters worse, he was the one who had to look into it behind her back. She hadn't asked him to do so. All she'd said was that she was a little worried. Did that give him permission to go call the man in Charlotte and find out Dakers had left town?

If he knew, he could have kept it to himself. The board's attorney would find out sooner or later. But no. Mr. High-and-Mighty Bell had to round up Calvin and Alana and come to her office to tell her the good news.

Did it make him happy to see her faint?

Did he remember at all that a few days before, at Calvin's dinner party, he, Gabe, had honored her by telling the group that the board had signed the contract? People had cheered and congratulated her.

Did he realize how humiliated she felt to learn it had all blown up in her face?

Stupid man. He thought he was doing her a favor to come to the center to tell her, and with an audience.

She would never forget nor forgive the humiliation he had brought on her. Never!

Chapter 30

Lawrence left the center whistling. He'd volunteered to help Jimmy wax the floors. A hard and long job but it was over. The weeks of being the guy who was ready to pitch in wherever needed was paying off and he couldn't wait to tell his partner.

He picked up some food from a hamburger stand for dinner, drove to the motel and parked the car. Hakim opened the door. "I wondered when you were coming," he said.

"The job took longer than I thought it would but it was worth it." He divided the food and took a bite of his burger.

"You found out something?" Hakim held his food, eager to hear what Lawrence had to say.

"Jimmy said he's lived here all his life and has always heard that there's a treasure hidden in Mr. Zeke's trees. That's why there's a six-foot-high fence around it with barbed wire on top. He said it's supposed to be haunted." He stopped to eat some French fries. "I don't know how much stock to put in the haunted part, but all the boys try to climb the fence. Apparently no one has succeeded, not even the bravest boys. He tried it when he was about ten." He stopped to take a drink of coffee.

"What did he say happened?" Hakim asked.

"He got halfway up with some other boys urging him on. This is always tried at night, of course. Then he got scared. 'Scared of what?' I said. 'I'm not sure, but I fell back down and ran away,' he said. When I tried to press him, he changed the subject so I left it alone."

Hakim ate the rest of his food in silence. Intuition told him he was close to the object he'd been seeking for two years. He just needed to be patient a while longer.

"What's the next step?" Lawrence asked as he threw the hamburger paper in the trash.

"We have money for another two or three weeks. By that time we'll have what we've come for and we won't have to worry about money again."

They'd met several years earlier and recognized in each other the ability and desire to make money any way they could, even if it meant skirting the law. Lawrence knew Hakim had been involved in illegal transactions concerning African artifacts but this present venture seemed particularly significant for him.

"How can you be so sure?" Lawrence wanted to know.

Hakim's voice became resonant, his eyes closed, and his face took on a rapt expression as he described the treasure he'd seen and the power that would soon be his. "I had a vision. I saw myself holding the chest that has the amulets in it. They protect the wearer from all kinds of danger, increase their knowledge and seek the favors of superior powers in all circumstances. There's a legend that they belonged to a holy man of great spiritual talents, faith and power. The power of the amulets increases the length of time they've been buried and that power, the prophecy says, is granted to whoever holds them."

"So I should keep going to the center to see what else I can learn?" Lawrence asked.

"It won't be for much longer. Keep yourself vigilant."

Makima was still at her parents' home. They refused to let her go until she demonstrated to their satisfaction that she had enough strength and energy to take care of herself.

Her mother brought in some boxes and set them on the dining-room table after breakfast on Tuesday morning. "I know you're bored, honey. Maybe you wouldn't mind going through these boxes of old clothes I've been meaning to get rid of for ages."

Makima was determined to go to the Wednesday staff meeting even if she had to come back here afterward. Maybe if she showed energy in working with her mother now, she wouldn't have to argue about going to the center tomorrow.

She dug into the carton nearest her and brought out a pleated skirt with a matching blouse.

"I used to wear this in high school," she recalled. "It was a favorite of mine."

"I made that for you and you looked so nice in it," her mother said nostalgically.

Makima pulled out several more outfits from earlier school days. They brought back memories and as she emptied the box and started on another, the reminiscences she shared with her mother took her mind away from her present troubles.

She was laughing about an incident in grade school when her hand touched something hard. Out came a carved box, flat on the bottom with a rounded lid. Even before she opened it, she blurted out, "Look, Mom. Remember this?"

"The gift from Mr. Zeke for your eighth birthday! I'd forgotten it."

"So had I," she said, tracing the carvings of childrens' faces on the lid. "I used to make up stories about each of these children. They were my play brothers and sisters in Africa. When I told Mr. Zeke the stories he laughed like he was pleased."

"I'll bet Gabe would like to see that," her mother said with a glance at Makima.

Makima ignored the comment as she opened the box and took out the figure that was inside. The girl, carved from a single piece of wood, had the features of the eight-year-old Makima wearing an African dress. Hanging from her finger was a small metal key with the number 2 on it.

"What a worrywart I must have been to Mr. Zeke," she reflected aloud, "always hanging around and pestering him with questions. That's why he put the key on my finger. 'A key unlocks the answer to questions,' he said. That makes me remember something else. He made me promise not to lose the key. Naturally I asked why. 'You'll need it someday,' he said."

Her mother looked at her fondly. "They talk about the terrible twos but with you it was when you were eight. You wanted to know the reason for everything!"

Makima set the box aside. "I'm so glad to find this. I'll take it home with me. It gives me something to remember Mr. Zeke by."

Alana took Makima home to her own apartment after dinner and helped her wash her hair. Assured that Makima was well enough to go to the center the next day, she called their mother and told her not to worry.

It took Makima some time to dress the next morning. She'd lost weight and it was hard to find an outfit that made the statement she desired. She decided on a jacket and pants she'd bought because the color reminded her of a field of poppies. A white silk blouse and suede slides the color of the suit completed the look she wanted. She had to put on a little more makeup than usual as she was still pale. She put silver hoops in her ears, gave her hair a final brush and left for work.

She walked into the staff meeting with her head held high, a little late as she'd intended to be.

"Makima! How good it is to see you again," Dr. Cook said, rising from his chair. "Are you sure you're well enough to come back to work?" He seated her in the chair next to him.

"I'm much better now," she assured him. She looked around the table, smiled at Eugenia and Jimmy, who both said they'd missed her. She took a deep breath and looked at Gabe.

"Good to have you back, Makima," he said as his eyes slid right over her.

Gabe couldn't trust himself to look into her eyes directly. He'd never been so deeply hurt in his life. Even when he'd broken up with Olivia it hadn't made him feel like this. He'd had time in this week when Makima had broken off communication with him to analyze the difference in how he felt about the two women.

He and Olivia had socialized in the same group. She was pretty, fun to be with, good to talk to and let him know she found him attractive. Over a period of months their friendship became deeper and eventually they spent most of their social time exclusively with each other. They were at a marriageable age and Gabe decided to ask her to marry him. Fortunately before he did, Webster had told him about the affair she was having with a guy in New Jersey.

His pride was hurt. Close friends commiserated with him and said how lucky he was. He agreed and Olivia faded out of his life.

With Makima, the first time he'd seen her in the restaurant, an awareness had been established which even the subsequent spilling of salad hadn't been able to dim. The awareness had become a connection.

They'd both felt it and it had held when he'd refused to give her land for the clinic and when Alana had pursued him. It had held despite the different way they looked at religion. It had held and grown stronger until they could no longer deny it.

He'd invested so much more in their relationship than before with Olivia. Thinking of it now, he realized he had grown in maturity since Olivia. Being left with Drew had helped in that process and he was thankful.

"Gabe," Dr. Cook said, "have you any ideas about the major fund-raisers for next year?"

"Yes, I have." He opened his notebook and began to talk. He wondered if his name had been called twice, because Jimmy and Eugenia were looking at him sideways.

He ignored Makima completely and when the meeting was over was the first to leave the room. If it caused speculation, he didn't care. There was too much emotion boiling up in him to be near her.

Last night he'd wondered what he'd do the next time he saw her. Now he knew. He'd stay as far away from her as he could.

Makima settled in her office chair with a sigh of relief. The worst was over. She'd survived seeing Gabe. He'd not met her eyes but that was fine. She hadn't wanted him to. She hadn't wanted to deal with any negative feelings or outbursts from him. She was strong; actually, she was tough from having to work with the clinic project. So she could deal with Gabe if she had to, but she'd rather avoid it.

There was a knock on the door and immediately she felt a lump in her throat.

"Come in," she said and was so glad to see that it was Lawrence. She gave him a big smile.

"Makima!" he said as he came over to grasp her hand. "How are you feeling? You've had a rough week."

"I thought the flu would never go away but I'm much better now," she said.

"I figured the work has probably piled up since you've been gone." He looked around. "Got anything I can do?"

"The thank-you letters to the volunteers and to people who

donated items for the fund-raiser still need to go out. You might start on them."

"That fund-raiser was phenomenal, wasn't it? I've never seen such a successful one."

"It did go well."

"You had it so well organized, even what to do if it rained. I was helping some guys to bring the tables in from outside. They were laughing about a supposedly haunted house they'd been to last week. Seems they went there on a dare. One of them said that Gabe's trees are haunted and that's why the fence is so high and has barbed wire on it." He looked at her guilelessly. "You ever heard that?"

She glanced up and noticed that no matter the expression on his face, his eyes were always watchful. Maybe that's why she'd told Alana there was something about him that didn't sit right with her.

Suspicious now, she said, "I think that's nonsense. People make a lot of things up out of ignorance," and went back to work.

Gabe had been sitting at his desk for half an hour going over the same figures without being aware of what he was doing. He suddenly got away from his desk and began pacing. He wished he had a window so he could stand at it until it was time to go home.

He couldn't get any work done. There was nothing in his mind except Makima. How did she dare to come back and say nothing to him? She at least owed him an apology.

Unable to contain himself any longer, Gabe caught up the notebook he'd taken to the staff meeting and hardly knowing what he was doing, swirled out his door and walked down the hall to Makima's office.

He knocked once on the door and before she could answer he stepped inside.

There at a side table sat Lawrence, who looked at Gabe speculatively.

"Could you leave us for a while, Lawrence?" The authority in Gabe's voice made Lawrence get up immediately without checking with Makima and walk out.

Gabe made sure the door was tightly closed, then he turned his burning gaze on Makima, who was rigid in her chair, watching his every move.

He pulled up a chair and placed it opposite her so they were eye to eye.

"I told myself to stay away from you, Makima, but I have to know, why did you refuse my calls?"

"I was sick with the flu," she said expressionlessly.

"Don't play with me. You weren't sick the whole week. Why did you refuse my calls?"

"You really want to know?" A little color came into her face and she stiffened.

"I've asked you twice," he said grimly.

"I was angry with you."

"Angry with me?" He was incredulous. "What did I do?"

She leaned across the desk. "If you'd let us have some of Mr. Zeke's land like he promised me, we wouldn't have had to get involved with Dakers and Sons."

Gabe looked at her in astonishment. "I told you why that wasn't possible. I explained Great-Grandfather's will to you, Makima. You said you understood and thanked me for taking you into my confidence. Or do you want to forget that bit of truth?"

Makima's mouth took on a mutinous curl and her eyes were blazing. "You could have negotiated something if you'd really wanted to," she insisted.

"I can't believe I'm hearing this." Gabe got up and paced a few steps away then came back and put his hands on her desk.

"You're trying to make me the reason your clinic money has

disappeared when I'm the one who tried to find out what happened to it."

"I didn't know you were going to do that." She spit out the words. "Then you had to include Calvin and Alana when you told me. It's a wonder you didn't sell tickets so everyone could see my humiliation," she said bitterly.

Gabe looked at her as if he hadn't seen her before. Who was this woman making such ridiculous statements? She'd gone from pale to flushed cheeks, her lips were stretched thin and her eyes were angry. She wasn't making any sense. Maybe the flu had stolen her reasoning ability.

"What's happened to you, Makima?" he said. "You're not being logical."

"Where is logic when what you did made us lose the money and betray the trust of people who sacrificed to give us their dollars when that money was needed for their children?"

"You want to talk about betrayal? How about when I took you to the praise house that no one else has seen except Drew and Calvin, and I asked you to keep it in confidence. 'You can trust me, Gabe,' you said. What happened to that trust?" Gabe asked through his teeth, his eyes locked with hers as they faced each other across the desk.

"What you did—"

"Don't...you...say...that...one...more...time," he interrupted, spacing his words in the authoritative tone he'd used with Lawrence. "All I did was try to be your friend. What you and the board did was your decision. I had no part in it and I refuse to accept the blame you keep trying to put on me."

He straightened and gave her a final look compounded of despair, weariness and pity. "You are suffering from delusions, Makima, and I'm sorry for you," he said.

He turned away, opened the door and left the room.

Chapter 31

"Calvin?" Gabe called when he got home.

"Up here in the office."

Gabe found him sitting in a chair with his computer on his lap instead of on the desk.

"Is that comfortable?" Gabe could never get his laptop to work fast for him except on a hard, level surface, but his legs were longer than Calvin's. And thinner. Maybe that made the difference.

"This is my favorite way to work when I'm beginning a new book," Calvin said.

"A new one? That's great, Calvin. Is it laid in the South?"

"Of course," Calvin said, but Gabe had been around his writer friend enough to sense the excitement under his surface calm. Gabe also knew that when and if Calvin wanted to tell Gabe more, he would do so. Until then the subject was banned except for superficial comments.

"I was going to ask if you wanted to walk in the forest. I want to see what's beyond the praise house and thought I'd spend the rest of the afternoon exploring."

Calvin looked at him thoughtfully. "I'll go another time, Gabe. You look like you need the forest to yourself today. I'll see you when you get back." His fingers began to move on the computer and Gabe left the room.

A few minutes later he had begun his walk. The day was warm and sunny. Patches of flowers whose names he didn't know were springing up around trees. Grasses were growing tall and he could hear little creatures scrambling through the bushes as he walked along. He carried a long stick and occasionally swished vegetation out of the way. When he came to the pond which had been such a surprise to him, he detoured to it and stood for a while watching the turtles sunning themselves.

He was so still that a doe came to drink from the pool. She looked at him with her big, brown eyes. He scarcely breathed. She dropped her head, drank again and was gone with a graceful leap. The last he saw of her was the flick of her white tail.

He came to the area where the praise house was hidden and kept walking. He might stop in on the way back. What he craved now was the beauty of nature spread out all around him. He needed its healing properties to restore calm to his wounded spirit.

The forest was large. Ms. Frye had said something that he'd translated into fifteen acres. That wasn't much for people who had huge tree plantations, but it seemed large to him. If he came into his full inheritance, he'd have the house, one hundred thousand dollars and this forest.

The sale of all these trees would bring in a sizable income and he could move back to New York with a healthy nest egg for his and Drew's future.

He looked around as he walked, trying to picture how this would look with all the trees gone. With the trees sold for lumber, he'd still own all the land. How ironic that would be!

There'd be land enough for more clinics than Makima could ever build and more church classrooms than Reverend Givhan would know what to do with, not to mention whatever else the townspeople would find themselves suddenly wanting. The one thing he'd build himself would be a state-of-the-art community center and name it for his great-grandparents. The Sarah and Ezekiel Bell Community Center. He felt a little tingle just saying the names.

Children for generations to come would benefit from it. He'd establish a foundation to keep it up to date. He and Drew wouldn't be able to see it all of the time but they could visit Grayson as needed.

Drew talked about being on the swim team next year. He was doing so well here. It would be a shame to take him away, but Gabe couldn't leave him here by himself. They were family, closely bonded and necessary to each other. Nothing would make Gabe abandon him. Other people Gabe knew could abandon people they were supposed to care deeply for. They could betray trust, but not Gabe. It would be hard on Drew at first, but he'd make new friends at home and visits could always be arranged between here and New York.

A snake slithered through the leaves, startling him, and before he knew it he'd used his stick to slash out at it.

He wouldn't talk to Drew yet. First, he hadn't discovered the treasured destiny he came to find and he wasn't going to let Great-Grandfather down. In fact, this evening he needed to call Moultrie and see what else was required. Having found the praise house, his intuition told him he was nearing the end. He'd get on to that. It would help take his mind off Makima.

Once the will specifics had been cleared up, he was returning to New York. He could not stay here so close to Makima. It hurt his heart unbearably.

A glance at his watch told him he'd been walking two hours.

It was time to start back, but he just stood, looking all around him and at the tops of the tall trees. The forest was majestic and moving; it was a living entity providing life to all the forest creatures and many benefits to man as well.

Ms. Frye had told him about private owners who subscribed to the sustainable-forestry initiative which worked on the principle of meeting the need for wood products now, while ensuring healthy forests for the future. That's what he would have done had he decided to stay.

Too bad, he thought. Life goes on from day to day and unexpected changes occur to which one has to adjust.

On the way home he focused his thoughts on the beauty of the trees, the birdsong he heard, the rabbits he saw and the way the warm breeze felt. He kept his mind away from Makima.

Calvin was waiting for him on the bench. " I see the walk gave you some peace of mind," he said.

"It's much larger than I realized. When you get stuck for an idea it's a good place to go."

"Does it beat walking in Central Park?"

"It does if you want absolute solitude." It was on his mind to mention the conclusion he'd come to in the forest, but something told him to wait. He needed to get closer to the end and in all fairness, he should discuss the future with Drew before he spoke to Calvin.

After dinner, he called Mr. Moultrie.

"I need to know what remains to be found. I have two scrolls, key number one and the praise house."

"There's one more item to be uncovered and key number two. That's all. Remember that intellect alone isn't necessarily the answer."

Did that mean another meditation on the bench? he pondered. Maybe another time. He had no appetite for it now.

At work the next day he made it his business to stay in his

office and catch up on his work. He said goodbye to Eugenia as he left because she was in the hall. Friday was the same.

Saturday, Drew held a barbecue for sixteen of his friends. Gabe helped with all of the preparations then left the yard to Drew as host. He spent a lot of time upstairs, overseeing activities so he could respond at once if needed.

He was especially concerned about the grill, but Drew handled it like a pro. He called upstairs to invite Gabe and Calvin to come down and eat. A softball game followed, then another round of food. Gabe was eating a well-grilled hot dog when Arnold, a boy about Drew's size, came over to him.

"Can I go through the locked gate, Mr. Bell?" he asked.

"Did you want something there?" He'd had an understanding with Drew that no one was to go into the field.

"I just wanted to see in there."

"You can look through the fence and see there's only grass, flowers and shrubs," Gabe said pleasantly.

"Then why do you keep it locked?" Arnold asked.

"Because it's private," Gabe said.

"Hey, Arnold, come on," another boy yelled.

"Was that as innocent as it seemed?" Calvin asked.

"I'm not sure. I was expecting someone to try to get into the trees. That was so straightforward, it probably was innocent."

Jeff, Angela and Penny stayed to help Drew clean up then Jeff drove the girls home after they all planned to meet at church the next day.

"That was so cool, Gabe. Thanks for letting me have it." Drew was beside himself with excitement later when they gathered in the kitchen.

"That was your first big party. What'd you think of it?" Calvin asked as they sat around the table drinking chocolate shakes.

"It couldn't have been better. I got to invite the kids I really like and we all had fun. No fights, no drinking. The two of you were on hand if there was any trouble but there wasn't." He looked at Gabe. "Did you know that the parents here keep a list of the houses where their kids can go and be safe?"

"No, but it's a pretty good idea. You're big as a man but I still wouldn't want you to go to a party where fights and drinking go on."

"I bet our house goes on that list after tonight." Drew seemed happy at the prospect.

"Did that kid named Arnold ask you if he could go through the gate, Drew?" Gabe asked.

"Yeah, and I told him no. Why?"

"He came and asked me," Gabe said.

Drew was puzzled. "Why would he do that?"

"I wondered why, too. Is he slow or something?"

"He's not the brightest kid in class but still that's strange."

Sam Williams called Gabe the next day as Gabe was getting ready for church. "Thought you'd like to know someone was snooping around your fence last night. I don't sleep well and I often get out of bed and look out the window. I sleep upstairs and I can see a good part of your fence. Couldn't see who it was. Person had on dark clothes but I saw their flashlight going up and down the fence."

"Thanks, Sam. I'll come over this afternoon and you can show me where it was." On the way to church they discussed the snooper.

"Do you think it was Arnold?" Drew couldn't believe it.

"Maybe, maybe not. Do you see him at church?"

"No, but I'll see him at school tomorrow."

"Can you find out without asking him outright?" Calvin said.

"I'm not sure."

"I'll give you some ideas this evening," Calvin said.

Gabe was considering who else it might be. Somehow Arnold didn't seem to fit the bill of a midnight snooper.

He hadn't felt like attending church this morning but pride

told him not to let Makima keep him away. Drew and Calvin were going and his absence would be noticed by their group of friends. Also, he wanted to speak personally to some of the volunteers who'd worked at the fund-raiser.

After the service, he spoke to the Grays. He was leaving when Valerie and Bobby came up to him. "We have something to show you," they said. Valerie extended her hand with a stunning diamond ring on her engagement finger. He hugged Valerie and shook Bobby's hand. He was genuinely glad for them.

As the others gathered around the smiling couple, Gabe couldn't help seeing the irony of the situation. The last time they'd all been there, it was Alana and Calvin who hadn't been speaking to each other. Now it was Makima and he who were ignoring each other so fiercely that it created an air of tension. He excused himself and talked to the volunteers until Calvin came to find him.

The last thing Makima wanted to do was to go to church. Common sense and experience told her that the longer she put it off the harder it would be. She armored herself by wearing an ankle-length cream knit with a short-fitted jacket, and turquoise accessories.

Sitting in her usual place with her parents and Alana made her feel supported and secure until the pastor said, "Let us pray."

How could she pray? What was she doing sitting here in the house of God all dressed up as if she was honoring Him and bowing her head? There had been times before when her faith had been tested. Everyone went through trials and she'd not been immune to them. Yet somehow she had come through them, her faith made stronger.

This time was significantly different. She had dared to be angry at God. She was such a hypocrite! The urge to get up and

walk out of the church was so strong that she clutched her bag
and tensed her muscles to stand up.

Her mother's warm hand took hold of hers and held it. The
affectionate gesture brought Makima to her senses and she sat
through the rest of the service with that hand as a sanctuary. She
kept biting her lip to keep the tears away and was deeply grateful
when the service ended.

Miss Selina was the first person she spoke to as she left the
pew. "Now don't you feel bad or guilty about what those bad
people did with the clinic money, Makima," Miss Selina said as
she clutched her hand. "You meant nothing but good with that
money and God's going to make it all right. You wait and see."

Makima couldn't keep the tears back. She kissed Miss Selina
and thanked her.

All the way down the aisle people offered their sympathy for
what had happened. Over and over she heard the phrase that the
clinic money had been raised to do God's work and one way or
the other it would get done.

Outside in the churchyard she heard the same sympathetic
comments. All she could think of was how wrong she'd been in
her estimation of peoples' reactions. *O ye of little faith,* she
chided herself.

When she saw Gabe, she wanted to shrivel up from embarrassment and shame.

You brought it on yourself, she thought. *You can attract men
but you can't hold them. What is the matter with you?*

She had delusions, Gabe had said. Delusions of pride. She
hadn't wanted him to see her vulnerability, that she, Makima
Gray, could have made such a terrible error in judgment about
Dakers and Sons.

She who was so respected in the community and had almost
single-handedly established the clinic project. The Makima who
Gabe had honored on Saturday night by seating her in the place

of his hostess and later had told the crowd about the signed contract. Makima Gray who apparently must be perfect.

Other people could have faults but not her, especially in the sight of the man she'd told had made her understand what desire felt like for the first time. She hadn't actually used that word. Yet her actions with him had told him beyond doubt that's what she meant.

Now what was she to do? She didn't want to inflict herself on him. He'd made it clear that he was through with their relationship. He'd been at the center Thursday and Friday but she hadn't seen nor heard him.

She approached the family and stood beside her father, spoke to Calvin and to Gabe. Then Valerie and Bobby joined them and after she'd kissed Valerie and admired the ring, Gabe was gone.

Taking her heart and her future with him.

Chapter 32

"When Zeke had this fence up he told me he didn't want it too close to the trees," Sam told Gabe and Calvin as the three of them walked along outside the fence.

"Why was that?" Calvin wanted to know.

"Didn't want snoopers to be able to catch on to a big branch and get into the trees that way."

"Then he had the idea of putting the loops of barbed wire on the top of the fence. That's pretty discouraging, you know," he chuckled.

The strip of ground outside the fence was narrow and covered with weeds. It sloped down gradually to the road that ran beside Sam's house.

"Can't see any footprints here," Gabe complained.

"That's true. Here's the first place I saw the light. He started here and walked for about ten minutes, so let's see if there's any clue in the weeds."

They walked on the very edge of the strip and examined the grass intently but saw nothing. "He probably wore tennis shoes," Gabe said in disappointment.

"The fencing is exactly the same all the way around so what was he looking for?" Calvin asked.

"What do you think, Sam?" Gabe wanted to hear his opinion to see if it was the same as his.

"I'd say he's figuring on cutting through the fence," Sam said.

"Just what I'm guessing. Is it easy to get wire cutters that strong around here?" Gabe asked.

"Sure. Farmers use them all the time."

"Any idea when he might be back?" Gabe looked up and down the fence, trying to get into the mind of the snooper. What was he after? It must be that despite their best efforts, a rumor of the praise house had slipped out and some vandal was anxious to get in the trees and find it.

"I'd say pretty soon before the moon gets bright. I'll keep watch and call you the minute I see anything."

"Really appreciate that, Sam," Gabe said.

"Glad to do it. Put some excitement in my life."

As it turned out they didn't have to worry about that night. The clouds moved in at dinnertime. The rain started soon after and the hard steady rain the farmers had been praying for lasted through the night.

"When you get home, Drew, we need to go to the praise house," Gabe said at breakfast.

"Why?" Drew asked, finishing his orange juice and reaching for a second toasted English muffin.

"To clean up the clearing. The last time I was there I noticed some weeds that need taking out by the roots. Last night's rain probably washed in some debris."

"I'll go, too," Calvin said.

It was bound to be muddy after the rain, they agreed, so they all wore old clothes and shoes. They armed themselves with rakes, a shovel and a couple of other tools from the shed. The leafy weeds Gabe had noticed seemed to have shot up at least a foot. He attacked them with the hoe, chopping deep to get at the root, which came away easily from the rain-softened earth.

Drew was using a rake around the perimeter of the clearing while Calvin used a long-handled mattock to rid the praise house of the leaves that the rain and wind had piled against its foundation.

"Gabe," he called, "come look at this."

His pick had hit something that shouldn't have been there. "I was digging here at the corner where a lot of water had seeped in. The ground was soggy and after I got the leaves and muck out, I hit something hard instead of the soft ground."

Calvin passed the mattock to Gabe, who handled it carefully. "It doesn't feel like a rock or a piece of concrete."

Drew had come to see what they were doing. "Can I try?" Gabe handed the pick to him. Drew moved it around. "Feels like a box but I can't get a hold on it with this."

Suddenly he threw the tool aside, flung himself on the ground and stretched his arms until he felt the box. "I bet it's the treasure!" he cried. "I just know it is."

Gabe and Calvin held their breaths as Drew wriggled until his fingers had a purchase on the box. He scooted backward, getting his clothes muddy as he emerged far enough to bring both long arms out from under the building.

The box was flat on the bottom with a rounded lid, about fourteen inches long and six inches wide, Gabe thought. Probably four feet deep.

"Open it, Gabe," Drew begged, handing it to his brother.

Gabe accepted it reverently. He knew beyond a doubt that this was the treasure his great-grandfather had designed for him.

How would it affect his and Drew's lives? He was almost afraid to open it.

Calvin had been watching him intently. He laid a hand on his shoulder briefly. "Courage, my friend," he said.

Gabe put his hand on the lid and pulled. Nothing happened. He looked at it clearly and saw the keyhole, which had been covered with mud.

"We all have to wait, Drew," he said. "It's locked, so we'll take it home, clean it off and see if the key I found will fit it."

Then he remembered about the second key Moultrie had mentioned. Was it to this box? He searched it again but couldn't find another keyhole. He'd ask Moultrie about it as soon as he got home.

"Maybe there's something else under here," Drew said and went around the building, searching. Meanwhile, Gabe and Calvin decided the reason that corner had been vulnerable was because Great-Grandfather had checked the box over the years that he had been guardian of it. Evidence of repair and reinforcements could be seen in that corner.

"We need to fix it up as best we can now until we can do better," Gabe said.

When that was done they hurried home, hoping Gabe could get to the safe-deposit box for the key before the bank closed. He was too late.

At least he could talk to Mr. Moultrie.

"You found the box? That's hard to believe, Gabe. It's hardly been twenty-four hours since you called to ask what was left to do. Tell me how you found it."

Gabe related the sequence of events. He couldn't see how intellect or intuition had guided him. He was just thankful he'd found it.

"I truly congratulate you. The only thing that's left is for the second key to reveal itself."

Gabe frowned. "To reveal itself? Don't understand."

"You will when it happens so don't worry. However, Gabe, I must warn you that when the two keys open the box you must take great care."

His voice was so full of warning, Gabe frowned again. "Why?"

"You and the box will be in danger. I can't explain more than that but please believe that I am serious. I hope to hear from you very soon."

When Gabe relayed this information to Calvin and Drew, they were as bewildered as he.

"The box must hold diamonds and other jewels just like I predicted," Drew said.

"You might be right after all," Gabe said thoughtfully. "Yet that doesn't fit in with the kind of man I think Great-Grandfather was. I think it has to do with Africa."

"The diamond mines are in Africa, aren't they, Uncle Calvin?"

"They are but I agree with Gabe. What would the scrolls have to do with diamonds? If he had diamonds to give you and Gabe, I think he would have put them in a vault."

"Diamonds or whatever, I think we need to put another box under the praise house that looks as much like this one as possible. Use it as a decoy and ask Sam to be especially watchful."

"I'll help you when you get off work tomorrow," Calvin said.

Makima was miserable. She'd made the biggest mistake of her life and she didn't know what to do about it. Even if she got up the courage to go to Gabe and look him in the eye and apologize, what good would that do? She couldn't believe that he'd accept the apology and go on with their relationship. The accusations she'd hurled at him in her anger had been too severe and completely unjust. It had been wicked of her to mistreat him so.

Expecting his forgiveness was out of the question.

At the time when she'd thought there might be an affinity between Alana and Gabe, she'd given serious consideration to moving away from Grayson. How she wished now that she'd done so. Anything would be better than this situation.

She'd never thought that the time would come when she'd lose interest in the work of the center. There was still much to do under its aegis to enrich the lives of the men, women, children and infants of the Grayson community. She had a folder half-full of ideas for the future when they had the money. Any program in the country that came to her attention went into the folder.

Yet now she could barely get through the routine jobs and the other ones Dr. Cook gave her. She and Eugenia used to fantasize about how they could modify some of the plans in the folder to fit into their budget and space.

She hadn't touched the folder nor talked with Eugenia in weeks. Today at work she'd looked to see if Gabe's car was in the parking lot. That was the only way to know he was at work.

The hours dragged by and with each one she became much more depressed. She wondered how she was going to get the energy to come to work the next day.

As soon as she arrived home she changed into her gown and robe, made some tea and drank it sitting up in bed looking at the evening news.

She was startled when the doorbell rang. Thinking it must be a salesman, she ignored it. Her phone rang and it was her mother. "I'm outside, Makima. Let me in."

"I'm sorry, Mom. I wasn't expecting anyone and I was in bed watching the news," she said as she opened the door.

Her mother looked at her intently and shook her head. "Go back to bed, honey. You look pale and tired. I brought food over and we'll eat together as soon as I warm it up."

"You didn't need to do that," Makima protested.

"Yes, I did. Now get back to bed."

The plate of roast chicken, mashed potatoes with gravy and a dish of greens tickled Makima's appetite. "This looks wonderful."

"You'd had enough soup. You need food that will put flesh on your bones," her mother said. "I hate to ask when the last time was you ate a full meal."

Makima didn't answer, letting the food in her mouth be an excuse. After she'd swallowed it, her mother said, "Was your last meal at my table?"

Makima gave a shamefaced nod.

"I don't want to have to take you back home with me," her mother said firmly when she'd finished her meal. "You cannot go on this way, Makima. You're a grown woman and you have to stop acting like a child. I watched you yesterday at church, you and Gabe. You wouldn't talk to him the week you were home. Yesterday you two hardly spoke, where before you couldn't stop looking at each other. He seems to be a fine man, Makima, better for you than Reggie Powell ever was. Is there something he's done that your dad and I should know about?"

Makima looked horrified. "No, Mom, no. It's nothing like that."

"Do you care for him?" Her face was uncharacteristically sober as she waited for her daughter's answer.

Makima looked at her steadily. "I do care for him, very much."

Her mother's face cleared. "Then act like a woman, not a child. Go to him and whatever it is, make it right."

Later, as she turned out the lights, Makima went over and over her mother's words. They sounded so simple, but this didn't fall into the category of kissing and making up when you'd pushed your six-year-old playmate and made her fall.

Still she had to make it right some way. The only way to begin was to pray to God and seek His forgiveness for her arrogance and pridefulness.

When she drifted off to sleep, she was still praying for forgiveness, humility, and for God to show her the way to make it right with Gabe.

Chapter 33

The sun peeked in and out of the clouds as Makima drove to work. The weather forecast flirted with the possibility of rain showers in the early evening. Makima didn't care, she'd be home by then.

She'd enjoyed her first sound sleep in a long time and she was going to work without the dread that had accompanied her yesterday. She was grateful that her prayers had been answered. She felt that forgiveness had been granted her and a mountain had been lifted from her spirit.

When she parked at the center she saw Gabe's car. Maybe today she'd see him and could tell him good-morning. Her heart beat faster at the mere idea. Something had told her to bring with her the box Mr. Zeke had carved for her eighth birthday. If for some miraculous reason Gabe came to her office he would see it. It might make a bridge for them since they both loved Mr. Zeke.

She didn't know. She could only hope.

She heard a door open and quickly stepped into the hall,

hoping to catch Gabe. It was Eugenia who came over to hug her and ask about her health. "Any time you want a break just let Gabe or me know. We want you to be completely well before you do all that hard work."

"I'm getting stronger every day and by next week I should be up to par," Makima said.

It was Tuesday, which meant a bridge club, some quilters and a children's play group used the center. The volunteer facilitators all came to see her but not Gabe. Twice she picked up the box, but her courage failed her each time.

Then it was one o'clock and Gabe had left the building, but just to be sure she knocked on his door, then opened it. The room was empty. She scolded herself for being a coward and went back to work disheartened.

Gabe had spent another workday holed up in his office seeing no one. Once, he'd heard Eugenia go into the hall and a moment later he heard Makima's voice.

Motionless at his desk, he'd listened to the muffled tones of the two women and wondered if they were coming his way. If Makima came to see him, how would he feel?

Maybe he should go out casually and join their hallway conversation. That's what you did in the workplace. She hadn't looked well at church on Sunday, probably wasn't eating enough. Was she looking any better this morning?

The voices ceased and Eugenia's footsteps went into her office next door. The hall was quiet. Gabe sighed and returned to his figures.

When he left work he went immediately to the bank to retrieve the key and the scrolls from the safe-deposit box. He expected something in the box to explain the scrolls, so he might as well have them on hand. A call came in from Mr. Moultrie soon after he reached home.

"Any more news, Gabe?"

"I just got the key from the safe-deposit box, and as soon as Drew gets home from school, we'll open it. Also, Calvin and I decided to put another box where we found this one, as a decoy. Sam Williams saw someone searching along the fence late at night. We think he'll be back with wire cutters. Apparently a rumor got out about the praise house."

"I did warn you about danger, didn't I?"

"Yes, you did."

"I think it's best if I come down there. I'll leave from work and get there in the early evening. And Gabe, hold off on the decoy until I get there, please."

"Sure. We'll be glad to see you again, Mr. Moultrie," Gabe said.

He repeated the conversation to Calvin and they both tried to figure out why the attorney wanted the delay in setting up the decoy.

"I think he knows more than he's told you about this whole setup," Calvin said.

Gabe gave a short laugh. "If he doesn't, we're in real trouble."

The box had been thoroughly cleaned and placed on the kitchen table. Drew came running down the street from the bus, up the sidewalk, jumped the steps to the porch, flew across the porch and in through the door.

"I could hardly wait for this day to go by," he said. "You got the key?" he asked Gabe eagerly.

Gabe opened his hand to show him the key. He was getting ready to call Calvin, when he appeared in the doorway.

The three of them crowded around the table as Gabe inserted the key, praying the lock would work after being underground so long. It worked smoothly and Gabe held his breath as the lid slowly began to open. It opened one-third of the way and stopped. Gabe touched it gingerly to try to open it farther but without success.

"Feels like the lid is hinged," he said.

"Can't you force it?" Drew put out his hand to take hold of the lid.

"No, Drew," Calvin said. "It's a good thing Mr. Moultrie is coming."

"The box needs the second key to get it to open all the way," Gabe said. "See where this tiny keyhole is? It wasn't apparent until the box was partially opened."

"Can I hold it to see if there's anything in it?" Drew asked.

"Of course." Gabe had been about to do the same thing, but Drew was as involved in this as he was. Drew picked up the box and held his eye to the opening. "I can't see anything," he complained.

Calvin looked and then Gabe. Nothing was visible.

"Hopefully, Mr. Moultrie will have the second key," Calvin said.

Gabe said nothing but he kept thinking of the peculiar words the attorney had always used when talking about key number two. Just last night when Gabe told him about finding the box under the praise house, Moultrie had used the phrase "the only thing left is for the second key to reveal itself." That didn't sound to Gabe like Moultrie was bringing it with him.

While he prepared dinner Gabe pondered why Great-Grandfather had fashioned the treasure box with two locks, especially with the first key opening it just enough to be tantalizing. What would happen if you were the kind of person who didn't wait for the second key and yanked the top off those hinges? He speculated that only a part of the contents would be available. If you smashed the box to pieces to get at what the second key revealed, would you be destroying whatever that was? He wouldn't be surprised. You had to have patience to access what Great-Grandfather had in store for you.

They were sitting at the table over apple pie and coffee when the doorbell rang.

"He made good time," Gabe said, referring to Moultrie. "Cut a piece of pie for him, Drew, while I go open the door."

He swung the door open and there stood Makima.

They stared at each other, then Gabe remembered his manners. "Would you like to come in?"

"Yes, thanks. I'll just take a minute of your time," she said.

He opened the door and she stepped inside. She looked him in the eye and started speaking immediately before she lost her nerve. "I had something to give you all day at work but I never got the courage to take it to your office. First, Gabe, I want to apologize for my awful behavior and I pray that someday you can forgive me." She took from a bag the carved box and held it out to him. "I need to give you this. I was going to wait until tomorrow but I had an urge to bring it over now."

Gabe had been looking at her, dazed at the fact that she was here and had apologized. When she first held out the box, he still looked at her. When it came into his hands and he glanced it, a shiver ran through him.

"It looks like one I have that my great-grandfather made, only it's much smaller," he said.

"Are you busy? May I tell you about it?" she asked hesitantly.

He wasn't sure he wanted to hear what Makima had to say. It was kind of her to bring Great-Grandfather's box even if she was using it as an excuse to see him. At least she'd offered an apology.

Apologies were just words unless offered with true regret and remorse for the pain the other person suffered. He didn't know if she felt that. How could he trust her again? Makima saw his uncertainty. "I'll see you tomorrow," she said and turned to leave.

"No, stay." He couldn't be so discourteous. "We're all in the kitchen, come on back." Calvin pulled out a chair for her while Drew served her a piece of pie, and Gabe put on water for tea. Then he set the box in the middle of the table. "Does this look familiar?" he asked Calvin and Drew.

"It's shaped the same as the other one," Drew said.

"Surely there's a key in it," Calvin said.

"Yes, there is." Makima looked astonished. "How did you know?"

"Tell us about it, please," Gabe told her.

Drew, Calvin and Gabe gave her their rapt attention as she began with her eighth birthday until an hour ago when the urgency to show Gabe the box came to her.

Opening the box, she took out the carved figure and handed it across the table. "This was intended for you," she told Gabe and put it in his hands.

"Thank you," he said solemnly. He made room on the table for the larger box from the praise house.

"We found this yesterday under the praise house. You can see it's partly open. That's because I have one key for it but I needed a second key and we didn't know where it was coming from. You've just given it to me."

Makima felt her eyes couldn't get any wider. This story of the two keys and something under the praise house was too fantastic to believe. Suppose she hadn't found the key at this crucial moment. She couldn't think that way. To her, the hand of the Almighty was apparent all the way through this chain of events.

Gabe inserted key number two and the top slowly rose up until it reached its limits. The top part of the box held a tray. Whatever it was designed for had been removed. Although there was nothing visible in the tray, a faint emanation from it reached Gabe. Glancing up, he saw the same awareness in Makima.

In the bottom section of the box was a packet of papers in a watertight seal.

Gabe took the packet out. Drew looked in the box, put his hand in and felt around to be sure it was totally empty. "Where's the stuff that was in the tray?"

"I'd bet Mr. Moultrie has it for safekeeping. He should be here any minute now," Gabe said.

He began to break the watertight seal. There were several layers of it and Calvin handed him a sharp knife to cut through them. When the doorbell rang this time, Drew ran out and was back in a few moments with Mr. Moultrie.

After the greetings and introductions, Drew said, "I told him he was just in the nick of time. He wanted to know why and I said you'd tell him, Gabe."

"As you can see, the box is open and we found the top tray empty. I assumed that you have its contents." He looked at Moultrie questioningly.

"Your assumption was correct." Mr. Moultrie smiled warmly, his eyes gleaming through his glasses.

"Please have your pie and coffee. We've waited this long, a few more minutes won't matter." Gabe made another pot of coffee, gave Makima fresh tea and asked about Moultrie's trip from Charlotte.

"Drew," Moultrie said, pushing his empty plate away and reaching down for his briefcase. "I remember the first time I talked with you and Gabe in your apartment. You used the term *buried treasure* as if you were thinking of diamonds and other jewels. Those are commonplace, you can buy them all over the world. This treasure you've uncovered is extremely rare and almost priceless!"

From his briefcase he brought forth a suede bag, laid it on the table and carefully drew from it seven pieces of cord, each one holding pieces of leather formed into squares.

As the pieces lay on the table, the atmosphere in the room began to change. There was a pulse in the air accompanied by a nearly subliminal hum. Gabe glanced at Makima and Drew, who had a startled expression on his face. His eyes were wary and fixed on his brother.

"Perhaps we could put them back in their bag," he told

Moultrie, who nodded. The room returned to normal as soon as the cords were covered.

"We saw these on the carving of the man in the praise house," Makima remembered.

"That was certainly interesting," Calvin said. "I've never experienced that kind of power. What are they?"

"Jujus or amulets. They are made to protect a person from harm. Inside the small leather squares are scriptures from the Qurán. The wearer has absolute faith that they will keep him safe from a variety of dangers. It's a little different for the holy men. They devote their lives to increasing their knowledge and their faith, to helping people. And with a pacifying attitude, seeking the favor of the superior powers under all the circumstances of life. They become men of great spiritual power, men who could prevent harm from coming to anyone if they choose to."

"Who did these amulets belong to?" Makima asked, her eyes on the bag as if she expected them to come out any time. Their power had been real to her.

"His story is on the first scroll that you found, Gabe. In your papers is the translation from the Gambian dialect."

Gabe found the paper and began reading.

The holy man was walking from one village to another to heal a boy who had broken his leg in several places. He had been walking a long time without food or water. In the heat of the day he came to a large tree where he laid down to rest. The poisoned dart of the bowmen pierced him. The slavers took away his amulets, tied him up and made him walk to a place where many more captured people were imprisoned. They shaved his head and put him on a great ship. In the strange country he made himself other jujus. They will be buried with him to gather the power that will be a benefit to his people in the future.

"That particular holy man ended up here in Orangeburg County, South Carolina, Gabe. You've another story from Mr. Bell's great-grandfather, Elijah, and he explains more." Moultrie pointed to another paper.

Gabe glanced at it, then told Makima, Drew and Calvin that this had been written by Ezekiel Bell, Sr., on behalf of his father, Elijah Bell. "Elijah is our great-great-great-grandfather," he told Drew.

My father, Elijah Bell, was born in the Gambia on the coast of West Africa. I heard stories from him and other elders about a place they called De Land. It was sacred ground to all the slaves from parts of West Africa and was watched over by "sperrits." The following are my father's words: Dose ol souls, all we people dem watch over she, dey tell us what to do. In deep trees is treasure, waiting for man time six named Bell and woman time six with two keys open it. The Gambia waits for return of treasure, the prophecy say.

Gabe laid down the paper and drank some coffee. The room was silent. Gabe glanced over the rim of his cup at Makima and Calvin. They were in deep thought. Moultrie was composed and relaxed. Drew was a combination of interested and impatient. When he caught Gabe's glance, he asked, "Where was Elijah? Wasn't he living here?"

"No," Mr. Moultrie answered the question. "According to Mr. Bell, the early family members lived somewhere else in South Carolina."

Drew was even more puzzled. "How'd they know about this place?"

"There was a prophecy about it in their tribe in the Gambia," Moultrie explained. He could see his young friend struggling with that idea.

Gabe's thoughts were immersed in all he'd read. This had all begun in the Gambia, that small country between Senegal and Guinea-Bissau. All he remembered was that it had heavy forests and was in the West Atlantic coastal region of Africa. He had lots of questions about it now. Great-Grandfather's library would provide the answers.

The last paper in the packet was a note from Great-Grandfather to him.

To my great-grandson: Dear Gabriel...

Gabe read that far and had to stop. This was his first communication from the great-grandfather he'd grown to admire and respect although he'd never seen him or his picture. He swallowed hard and resumed reading.

The other scroll you have shows the slave cemetery. I put my bench there so I can feel close to my African kinsmen and meditate on their fate. The second key for the opening of the treasure will come from Makima Gray, who is also a sixth-generation Gambian descendant.

The amulets have accumulated extraordinary power and value from being with the spirit of the holy man and his enslaved countrymen for six generations. You will feel the evidence of this when they are uncovered. Now you have completed the first part of your destiny. The second part will be the return of the treasure to the Gambia where it can be put to use for the education and betterment of its people. You will accomplish this with the help of Drew, Makima Gray and Jasper Moultrie.
Ezekiel Bell Jr.

Where before there had been only the sound of Gabe's voice, suddenly it seemed everyone was talking at once.

"I'm a sixth-generation descendant of someone from the Gambia?" Makima looked at Moultrie. "How'd Mr. Zeke figure that out?"

"Your mother is Olivia Lines Gray. If you go back five generations on her side, you'll see a slave from this area."

"That's a cemetery we've been walking on all this time?" Drew said.

"It's no wonder I always felt so close to Great-Grandfather, sitting on that bench. Sometimes I almost felt I heard his voice," he mused.

"You probably did," Calvin said.

"I've no idea about the second part of this destiny, returning the treasure to the Gambia. I hope you have some thoughts on it," Gabe told Moultrie.

Everyone looked at the attorney. What were they supposed to do next?

He looked at his watch. "This has taken longer than I thought it would. What we have to do now is get this box back to the praise house."

"Why?" Makima was bewildered. When the snooper and the decoy were explained to her, she looked across the table at Gabe. "This makes me think of Lawrence."

"What about him?" Everything in Gabe was alerted.

"I don't trust him. He's always trying to find out about you. Just the other day he asked about the fence, why it was so high and had the wire on top of it. That people said your trees are haunted and had I ever heard that. I told him people make a lot of nonsense up out of ignorance. His eyes are always watchful. Have you noticed that?"

Gabe and Calvin exchanged glances. They both nodded.

"I don't think they'll come tonight. The rain had begun when I arrived and it's supposed to get heavier. I suggest that we use what Makima said to lure him to the praise house tomorrow night."

How to make that happen took up the next half hour, at the end of which everyone was satisfied with the plan they'd devised.

At the door, Makima and Moultrie were saying their good-byes when Gabe said, "One more question, Mr. Moultrie. Why weren't the amulets in the tray?"

"Mr. Bell took them out shortly before he died. He was uneasy about them because he couldn't be sure how soon his heir would get here after he died. He gave them to me for safekeeping. I was reluctant to take them as I wasn't the assigned guardian, as he was. But in the end I assented and promised to keep them until the entire will is carried out." He shifted the briefcase in his hand.

Gabe extended his hand. Moultrie looked surprised but grasped it. Gabe shook it warmly. "We thank you for all you've done, sir. Great-Grandfather knew you were a man he could trust and so do we."

Chapter 34

Gabe had a restless night. Too much had transpired to allow him to sleep as soundly as he usually did.

The holy man's bag of amulets as the treasure he'd been hunting was a total surprise. He'd never have anticipated such a thing in a hundred years. He'd known vaguely that there were powers outside of one's normal existence. How else did people walk on burning coals, swallow fire or perform extraordinary feats of bravery when necessary? But he'd never been this close to that phenomenon.

He tried to imagine the life the holy man must have led. How the deep well of faith he possessed never ran dry. The way he'd learned to tap into that faith and access power not for himself but in the service of others.

He wished he had even a small portion of that kind of faith. His mother, he knew, had been blessed with a faith that had been tested through the trials of life and it had grown stronger.

Pop, on the other hand, had seemed to believe only in himself. Faith didn't seem to enter the picture with Pop, yet who was Gabe to judge?

He could only know about himself.

He twisted and turned in the bed trying to find a comfortable spot. After a while, he threw back the covers and got out of bed to stand by the window. Rain was falling steadily and he hoped it had discouraged Lawrence or whoever the snooper was. It would certainly be ironic if the box was stolen tonight after all. It hadn't taken the three of them long to put it back under the praise house and replace the outside boards and push leaves up against it.

His thoughts circled around Makima's unexpected presence at the kitchen table. He'd never told her how he had to find clues leading to a treasured destiny. He wondered what she thought as the papers from the box were read.

He knew she'd felt the power of the amulets. Despite their confrontation and anger, the connection between them told him the power was as real to her as it was to him.

But what about the rest of the story and the news that she was also a sixth-generation descendant of one of the slaves buried in the ground he could see from this window? Perhaps the fact that she'd been in Great-Grandfather's presence from childhood had somehow prepared her to comprehend the essence of the story.

All evening he'd tried to suppress his emotions concerning her while he dealt with the contents of the box.

Now as he stood at the window he came to no conclusion, except that he couldn't conceive working with Makima to accomplish the second part of his destiny as laid out by Great-Grandfather; returning the amulets to the Gambia.

On the way to the center, Makima prayed this was one of the days when Lawrence would show up for volunteer work. He came almost every day. But she didn't have to worry. She had been at her desk only a short time when there was a tap on the door and Lawrence stuck his head in. "May I come in?" At her "good morning" he opened the door and came in.

"You're looking better today," he said.

"I had a good night's sleep and my energy is coming back," she told him.

"Any work for me today?" His watchful eyes scanned her desk and the table where he usually worked. Both were empty.

"I will have some this afternoon," she said. "Eugenia asked me at the staff meeting if you'd be coming in today. I said I didn't know. She has a big job to do and could use some help, she said. Why don't you talk to her about it. What I'm going to do can wait until tomorrow if necessary. Okay?" she said pleasantly.

"Okay," Lawrence said. "See you later."

Makima looked at her watch. After forty-five minutes, she strolled down the hall to the staff meeting room, coffee mug in hand. She looked surprised to see the table strewn with brightly-colored folders. Eugenia and Lawrence were on opposite sides, each with a short stack of folders.

She stopped at the table. "That does look like a big job. You're lucky Lawrence came in."

"It's a job I've been putting off. Lawrence is helping me go through every folder and separate what's necessary."

"More power to you. I'm going to get my tea and leave you to it."

Makima went into the kitchen and put the kettle on. She selected her tea. Eugenia came in. "I think I'll have some, too." She called out, "Want some tea, Lawrence?"

"No, thanks," he said.

The kettle boiled and Makima poured the water into their cups. Eugenia lowered her voice but still spoke distinctly. "How are you and Gabe getting along?"

"We had an argument but we've made up. I was over there last night and he told me the most exciting news. He thinks there's a treasure hidden under the praise house and he's going to try to find it. It's all very confidential for now."

"You know I won't tell," Eugenia said. She raised her voice to its usual level. "I told Lawrence I'll take him out to lunch for helping me with this job. It's a real pain."

"See you both later," Makima said as she left.

Gabe came to her office before he left the center. "How'd it go?" he asked.

"Eugenia and I think it's a success." She told him what she'd said to Lawrence and what she and Eugenia had allowed him to overhear. "She was going to take him to lunch for helping her, but after our little play he told her he'd take a rain check as he had an errand to do before he came back to finish the folders."

"That sounds promising, and thanks, Makima. If it doesn't turn out to be Lawrence and Hakim, we'll have a problem on our hands," he mused, looking into space.

Her heart beat a little fast at the "we."

"I wish I could be there tonight," she said involuntarily.

"It's too uncertain. We don't know if the snoopers, whoever they are, carry weapons. If it's Lawrence and Hakim they may become desperate."

"There'll be you, Calvin, Drew, Mr. Moultrie and a policeman. That's four against two, so surely I'd be safe," she said.

"Perhaps, but I'm not taking a chance," he said firmly. "I don't even want Drew to go, but I can't refuse him." She was secretly pleased at his protectiveness.

"Will you call me when you get home, please?" she asked.

"It might be the middle of the night," he protested.

"I don't care what time it is. I won't rest until I know it's over and you're all safe." She wanted to say much more about how she'd feel if anything happened to him, Gabe, but had to be content with a statement that included all of the men.

The night sky was perfect, starless and dark. By nine o'clock Captain Powers had stationed Gabe near the entrance to the clearing. Drew was farther around the square in the back. Moultrie was on the right side of the praise house and Calvin was near the policeman, guarding the front in case the snoopers came directly from the road where Sam had seen the light. They would cut through the forest and would be easily heard if they came that way.

Captain Arnold Powers and Moultrie had been in school together and had gone their separate ways, to law school for Moultrie and to law enforcement for Arnold. He'd been happy to represent the police on this unusual setup. Everyone wore black clothing, black socks over their sneakers, black stockings over their faces with cut-out spaces for eyes and mouths.

"You'd be surprised how your face shows up if a light happens to hit you," he'd explained. "The thieves will have lights, so you must be absolutely motionless. Our lights are bigger and brighter than theirs but aren't to be used until I give the signal. When will that be?" he asked. They'd gone through all these details, but since they were rank amateurs he had to be sure they understood procedures. Even so with amateurs, there was always a risk of something going wrong. Especially when one was a fifteen-year-old kid, jumping with excitement and nerves.

"When will I give the signal, Drew?" he asked.

"Not until the box is actually being held by one of the thieves," Drew said.

"Excellent. Then what do you do?"

"We all shine our lights in their eyes, which will blind them for a minute, and if they try to run, run after them."

Powers had said they would instinctively try to escape capture by retreating down to the road by the same way they'd come. That's why he'd placed himself in that area with Calvin as backup.

"Remember, they won't know exactly where the box is, so they'll do some exploring. You must be absolutely quiet. Don't let them hear you breathe. Sam Williams will call as soon as he sees a light. Stay behind the trees and shrubs, so if they flash a light around they won't see you."

Captain Powers had given this last rehearsal of detail as they'd made their way silently to the praise house. They'd been settled in their places and Gabe was thinking that his life was becoming more and more like a B movie when his cell phone vibrated.

"Two men just cut the fence where I showed you," Sam said.

Gabe passed the message on to Captain Powers who went noiselessly to each man to alert him the thieves were on their way. The flickering of their lights was visible even before the sound of their passage which they made no effort to hide.

"I hope you know where we're going. I don't like being lost in all these trees." Gabe heard Lawrence's voice, loud and nervous, as the footsteps came closer.

"We're almost there. I can feel it." Hakim's voice was tense and his words clipped.

A moment later Gabe heard the rustle of branches as the man stepped into the clearing. Their lights shone on the praise house and Hakim drew in his breath. Then he said a rush of words and although Gabe didn't understand them he knew they were an expression of triumph.

"There's a lock on the door," Lawrence said. "The treasure must be inside under a floorboard." He pulled a hammer from his pocket and hit the lock with it several times. "I can't break it," he complained.

Hakim grabbed the hammer and gave the lock a mighty blow followed by an even stronger assault against the door by the force of his whole body. As the door gave way, Gabe clenched his hands at this wanton desecration to the ancient praise house. He could hear it continue as Hakim and Lawrence threw the benches around and tore up the floorboards. He gritted his teeth and stood motionless, vowing to erase every trace of this soulless destruction going on inside.

The light came outside and Gabe heard Hakim accuse Lawrence, "You told me Makima said it was hidden under the praise house. It wasn't there."

His words had a dangerous edge that made the hair on the back of Gabe's neck stand up. He thought Lawrence must have heard it, too. "She didn't say exactly where the treasure was hidden," he protested, "so it must be on the outside since we didn't find it inside."

Lawrence and Hakim disappeared around the side farthest away from Gabe. They'd be under the watchful eyes of Moultrie and Drew before they came around to where Gabe could see them.

Every nerve in his body was on the alert. Was this the way soldiers felt when they were going into combat? He'd never been in a situation like this in his entire life—one filled with anticipation, excitement, dread, determination and other emotions he couldn't even analyze.

The lights he'd been waiting for finally came around to where he could see them. He watched Lawrence use a long stick to clean out the leaves piled against the outer wall where it met the ground. Hakim began exploring several yards away. Gabe heard him breathe.

"Look! I see something back there!" Lawrence's light illuminated an empty space behind the leaves and far back in it was a box. He tried to bring the box forward by getting his stick behind it.

Hakim rushed over and knocked him away. The light in Lawrence's hand wavered as Hakim's lips pulled way from his mouth in a primitive snarl. "Get away from it. It's mine!" he hissed.

He flattened himself on the ground. Gabe watched as he grunted like an animal, twisting and turning until his hands reached the box. He began to back away and finally stood with the box clutched to his chest.

Suddenly the clearing was flooded with light. "This is the police. You're under arrest." Captain Powers began to close in on the two men. Lawrence immediately dropped his flashlight and put up his hands as Moultrie and Calvin approached him from each side.

Hakim took a step toward the policeman, his eyes startled and the box tight against his body.

"Give me the box and put up your hands," Captain Powers commanded.

With a movement almost too quick to see, Hakim feinted around Powers and fled in the opposite direction past where Gabe was posted at the clearing, entering the path through the woods to the house.

The sound of his pounding feet had barely disappeared when Gabe and Powers were on his trail.

"Does he know where he's going?" Powers asked, running easily and flashing his powerful light from time to time.

"Not to my knowledge." Gabe knew Hakim had never been in the house, but Lawrence had. He didn't think that was important at this point. Hakim seemed to have his head in another world where only the holy man's amulets with their immense power were real to him.

Powers flashed his light but the running figure it had shown once in a while had disappeared.

"I can't see him," he said. "Did he cut back into the woods to go down to the road?"

"I don't think so," Gabe said. In the distance he could see they were approaching the end of the trees. He led Powers to where the woods stopped and Great-Grandfather's bench stood.

Powers glanced around. "We lost him," he said disgustedly.

"Shine your light across the field," Gabe said.

There was Hakim on his back lying in the middle of the field. He'd broken open the box and it rested facedown on his chest. His staring eyes were fixed in awe and terror at something only he had been able to see.

It had sucked away his life spirit.

Powers knelt and felt his pulse, bewilderment on his face. "I've never seen a body like this before. Did he have a sudden heart attack?"

"I don't think so," Gabe said, his eyes on Hakim's distorted features. "How does he look to you?"

"As if he's deathly afraid of something."

"It was that fear that killed him. Hakim tried to steal something sacred."

When he saw Powers open his mouth to ask another question, Gabe turned away.

"Ask your friend Moultrie. He can explain it all to you."

Chapter 35

Makima stood at her bedroom window gazing out at the night sky. The moon was just a fingernail sliver and thin clouds left over from the weather front that had brought yesterday's rain scudded across the sky.

Earlier she'd run her tub full of hot water and sprinkled a few drops of fragrant bath oil into it. She'd lit the scented candles that sat on the corners of the tub, put on soft music and climbed into the welcoming water.

Not for her the usual shower tonight. She'd needed the bath to soothe her nerves, to quiet her emotions and to keep her from succumbing to fear for what the night might bring.

Now clad in a robin's-egg-blue gown with matching robe, she pictured the praise house and tried to imagine what was taking place there.

She should have insisted on going with Gabe and the others. The papers Gabe had read from Mr. Zeke had named her as having a role to play in disposing of the treasure, which it had taken her key to unlock. So why couldn't she be a part of catching the thieves who wanted to upset the plan?

Even as she formed the thought she could see the flaw in it. The box the thieves were after had been emptied, so she wouldn't have been protecting the true treasure.

She just wanted to be there. But her presence would have been an additional burden on Gabe, who was already concerned that all their plans would work and that Drew would come to no harm.

She leaned her forehead against the cool window in frustration. Was she never going to learn? She was reacting to her own emotional needs again. That was exactly what had caused the rift with Gabe.

All her life she'd seen herself as spiritually strong, as a person steadfast in faith who could stand anything. This was confirmed after June's tragic death. Nothing could be worse than that because death was so final.

She'd taken that pain and turned it into a positive action by planning the health clinic for Grayson.

Why had her faith failed her so suddenly and strongly when Gabe, trying to be helpful, discovered the contractors had stolen the clinic money?

She understood that the immodest pride of which she'd been unaware caused her to feel a high degree of embarrassment for personal failure. Was that the only thing that made her lash out at Gabe? If Alana or even Calvin had brought the same news she wouldn't have acted that way. What was it that made the difference?

Comprehension flooded her being and took her breath away. She loved Gabe!

That was the difference and she wondered why the realization had been so long in coming. Maybe it was the simple fact that she'd never been in love before and was unprepared for the many ways it affected a person.

She wouldn't have minded Alana or Calvin seeing her huge disappointment or resulting panic at the loss of the money. But she couldn't stand to appear that way in front of the man she loved.

Because she loved him she wanted his love, his admiration, his respect—not his pity. Her mother had asked if she cared about Gabe. She'd said she did. What she felt was so much more than caring.

Despite the problem between them, she felt joyous and exhilarated. Happiness ran through her veins and she couldn't wait to see him again and to hear his voice. She wanted to feel his arms around her, hear him say tender loving words. She wanted to tell him how much she loved him, how sorry she was for her ugly behavior and how she just now understood the reason for it. Distorted? Yes. His fault? Absolutely not.

Would he listen? Would he understand?

She prayed to have the opportunity to tell him the story, to pour out her heart to him and to promise to never make that particular mistake again.

When the phone finally rang she answered it eagerly, knowing it would be him.

"Gabe?" she asked on a quick intake of breath.

"Yes. I said I'd call." He sounded weary.

"Are you and Drew all right?"

"We're fine. It was Lawrence and Hakim. They found the box and when we turned the lights on them, Lawrence surrendered at once. Hakim took the box and ran. We expected him to go back the way they came but he ran through the trees with Captain Powers and me chasing him." He paused.

How drained he must be, she thought.

"Do you mean he ran in the direction of the house?" she asked.

"Yes. Then something really strange happened, Makima. You know where the bench is?"

Sacred Ground

"Of course." Her hand tightened on the phone. She could feel the connection between them begin to flow again.

"Hakim came out of the trees there. We thought we'd lost him because we couldn't see him anyplace. Powers has a very bright light and when he played it on the field we saw Hakim."

Gabe kept pausing and Makima knew this was not a story he wanted to tell. Maybe she could help.

"You and Powers found him dead, Gabe?" she asked softly.

"Lying on his back in the field. He had opened the box and it was on his chest. He died in great fear. Powers thought it was a heart attack but I know better."

Makima could see the picture clearly in her mind. How awful it must have been for Gabe.

"Hakim had violated the holy man's powers and he paid the price," she said.

"Yes. You do understand," he sighed.

"I do," she affirmed. "It wasn't the ending you anticipated for whoever the thieves were, but it wasn't your fault, either, Gabe. It was Hakim's greed for what didn't belong to him. Don't blame yourself," she urged, hoping to help him resolve any guilt he felt for Hakim's death.

"At least it won't go so badly for Lawrence and I'm glad for your mother's sake. He'll have to spend time in jail and maybe it'll help him straighten out his life, but the idea was Hakim's. Lawrence didn't understand about the amulets."

"Drew's all right?" His brother's safety had been Gabe's great concern. She wanted Gabe to think of him instead of the lifeless Hakim.

She was rewarded when he gave a little laugh. "Drew thought it was the coolest adventure he'd ever had. Of course, when he saw Hakim that was pretty bad, but we talked about it and I think he'll be okay."

"You're a wonderful big brother, Gabe," she said quietly.

"I'm glad you think so. Times like this I know he misses our mom."

"I expect he does and maybe you do also. But you have each other, Gabe, and—" She interrupted herself. This wasn't the time, yet the urge had been so strong to make the promise, to express at least a portion of the love that filled her heart.

There was a pregnant silence on the line. She was scrambling in her mind to fill it with something appropriate when she heard him take a breath.

"And what, Makima? What else were you going to say?" There was a new note in his voice.

Encouraged by the sense of intimacy that came to her across the wire, she said, "Dearest Gabe, I was going to say that you also have me. That is if you still want me." She rushed on with the request that was imperative if they were to erase the distance between them. "I haven't had the chance to tell you about myself and why I acted as I did. I need to do that. Is there a time tomorrow when we can get together? Please." She closed her eyes and said a little prayer that Gabe would know of her sincerity and would accede to her appeal.

"I want that, too. How about seven at your place?"

"That's fine. I'll let you go now. Thanks so much for letting me know what happened."

"It was good for me, too. See you at work tomorrow."

Gabe stood at the praise house the next afternoon. In the sunlight there was little evidence on the outside of the violent event that had taken place the night before except for the broken lock.

Inside was a different matter. On the front wall the figure of the holy man had been defaced by Hakim's ax. Every bench had been broken or chopped at by Hakim in his fury to find the treasure.

Gabe felt sick in his stomach. He sat on the floor and asked forgiveness for the destruction and the godlessness that had invaded the praise house after all the centuries. As a Bell he had failed in his guardianship and he was profoundly sorry.

His bond with the people who'd built this place and worshipped here was strong. It was their suffering and their endurance that had made it possible for the generations that came after them to produce a man like Great-Grandfather who was determined to unearth him and Drew so the family line could continue in full knowledge of their heritage.

He longed for their pure belief and that of his mother.

In the silence he gradually became aware of an inflow of certainty and a profound connection he'd never felt before to the universality of God. It's all the same. The God of the slaves, of the holy man, of his mother, the one Reverend Givhans preached about and Makima prayed to. It was all the same eternal source of good and faith.

His strong link through Great-Grandfather, and the first African in his line wasn't just chance, but a pattern, a destiny that could only have come from an omnipotent Being.

Gratitude and a peace he'd never known before surged through him.

He didn't know how long he sat in meditation before he opened the letter Moultrie had given him this morning when they'd met for breakfast before the attorney drove back to Charlotte.

He'd said, "I'll be back in a day or two to help wrap things up. Mr. Bell wanted you to have this note from him after the treasure was found."

Gabe had put it in his pocket, waiting for the place and the frame of mind to read it. He unfolded it now.

My dear great-grandson, Gabriel,

Although you may have found this journey difficult, even annoying at times, I have made it a challenge so that you and Drew would be good stewards of the destiny under the praise house, as well as of the property which I pray you will live on, nourish and enjoy the remainder of your lives and pass on to your heirs. I built the property to last for generations. I was denied the opportunity to do this for my own children, Elizabeth, Robert and Edward. May you pass it on to yours.

Your great-grandfather,

Ezekiel Bell Jr.

All Gabe could think as the poignancy of Great-Grandfather's plea hit him was how a few days ago he'd decided to sell the property, take Drew and return to New York. He'd thought he'd found someone he could love and trust and a future in Grayson had seemed a possibility. Then in a few blazing minutes, that possibility had been burned to a cinder when Makima had accused him of being the cause of the board losing their deposit for the clinic construction.

The idea that she could think such a thing of him cut him to the quick and demonstrated that the closeness he'd thought they had was a mirage. He'd never suffered such profound heartache before and yet at work he listened for her footsteps in the hall, the sound of her voice saying something to Eugenia next door. But how could she have misjudged him so? *That* he couldn't understand.

Then she'd shown up with the second key to the treasure and an apology. The key was genuine. Perhaps the conversation she wanted to have tonight would explain the substance behind the apology.

He wouldn't let himself hope. Not yet. Too much was at stake.

Makima tried on the fourth outfit in preparing herself for Gabe's visit. Maybe she should wear the jumpsuit she'd put on for the cooking party at Carolyn's. The effect it had produced on Gabe was the one she wanted to see tonight, flat-out admiration and an overwhelming desire for embracing. She took it out of the closet and held it up to her body.

No, that would not be fair. Tonight she was not playing games of any sort. She put all the gowns back in the closet and pulled out the skirt and blouse with the turquoise jacket she'd been wearing in the restaurant when they first saw each other.

That was the honest thing to do. If he could accept her full-blown apology when being reminded of how she'd embarrassed him in that restaurant, she would have won. Definitely.

When the bell rang at seven and Makima welcomed Gabe in, seated him opposite her and offered him coffee, she knew she'd made the right decision in what to wear. Gabe had not arrived in the mood she'd remembered from the cooking party.

His eyes were wary. He'd agreed to hear what she had to say but it wasn't going to be easy to convince him of her change of heart. Her hands were cold and her nerves were jumping as she tried to find the right words.

"Gabe, I might as well tell you I'm jumpy because this is very important to me and I'm not sure how to go about it. I did and said such horrible things to you! I've never done such a thing before, not in my whole life and it's taken me a while to understand how it happened."

She made herself look at Gabe and then keep the eye contact. It was hard to do at first because she was ashamed. But as she progressed, the need for him to understand how and why she felt as she did took over and she lost her self-consciousness.

"When I got over being sick and feverish, I found I was angry with everyone, even with God although I was afraid to say it that way. I thought, how could He have let poor, ordinary people work hard to give money so that it could end up being stolen by Dakers and Sons? I was angry at the board because we didn't take the time to make a trip up to Rock Hill to check the company out, and I was angry at you."

She saw him flinch and she yearned to put her arms around him and kiss the hurt away. It was too soon.

"It was so wrong, Gabe, such distorted thinking. Delusions, you said. You were right. When I got well enough to see more clearly, I saw it was pride that made it hard for me to accept that Makima Gray could have made such an error in judgment. I was the one who recommended Dakers, you see."

Gabe spoke for the first time. "Everyone makes wrong judgments sometimes, Makima." His voice had warmth in it and she felt a spurt of encouragement.

"But then you and I argued in my office and I twisted events around so as to make you responsible. I am so ashamed of myself, Gabe. I have to ask now if you can forgive me for that."

"Are you saying that you knew all along that I couldn't have done anything to hurt you?" he asked quietly, his eyes holding hers.

"Yes, I knew you weren't that kind of man. You're a man of honor and integrity."

Gabe leaned forward in his chair. Opposite him she followed his action instinctively. "Of course I forgive you, Makima," he said. "But you need to help me understand why you did it."

She leaned closer and took his hand. The current between them was flowing in force. "I asked myself the same question. Had it been Calvin who told me about the money, would I have felt that way? The answer was a big no. Calvin doesn't matter to me except as a friend."

Her voice softened. She let her feelings come out as she caressed his cheek and gazed at him with open emotion. "You are my beloved, Gabe. For you and in your eyes I wanted to be perfect. I didn't understand that until later because I've never been in love before."

Gabe's eyelids closed halfway, he took in a breath and his mouth curved. He gently pulled Makima out of her chair and into his lap. With his arms around her, he gazed into her eyes. "How do you know you're in love?" He kissed the corner of her mouth.

"Because just thinking of you gives me a joy I've never felt before and I long to see you and hear your voice and touch you." She kissed him on his eyes. She wouldn't ask him but she yearned to know how he felt.

He tightened his grip on her and began kissing her all over her face and neck.

"How else do you know?" he asked in a hoarse voice, his eyes ablaze with desire.

"I want to be with you all of the time," she murmured, kissing his neck.

"Anything else?" He kissed her mouth with exceeding tenderness.

"Because even when we were mad at each other, I still thought of you all of the time." She caressed the nape of his neck and pulled his head down for a gentle kiss.

"My dearest Makima," he said. "I asked you all those questions because those are the reasons I know I love you." His voice was serious and firm. "I have one more question for you."

"What is it?"

"Will you marry me, Makima?"

Makima hadn't anticipated that particular question, hadn't dared dream that far.

"What about Drew?" she asked. "Will it be all right with him?"

Gabe grinned suddenly, like a lighthearted boy. "To have a chemistry teacher right in the house for the rest of his school years? Of course it'll be okay with him, especially since he already likes this chem teacher. Any other questions before you answer me?" He was serious again.

"Are you sure, Gabe?" Her eyes were anxious. "Do you think you can trust me again?"

"We will trust each other and promise to always talk out any problems. Will you marry me, Makima?"

"Yes, I will, Gabe. I love you with all my heart and soul."

Gabe held her close and laid his cheek on her hair. "Thank you, Great-Grandfather," he murmured, "for bringing me here where my heart's love was waiting for me."

For an instant he felt the presence of his great-grandfather and for the first time saw his face. He was smiling.

Epilogue

Calvin and Drew had been watching a late show on television when Gabe had come in from Makima's that night. Calvin had given him a searching glance, and come to a conclusion. He shook Gabe's hand.

"Congratulations, my friend," he said. "Have you set the date?"

"Date for what?" Drew had asked.

"Makima and I are getting married," Gabe told him, watching for his reaction.

"Good," Drew said. "I like her a lot. Can I be your best man at the wedding?" The appeal in his eyes touched Gabe's heart.

"Who else?" he said. "I'm going to break the rule and have two attendants, my best brother and my best friend."

Moultrie had been pleased with the news when he'd seen Gabe and Drew the following weekend to hand them a package from the safe-deposit box.

"This couldn't have come at a more opportune time," he'd told them. "Gabe, Mr. Bell wanted you to have this diamond wedding set he'd given his wife, and Drew, my young friend, you'll be especially interested in these." Inside a chamois bag were eight uncut diamonds. "Mr. Bell bought these over the years from Africa. Now they're part of your inheritance."

"I always thought there'd be diamonds," Drew said with a huge smile.

"These are yours also." Moultrie gave them a large manila envelope. Gabe pulled out from it the family photographs that had been missing from the house. There was Great-Grandfather just as Sam had described him.

In Great-Grandmother Sarah's countenance Gabe saw patience, kindness and a definite sense of humor about the eyes and mouth. There was an early portrait of the parents with Elizabeth, Robert and Edward as schoolchildren.

The last photograph was of a small ebony man with deep-set eyes, broad nose, generously molded lips set in a face that had lines running from nose to chin, seeming to end in a white goatee. He wore a knitted cap that had fitted his head closely. He looked out at the world with a serenity born of endurance.

"That has to be Elijah," Gabe said. He turned it over and there was the name in Great-Grandfather's writing.

"Mr. Bell said to tell you that images can be powerful and he didn't want these to distract you from what you had to do," Moultrie had explained.

The weeks before the wedding had been busy. An archaeologist from the university had begun exploring the slave cemetery, which had engendered a great deal of media attention.

Moultrie had had several more sessions with Gabe to get the legal matters straight in the transfer of property and assets. He'd also been instrumental in helping Makima and the board find Dakers and Sons and retrieving the five thousand dollars.

Calvin had cornered Gabe one day. "Remember when I first

arrived and spoke to you about the elements of the hero's journey as it applied to you and your search for what Mr. Zeke had left you?"

Gabe grinned. "I've been meaning to tell you that you might have been right, because in the letter Great-Grandfather left me, he mentioned journey and difficulties."

"So what do you think? You've been through a lot, has it changed you?" Calvin had given Gabe one of his soul-searching looks that made Gabe think seriously about the question.

"I guess it has changed me," he mused. "It's changed my idea about faith, forgiveness, the importance of family lineage and love."

These had been uppermost in Gabe's mind on the third Sunday in May when he'd stood, with Drew and Calvin, and watched a radiantly beautiful Makima come down the aisle to him.

He'd slipped the Bell wedding ring with its African insignia onto her finger and repeated his vows not only in front of the packed church but also in front of Mom and Pop and Great-Grandfather and Great-Grandmother.

They'd spent one week of their honeymoon exploring the Gambia and had gathered firsthand information for carrying out the destiny of the treasure. The second week had been spent on an island in the Caribbean where they could ignore everyone except each other.

Moultrie had gone with them on the second trip to meet with the cultural affairs department of the government. Matters had been arranged for the Gambian Education Foundation with its administrative site in Grayson, South Carolina.

The sale of a portion of the forest had provided funds and land for the Grayson Health Clinic, one building of which was already under construction, and for several classrooms for the church.

Gabe was involved with Marie Frye in learning more about sustainable foresting, and in drawing up plans for the new community center.

Public interest in the praise house had been fierce. People wanted it moved out of the forest. Why not put it close to the final resting place of the slaves who had built it, they said.

"I understand what they're saying." Gabe and Makima were walking hand in hand to the praise house one summer evening. The air was still balmy and it wasn't even dusk yet since it didn't get dark until around eight-thirty.

"But you still want to keep it private," she said.

"I admit to being selfish about it. This place means so much to me." They arrived at the clearing. He unlocked the door and they went in.

"It brings such peace to me. I think it's because I feel surrounded by my ancestors. I like to tell them all the things that are happening. Like about the clinic and the church classrooms and that there's going to be a monument to them at their cemetery." He grinned a little self-consciously. "I even came to share the news that Drew won the swim meet this year."

"You have time yet, honey. Eventually you might want to make it more accessible to the public but you don't have to hurry." She glanced at him lovingly and squeezed his hand. "I have some news to share with them."

"What is it?"

"We're having a baby to add to the Bell lineage."

This time when Gabe whooped with joy and hugged his wife, the person he saw was a slight ebony man with a goatee whose eyes smiled at him.

Sometimes love is beyond your control...

Bestselling author

ROCHELLE ALERS

The twelfth novel in her bestselling Hideaway series...

Stranger in My Arms

Orphaned at birth and shuttled between foster homes as a child, CIA agent Merrick Grayslake doesn't let anyone get close to him—until he meets Alexandra Cole. But the desire they share could put them at the greatest risk of all....

"Fans of the romantic suspense of Iris Johansen, Linda Howard and Catherine Coulter will enjoy this first installment of the Hideaway Sons and Brothers trilogy, part of the continuing saga of the Hideaway Legacy."
—*Library Journal*

Coming the first week of April wherever books are sold.

ARABESQUE®

www.kimanipress.com

KPRA0080407

"A relationship built within the church is a concept not too often touched upon and it made for a nice change of reading."
—*Rawsistaz Reviewers*

CAN I GET an *Amen* AGAIN

JANICE SIMS • KIM LOUISE
NATALIE DUNBAR
NATHASHA BROOKS-HARRIS

Follow-up to the ever-popular
CAN I GET AN AMEN...

The sisters of Red Oaks Christian Fellowship Church are at it again—this time there are some new members of the church looking for love and some spiritual healing...

Coming the first week of April
wherever books are sold.

ARABESQUE®

www.kimanipress.com

KPCIGAAA0670407

KPJT0280407

The fourth title in the
Forged by Steele miniseries...

USA TODAY bestselling author

BRENDA JACKSON

risky**PLEASURES**

Unable to acquire Vanessa Steele's company, arrogant
millionaire Cameron Cody follows Vanessa to Jamaica,
determined to become the one temptation she can't resist.
But headstrong Vanessa is equally determined to prove that
she's immune to his seductive charm!

Only a special woman can win the heart of a brother—
Forged by Steele.

Available the first week of April
wherever books are sold.

KIMANI™
ROMANCE

What a sister's gotta do!

At First
SIGHT

Favorite author

Tamara Sneed

Forced to live together to get their inheritance,
the Sibley sisters clash fiercely. But when financier
Kendra and TV megastar Quinn both set their sights on
wealthy Graham Forbes—sweet, shy Jamie's secret crush—
Jamie unleashes her inner diva.

*Available the first week of April
wherever books are sold.*

KIMANI
ROMANCE

www.kimanipress.com
KPTS0140407

Some promises were just made to be broken...

Other People's Business

Debut author

PAMELA YAYE

Stylist Autumn Nicholson looked like the kind of uppity, city girl L. J. Saunders had sworn off. And Autumn wasn't interested in casual flings, especially with a luscious hunk who'd soon be leaving. But fate, well-meaning meddling friends and a sizzling, sensual attraction all have other plans....

*Available the first week of April
wherever books are sold.*

KIMANI™
ROMANCE

What happens when Prince Charming arrives...
but the shoe doesn't fit?

THE Glass SLIPPER PROJECT

Bestselling author
DARA GIRARD

Strapped for cash, Isabella Duvall is forced to sell the
family mansion. But when Alex Carlton wants to buy it,
her three sisters devise a plan to capture the handsome
bachelor's heart and keep their home in the family.
The question is...which of the Duvall sisters will
become the queen of Carlton's castle?

*Available the first week of April
wherever books are sold.*

KIMANI
ROMANCE